KING OF FLESH AND BONE

THE PALE COURT BOOK ONE

LIV ZANDER

INK HEART PUBLISHING

Copyright © 2022 by Liv Zander

ISBN-13: 978-1-955871-01-3

www.livzander.com

info@livzander.com

Cover Art: Darling Cover Design

Editing: Silvia's Reading Corner

All rights reserved.

No part of this book may be reproduced in any form or by any electronic or mechanical means, including information storage and retrieval systems, without written permission from the author, except for the use of brief quotations in a book review.

This book is a work of fiction. Names, characters, places, and incidents are either the products of the author's imagination or are used fictitiously. Any resemblance to actual persons, living or dead, businesses, events, locations, or any other element is entirely coincidental.

Warning: This book is intended for mature audiences.

CHAPTER 1
ADA

"The dead are restless." I glanced out the rain-blurred window toward the cemetery, the air inside the house thick with sweat and the sweetness of amniotic fluid. "You better start pushing now or my husband will dig out of his grave."

As would the other corpses with the ground this soaked and soft. But my John as one of them…? Trudging across the village square with his skull exposed where he'd hit the rock two summers back, waterlogged skin swollen against his leather breeches? No, I would make bloody certain he stayed in the ground.

After all, I'd put him there.

"No. Not yet!" Sarah squatted at the edge of her bed, tears running down her red-veined cheeks, and dug her fingers into the straw mattress. "I can hold it in 'til the morning."

Brushing blonde wisps from my forehead, I kneeled on the pounded dirt floor for a better look. No trickles running down her thighs, skin puffy-red and swollen, a thatch of dark hair crowning between her legs with no progress… By

Helfa, had she shoved at the head all evening just to keep the baby in?

"No more stalling." I stroked Sarah's back through her sweat-soaked chemise, gathering the fabric higher while my other hand prodded her legs wider. "This child is coming, whether you want it or not."

Ransacked by trembles, Sarah's voice faded into a whimper against the straw. "Ada, I can't bear the thought of not knowing if it's dead or truly alive. How many hours 'til morning?"

"Too many to escape this fate." Everyone dreaded the full moon, but none more than women cursed to birth a child on such a night. "Instead of weighing down my husband's grave as I'm supposed to, I came here when you asked for my help."

"To keep it in... not to get it out!"

A fool's idea, risking both mother and child. The scalp had already turned more purple beneath the white film crowning its head. Was it dying? Already dead?

I'd only ever delivered four babies during the full moon —all alive the next morning—but I'd heard from other midwives who hadn't been so lucky. *Dead babes scream inconsolably,* they reported, *wailing in the same way the other corpses groan in the groanpits.*

The groanpits...

I shuddered at that word.

The corpses we'd collected over the last month already resonated Hemdale with their ragged wheezes. We'd found most of them around the village, though they also had a habit of falling into the river on full moons, catching on the fish cages.

I looked back at Sarah. "Get the child out now and it might live to see the morning. Leave it stuck with the head like this... and it *will* be cold in its cradle once the sun rises. With you bleeding out next to it. You want to join the undead so soon?"

"No," she cried, her voice as thin as my fraying patience.

No, none of us wanted that.

But it was what we all had coming.

Husbands. Elders. Mothers.

Everyone.

Even this child.

The thought of the dead resting and rotting in the ground was nothing but humbug in my ears. An evil curse upon the lands—old wives' tales had it—cast by an enraged god. Internally, I scoffed. Nothing but a story where we all knew who was to blame.

Or *what*.

The constant patter of rain against the window tensed my muscles. "Sarah, please. No widow should chase behind her dead husband, but certainly not during such a downpour. Push!"

Her groan filled the house, mingling with the hiss of flames from the hearth and the occasional pop of poorly seasoned wood. At last, Sarah held her breath and labored, gaining a precious inch. A stubby nose appeared—Oh, pink!

Pink was promising.

"Again!" When the child's head slipped into my hand, I angled it so one shoulder might pass first. "Only a few more. The head's already out."

The next contraction came with a yelp.

That, and the squeak of rusty hinges as the door opened, letting in a whiff of heavy smoke from the street. A monotone cadence of mumbles resonated outside. The priests, probably, calling for villagers to take up arms beside Hemdale's groanpit.

"What's this?" William pushed the door shut, the brim of his black felt hat barely hiding the anger glinting in his eyes. "What's she doing here?"

Since Sarah screamed through yet another contraction, I answered in her stead, "Getting this child out."

"I don't want you near my wife." He hurried over to Sarah, kneeled, and took her shaky hands into his. "It's bad enough you got my brother killed over that curse of yours."

I flinched. "She sent the neighbor over to my house, asking for me to come."

"And I'm asking for you to leave, unwoman."

Unwoman.

Stabbing pain grew in my chest until the laces of my dress strapped my lungs tight. Barren, punished by Helfa himself, blighted with a twisted womb... Of all the things some people called me, unwoman was the worst—and the truest. What else would you call a woman incapable of giving her husband a son?

A child was a blessing from Helfa.

I'd never even managed a daughter.

Clearly, I was cursed.

I blinked the stinging burn from my eyes and rose, feigning as much pride as my rounded spine would allow. "You want me gone? Serves me just fine."

My mule already stood harnessed in the stables in case I needed the old, stubborn thing to pull the cart onto John's grave. But what good was this precaution if I wouldn't get there before the rain made certain the wheels got stuck? None.

Sarah screamed as the baby's shoulder dislodged. A gush of amniotic fluid soaked the dirt beneath my feet, splattering the hem of my dress, thickening the air with moisture.

I quickly bent over and caught the child, then whispered, "Please don't scream."

The boy arched his back, his limbs slippery, his skin coated in a white wax. Little eyes blinked up at me—blue like mine—taking in their surroundings ever so curiously. Warmth swelled in my core with how his mouth rooted toward my chest as if... as if he were mine.

I extinguished it with a deep inhale. Because he was not mine, and no child ever would be. "It's a boy."

Grave silence settled into the room.

Sarah dug her face into the mattress, shaking her head until the straw crunched beneath the motion. Her haunches sunk to the ground, letting the umbilical cord drag over the dirt.

William frowned at the child, relief and terror letting the corners of his mouth hike and fall. "Is he... alive?"

My mouth turned dry.

Was he?

The longer William stared at me and Sarah remained utterly still, both waiting for an answer, the more the air cooled around me. As a midwife, I'd watched my fair share of mothers cradle their still baby. Watching them rock their crying baby on a full moon, only to find it cold and still the next morning. What curse could be more evil?

Cradling the boy in one arm, I grabbed a knitted blanket from a stool beside the bed and draped it over him. He might not need the warmth, but I would damn well provide it until we could be certain. A first scream built at the back of his throat, like a wet gargle from the remaining fluids in his lungs, running a shiver up my spine.

It meant nothing.

All babies cried.

"Can't say until the morning." Neither did I want to.

"Pray that he'll want to nurse, but... prepare yourself for the fact that the dead have no hunger."

William rose, lifting his arms as if to take his son, only for them to drop by his sides again. "But he... he's trying to wail."

Wail. Wander.

Corpses did it all during a full moon, ever so restless in their pursuit of reaching the Graying Tower in the south, only to cry when it denied them entry. It called to them like a cruel siren, the stony castle surrounded by piles of corpses, where the devil responsible for our plight lived. Evil in flesh, the priests called him, an unearthly creature from a wayward realm.

The King of Flesh and Bone.

I handed William the child, no matter his reluctance. "Cut the cord, wait for the afterbirth, keep him warm until the morning... and pray. I have to weigh John's grave down."

Letting my head retreat into the hood of my cloak, I stepped outside, raindrops pelting the felt in hurried *thud-a-thud-thuds*. The occasional grunt resonating from the groanpit mixed into it, filling my veins with a restless tingle. That thing had gotten overly full this month. Had corpses truly burned in the past?

Probably just another story...

I turned the corner of the courthouse and passed the brick archway into the cemetery. Rivulets of water trailed between the graves, glistening with the soft sheen of a full moon glowing behind clouds. Sacks of grain lined the wrought-iron pickets, though villagers had moved some onto the graves.

"All that grain would have fed me for a year," I

mumbled, heading toward the oak door which leaned against the fence.

I gripped the edge, dug my heels into the soggy earth, and... Devil be damned, this thing was heavy. The door dragged slowly, corners ripping bushels of sod from the ground. Sweat formed at the nape of my neck and muscles soon ached. Just a little more...

The door hit the ground with a *slosh*, burying my planted violets underneath the incessant drum of rain on wood. A sound loud enough it quenched what had now turned into a chorus of groans from the pit, but by Helfa, it did nothing to muffle Pa's protest.

"Drenched to the bone, but she has to weigh the damn grave down." He wrapped gout-gnarled fingers around a sack of grains, his graying hair pasted to his skull, cursing the weather as he dragged it onto the door. "You can't hold him forever, Ada."

"Twenty-three months and counting," I said, my cheeks tingly from the cold dampness. "Twenty-four if you help me put the mule before the cart. Ground's too soaked to keep him from digging out, so I best put the cart on the door."

"If the wheels get stuck, we won't get the cart back to the stable 'til spring."

"If John gets out, I'll have to chase him, bind him, and still get the cart to drag him back to his grave," I said, my eyes going to Pa's crooked digits as they fumbled with his red-smudged handkerchief. Had he coughed blood again? "The wheels will get stuck no matter what. Preferably atop my husband."

He quickly pushed his handkerchief into his leather vest pocket when he caught my eyes on the stained fabric. "Your eyes are red, the tip of your nose shiny. You've been crying."

Just almost. "Sarah had a son."

"Dead or alive?" When I shrugged, he slowly shook his head. "William paid a coin for your help?"

"No, but I bet he would have paid a coin for me to leave. Too bad I was in a rush."

"Wretched man," he grumbled. "You're too good, and that's not a compliment. Always taking on the problems of others. Always weighing down the grave of a man long cold."

"A person's only worth as much as his promise," I recited Pa's words like the prayer they'd been all my childhood. "I disappointed John in life, but I won't fail him in death."

Five winters ago, I'd sworn an oath inside the Tarwood Chapel, promising John the obedience of a woman, the fruitfulness of a mother, and the dutifulness of a wife.

Three promises given.

Two promises broken.

The third, I'd keep.

Pa tilted his head and frowned at me before he let his steps *splish-splash* over the flooding ground. "As stubborn as your mother."

We rounded the western corner where the bathhouse stood whitewashed and proud. Beside the building, two of the Fletcher boys squatted at the edge of the groanpit—nothing but a deep hole in the ground, reinforced by palisades lining the dirt edges.

Boar spear in hand, Gregory, the oldest, reached out and poked a corpse's head.

The dead man groaned.

The deep vibration, the desperation, the agony in its undertone—like a whooping cough rattling through a throat lined with weeping pox—put a sour tang in my gums. The corpse dragged fingers worn down to the knuckles over the sleek wood, which kept him from climbing.

Gregory thrust the spear into the man's belly. The wings carved a large enough hole that purple guts poured out, ripping a violent hiss from the dead man. Corpses usually didn't bother us unless provoked... but then they might maul you to pieces.

A nearby priest cut the boy a glare. "Do not disturb the dead."

"Nothing but a stranger," Gregory said with a shrug. "Never seen the man's face around here. I'm not poking anything that keeps him from wandering once you open the pit. If anything, the dead disturb *us*."

"And they will until we destroy this devil." The priest turned toward the village square, the hem of his black robes swaying about his naked feet as he let his voice shatter through the busy night. "Hear me! Your loved ones shall find no rest until the good people of this realm have helped us capture the King of Flesh and Bone!"

"Grandma said nobody can enter his kingdom, so it's not like we can drag him out," Gregory said, which earned him a few nods from idle bystanders and those preparing to open the pit's gate. "Met a trapper once who works around the Blighted Fields. Said he saw dead beasts go through the Æfen Gate, but never a man, dead or not."

"Pray to Helfa," the priest said, stretching his arms to the sky. "Pray that we will capture him soon."

I scoffed, hooked my arm into Pa's, and led him up the path toward the house. "As if the priests and temples haven't tried for... for what? The last hundred years?"

"Longer." Pa shuffled up the hill, the daub on the walls

of our home weatherworn. "The question is, what do you do with a creature of such power?"

I crossed the garden in the direction of the stable beside the house. "Someone once told me he's been captured before and contained with fire. Said there was a book—"

"Shh..." Pa glanced over his shoulder. "Don't speak of books this close to the priests. You know how they get with ungodly writings about this devil—"

Bang.

The entire stable shook at the violent kick of iron against wooden boards. Panicked snorts followed, letting my heart match each beat as it all repeated with aggressive fervor.

Bang. Snort. Bang-bang. Snort.

Another kick.

Wood splintered.

My heart clanked against my throat as a hoof shot through a wooden board. Was there no end to this miserable day? I ran toward the stable, cursing the damn mule—that animal couldn't have chosen a worse day to die.

Pa hurried up behind me. "That damned animal. You should've sold him to the butcher, like I said, when the beast refused to get up last week. He'll tear the entire stable down."

Should have, could have, would have...

None of it kept John in the ground.

I turned toward the cart. "I'll get ropes so we can hobble him."

"The beast will head toward the Blighted Fields the moment you open the stall."

"Serves me fine since the cemetery lies that way," I said and grabbed a set of ropes. "At least the stubborn thing will go in the direction I want him to for once. He can rest his bones with the King all he wants, but not before the cart stands on the grave."

I returned to the stable, stealing nervous glances through the gaps in the wood. "Stand aside."

The latch quivered in my clasp with each kick and trembled with each whinnied squeal that ended on the distorted *haw* of the mule. Old Augustine had been stubborn in life, and chances were, he wasn't any better in death.

"Easy now." Slow steps carried me to his stall, hands working one end of the rough rope into a catch noose. "You pull that cart for me one more time, and then when they release the corpses, I'll lead you to the village gate myself."

He flared his nostrils and pawed at the ground, eyes wide with panic, pupils staring at the open stable door with purpose. His leather harness hung crooked. A strap dangled loose where it must have caught on something before it had ripped.

I swung the rope over the beast's neck and lowered the noose to the ground where hooves trampled. "It's too dark, Pa. Open the door wider."

More moonlight filtered in.

Augustine's deafening squeal ran gooseflesh across my skin. When the damn thing finally stepped into the noose, I pulled hard and fast, tightening the rope around its pastern. I swung the rope to the other side and prepared a second noose. The mule stepped into that one fairly quickly. Hobbled like this, Augustine kicked with more fervor, and the stable moaned its age beneath the force.

"I'll bring him out now." I tied the rest of the rope around the mule's neck before I climbed the wooden partition and tied the end to the harness.

Pa's voice filtered in. "You'll get yourself killed."

Reins in hand, I led a hobbled Augustine out of the

stable, the beast hopping beside me toward the cart. "I won't let John escape just so some Fletcher brat in another village can carve him to pieces."

Pa hurried away, tugging on the shafts a moment later. "I'll turn the cart."

Augustine reared, the breath coming from his nostrils already so cold it no longer billowed. The reins burned inside the tight grip of my fist. I wouldn't let go.

"Hardheaded bastard." I righted the harness before I led the mule to the cart. "Come on now!"

Augustine's demeanor grew frenzied, whinnies taking on the wheezing qualities of the corpses in the pit.

He reared once more.

A hind leg slipped.

Augustine staggered.

Leather ripped with a *crrk-shk*, slapping my cheek like a whiplash. I stumbled back, my shoulder crashing against the mule's unforgiving rump. Heels sunk into the mud before I slipped.

The ground pulled out from underneath.

Thud!

Pain spread through my skull.

Darkness crept into my vision

Something tugged on my ankle.

"Help! Catch the mule before the beast drags her to death!" Pa's voice hollered around me, but it soon faded into the *clip-clop* of shod hooves.

That, and the incessant cries of a babe.

CHAPTER 2
ADA

Damp fabric clung to my skin.
Thud.
Something knobby prodded my spine.
Thud.
Pain ate away at me, inside and out.
Thud.
What had happened?

I blinked my burning eyes open, staring at a dark lavender sky. Was it... almost morning? God's bones, where was I? Another *thud* around my shoulder and my head tilted to one side, pupils catching on tattered clothes, gaping wounds, black-veined skin—

A scream formed at the back of my throat, but it lodged between raw muscles. Shocked into silence, I stared at the corpses lining my left and right.

They stared right back at me.

A young man missing a hand.

Thief.

A boy with blisters on his skin.

Pox.

Both stared, but not the soldier beside them, his breastplate edged with rust, his eyes pecked into a set of black, gaping holes. Perhaps by the crow sitting on what remained of his shoulder, arm dangling on little more than skin long dried around the shredded edges.

Something cracked beneath the weight of my shifting body. Twigs?

Muscles strained, aching, I glanced back over my shoulder, fighting against the darkness blurring the edges of my vision. A trail of mud and misery lay behind me, paved with crushed corpses poking from the ground where they didn't pile in heaps as tall as five men to each side.

My breath stalled.

Many heaps.

In fact, I'd only ever heard of one such place.

I lifted my head, glancing toward the slosh of hooves sinking into the mud before each one lifted with a wet *pop*. Hobbles gone, Augustine trudged along the parting crowd of corpses. He walked over those too dismembered to move, trampling them into the ground with blood-curdling cracks.

I was dragged over what was left.

Devil be damned, I had to free myself.

I reached for the piece of leather wrapped around my ankle. A little more... Almost...

Pain seized my muscles.

My head hit the ground and blood seasoned my tongue.

From the corner of my left eye, a gray structure rose above me, casting a cold shadow over my shivering body. The damn mule had dragged me to the Blighted Fields, but I couldn't pass the Æfen Gate into the Graying Tower. No human could enter—

Sloshing stomps turned to echoing *clip-clops*.

Sudden cold paralyzed my muscles. It accompanied me along a passage into darkness and crept into my veins as panic flooded my head. *I shouldn't be here.* Felt it in the marrow of my bones that I was in the wrong place.

The whistling of wind followed us for long moments but faded away the deeper we ventured. In its place, a violent *crshh* echoed from the surrounding stone.

"Wine. Always... wine." The voice was a low rumble, followed by another *crshh*, like shattering plates. "Did they all run out of mead? Wasn't there a single ale to be had?"

"If mead's what ye want, ye have to keep the rot from me body long enough so I can go another day past the nearest village. As if I dinnae have enough trouble already finding enough wine for ye muddled head."

The deep voice growled, "Mind your tongue, Orlaigh."

A final *clop* and Augustine stopped.

His swishing tail blocked most of my view, though I could make out white steps where pieces of clay jugs lay scattered. Wine dripped from them, red puddles on the pale alabaster surrounding it all.

"Ach, they worked ye poor animal to death, dinnae they?" Black boots appeared between my mule's four sturdy legs, and Orlaigh's voice came softer. "Dinnea bother taking the harness off, huh? What a fine animal ye are, bringing weary bones to rest with yer master."

Bones to rest with their master...?

A violent tremble grabbed my body, lungs heaving against the mounting desperation rattling through them. Was I truly inside the Graying Tower? No. This had to be a bad dream. A dream. Yes, only a dream. Just a dr—

The harness jiggled, sending such a stabbing pain into my ankle that I sucked in a sharp breath...

...and choked on it.

A gargle played around my ribs, expanded, swelled until my chest hardened against relentless pressure. Something warm and thick clogged my throat, bubbling underneath coughs until, turning my head, it all dislodged at once. It coated my gums, filled the gaps of my teeth, and dribbled down my chin like cod-liver oil as I heaved it all out.

Blood.

Too warm to be a dream.

Clop. Clop.

Footsteps.

"Ah dhia!" Orlaigh swung both hands to her chest, her pale features streaked with the same thin black veins that feathered across the white of her eyes.

A *talking* corpse?

But... how?

Gray braids shifted as she turned her head toward the stairs. "Ye best come see this."

The man sighed. "Does the mule carry mead?"

"Nay."

"Ale?"

Orlaigh shook her head, hands slipping down until they rested upon wide hips draped in a simple, green-checkered cotton dress. "It's a young lass."

Pottery crunched beneath slow steps, but the grind of soles upon clay soon made room for the rushing of blood in my ears. My heart ached with incessant pounding, but only until a man stepped around the mule... then my heart stopped.

No, it couldn't be...

Cold, colorless eyes locked with mine, set in a face with a straight nose and firm jaw, all framed by long black hair. It brushed over a white, untied shirt, barely hiding his well-thewed chest, hem shoved into black breeches.

No rich embroidery.

No gold chains.

No embellishments.

Nothing gave him away as more than a man—a wicked creature not of this world—yet I recognized him as who he was. Not from his proud posture, the arrogance on his arched brow, or even the liberties his eyes took as they roamed over me. No, what gave him away as the King of Flesh and Bone was the very air around him, like a chill coming off him in ripples and waves. That, and the twisted curl of disgust tugging on his upper lip.

He tilted his head, hands clenched into fists by his sides. "How did this mortal enter my court?"

Orlaigh scratched Augustine's rump and gave a one-sided shrug. "Kin tied the lass to the mule."

The King's gaze wandered to the leather straps which dug into my skin before his eyes snapped back to mine. "Is this a new trickery? You dare come to this court uninvited? Unwanted?"

My lips parted, mute, each apology drowning in the back of a throat already pooling with blood again. Specks of light and dark flickered around my vision. I needed to wake up.

Wake up. Wake up. Wake—

"Speak!" The King's shout shattered from the walls before it battered my bones. "You look at me from eyes still burning with a soul, and I demand this answer while you still have your wits about you." He walked up beside me, the tip of his boot brushing against my waist as he squatted down. "Is this a new trickery of your wicked kind? Tell me now, and I might show mercy by taking you outside before I snap your neck. Or remain silent and learn the damnation of eternal fealty."

"Now, now," Orlaigh mumbled, all straightness gone from her spine, "let the lass speak—"

The King silenced her with little more than his hand rising toward her face, eyes still fixed on me. "Shut your mouth before I sew your lips together and let you choke on your own tongue. The one I want silent won't stop pestering me, and the one I demand answers from won't speak." Sinking to his knees, he lowered his lips to my ear, his voice a whisper. "Listen to my words, mortal. You better answer before I find you employment at the Pale Court. If you believe wandering the Earth for all eternity is a dark fate, then let me assure you that serving me is the greater punishment for the wicked crimes of man. Ought I to refuse entry even to the beasts now?"

I swallowed past a lump of blood and fear. "F-forg... ough—"

A violent cough cut through my effort, crimson droplets speckling the King's loose shirt, the skin of the broad chest behind loose bindings, and even half his cheek.

Orlaigh shook her head, thick brows wrinkled, and a hint of pity hushed over her face. "Lass is drowning in her own blood."

The King reached for his face, wiping the blood off before he stared at his red-streaked fingers. Fingers he extended toward me, hesitantly, his lips now parted.

He cupped my cheek.

Skin connected with skin.

I flinched at the unexpected warmth.

So did the King.

He pulled his hand back as if I'd burned him, pushing himself up to stand, and stumbling back a step all at once. "So... warm."

He stared at me from those unnerving eyes, irises the

color of autumn clouds foreboding a storm. "Who sent you? Some mortal king? They no longer tie their harlots to the trees to lure me out, but now strap them to beasts?"

"Ye won't get answers from a lass half-dead," Orlaigh said. "From the looks of it, she hit every skull and was dragged over every sharp bone on the way in. Foot's twisted. Dinnae look like a trap to me."

The King stepped toward Augustine. "The looks of mankind are deceiving."

He grabbed the twisted leather strap tied around my ankle and pulled. With little effort, the strap broke and my leg hit the hard alabaster. Pain pricked my skin, seared my flesh, twisted around my body like ropes. I screamed loud enough that even the mule danced once more until the sound drowned.

"No mortal will die and find rest in my kingdom." The King's command resonated a chamber void of life, stripped bare to the white paneling on the crooked walls, the distorted ceiling, the very ground on which he stood. "Drag her outside and toss her onto one of the piles of corpses..."

His voice faded along with everything around me. Darkness invaded once more, and with it, another voice—a strange one, like the comforting embrace of a loved one, luring me toward where darkness paled into a path of the brightest light.

"Come to me," the voice beckoned. *"Let me take your breath."*

Limbs stiff, unmoving, I stepped toward the light. Brightness encapsulated all my being, chasing away the pain, the suffering, the—

"I forbid you to go to him!" the King snarled and a heavy weight settled onto my chest. "I'd rather mend your flesh and keep you alive than have you die and make me an oath breaker."

Pain returned twofold, choking me, ripping me away from the light. Lungs burning, legs kicking, back arching... I fought against death until, with a long, deep inhale, I filled my chest with the cold air of the chamber. It seared down my throat, through ribs, burning deep into a cavity now fully expanding. The tang of blood vanished from my mouth and the pain dulled into little more than faint throbbing.

My eyes fluttered shut.

"Orlaigh, leave through the Nocten Gate," the King said. "Buy food from the nearest settlement, and whatever else her... mortal needs require."

My body shifted, heavy limbs tugging on sore joints as they flapped about. Warmth pressed against my belly. Something was wrong with the scent wafting around my nose, like ash sprinkled over a layer of fresh snow.

"Your heart will beat for eternity, and no age shall befall your warm body while in my service, little mortal." The King's dark whisper hushed against my sweat-pearled temple. "Welcome to the Pale Court."

CHAPTER 3
ADA

D arkness hummed a melody, followed by a voice like teeth scraping over rock. *"Flesh and scar and skin and bone, feed her body to the throne."*

A shiver ripped me from sleep.

Above me, white, porous stone shaped like intertwined roots snaked around the arched ceiling, yellowed in some spots while others carried dark patches of moss. Rosemary and meat scented the air—so out of place in this naked room holding little more than my bed and a tub.

Orlaigh glanced down at me, her irises a pale green. "The living used to say ye slept like the dead."

With most of the pain gone, I propped myself up, the gray furs draped over my naked body shifting with the motion. "How long was I out?"

She shrugged and turned toward an outcropping of stone lined with jars, bowls, and flasks. "From the moment ye closed yer eyes to the moment they opened."

And how long was that? Dozens of questions tangled my brain. Did John break through the coffin and crawl out of the dirt? Limp toward the tower and collapse somewhere between there and here for some stranger to find and toss into a pit? What were the chances that Pa finished what I'd started, and—

Pa! He had to be sick with worry.

I glanced at where Orlaigh rummaged through pottery. "Hours? Days?"

"The dead dinnae care about time," she said. "A moment. A day. Forever. It's all the same for us. Pray, in time, it'll be all the same for ye."

The shiver returned, skin pebbling against a room so cold my breath rose in billows. "I have to get back home."

The blue-and-green-checkered skirt of Orlaigh's dress flowed with the motion as she turned back, a small jug clasped between hands, and sat beside me. "Stew's gone cold, but the bread's fresh. First, have a good swallow of this."

Smooth pottery pressed against my chapped lips, and cool water sloshed against my puckered gums before it gulped down a narrow throat. The water hit my stomach like a boulder, but I emptied it all.

"Yer stench is rotten, and that means something coming from a corpse." When she caught me staring at her, she lifted a bushy brow. "Wary around corpses?"

Only if they suddenly asked questions. "How come you move? Talk?"

"The Master had me soul bound to me body." A hint of dismay lingered in the undertone of her voice. "My thoughts are me own, but me body moves freely only if he wills it. Ach, he chases me poor bones across court as lordly as any man. Fifty-two years cleaning up after little lords and ladies; all of eternity cleaning up after him."

A cramp squeezed my stomach just thinking about the King. "Is it true what some say about him?"

"They say many things in many places."

"He's hundreds of years old?"

A low grunt resonated from her chest. "Older."

"He doesn't look a hair past thirty." A man in his prime, the memory of how easily he'd lifted me still fresh in my memory, no matter how fogged. "Where does he come from? Why did he curse our lands?"

"Never speak of it, lass." The woman placed the empty jar on the ledge before she pulled back layers of furs, exposing me to the biting chill of the room. "Cleaned ye up as well as I could, but what ye need is a good washin', lass. Up with ye!"

"It's as cold as winter. Is there no—"

"No fire. Never fire." The short, plump woman offered her hand, her skin void of those black veins she'd had when I'd arrived. "Dinnae bring it up with the Master or you'll put him in a foul mood that'll last for decades."

Interesting.

I breathed against the tension in my muscles, fighting the urge to run. King or not, I had no interest in serving him —least of all for eternity. But running with no notion about where I was or how I could get back home...?

A fool's errand.

I took Orlaigh's hand and rose, using my other to cover myself in a poor attempt at modesty. "What is this room?"

"Master's made it just for ye."

"Made? Whatever does that mean?"

Orlaigh waved her hand toward the alabaster vessel standing across. "Go on! Climb in."

My naked soles slapped over to a tub not made of wood

like in the bathhouse back home, but the same material as everything else in this room, this kingdom. Shaky fingers brushed along the elegantly rounded edge, smooth against my skin, save for the occasional chaffing of pin-sized holes.

Steam billowed on the surface of the water when I dipped my toe into the tub, and I immediately pulled back. "It's gone cold."

Orlaigh dived a hand into the water. "Feels warm enough to me, but I reckon a cold body is a poor judge." She turned toward a set of white carved doors at the end of the scarce room. "Best we call me Master—"

I gripped the edge of the tub once more and climbed in. "I'd rather freeze than face him." Taking a deep breath, I let myself sink to the bottom, arm draped over my breasts. "If you hand me soap, I'll wash."

Orlaigh retrieved a white bar of curd soap from the ledge but returned with a shake of her head. "Yer back's covered in barely closed wounds. They'll fester, awright. Mending flesh takes me Master great effort. Now dunk yer head and wet yer hair."

I did as I was told and let myself slip along the tub until my head submerged, fingers tousling through the tattered nest of hair. The moment I sat up, shivering, Orlaigh rubbed the bar over my scalp.

"What was the white room where you found me?" If I made it there, I might make it out. "My mule dragged me through an arch and down a dark passage."

"The throne room."

"Is it, um... is it far from here?" When Orlaigh's movements slowed, I added, "If you take me there, I'd like to thank your master for healing my wounds."

"Hear me, lass, there's no outrunning me Master. Not forever." The woman's freezing hand sent a chill through me as she tugged my shoulder to lean me back against the edge. "Corridor's cramped with corpses."

So was Hemdale. "I've known corpses all my life."

"Not this kind. They'll drag ye back to him each time ye try to run. Did ye reckon I never tried?"

There had to be a way... "How long have you been here?"

"Decades. Centuries. It's all—"

"The same to you," I said, my shoulders slouching as hope wanted to fade away.

Orlaigh's pat against my head told me there might be an ally in the woman or, at the very least, a friend. Would she help me? Perhaps distract the corpses so I could escape the King's punishment?

Harlot.

The word still echoed.

Would he employ me as such? If he looked like a man, did he have a man's needs?

My chest tightened at the premise.

John had once threatened to sell me to the whorehouse—as was his right as a husband when a wife proved barren. I'd slapped him in the face. He'd slapped me back harder, twice, but he'd never threatened it again. I'd avoided this fate then, and I wouldn't accept it now.

Not without a fight.

I scratched a nail over the material of the tub, pearls of water running down the digit, collecting in the notch forming there. Not stone. Who built all this if his throne room had been such an empty—

"She woke." The King's voice snapped my spine straight, amplified with each slow *thud* of a boot as he approached. "Leave us."

Behind me, Orlaigh turned unnaturally still, even for a corpse. "But—"

"Now."

The weight of the woman's hand on my shoulder turned heavier, colder, and in no way comforting. Worse was how it disappeared as she rose and walked off. "As me Master commands..."

Even after her footfalls faded behind doors long shut, the King didn't move, didn't speak—and neither did I. My heart did the talking for me, each beat sending a vibration whispering over the surface of the otherwise still water.

His long exhale cooled the surrounding air further, but his sharp command froze the blood in my veins. "Stand."

Breathing as shallow as I could to hide my fear, I rose to the deafening drips of water. Arm hugging my breasts tighter, I lowered my other hand to cover my crotch.

"I never meant to set foot into your ki-ingdom." My chattering teeth bit down on the words. "But thank you for mending my f-fl-lesh."

His silence was nothing but an extension of his disdain as the warmth of his body crept against my spine. If he resented us mortals so much, then why keep me? Everyone heard the stories of how lunatics tied virgins to the trees in the Blighted Fields to appease him. Most died strapped to the trunk. Why not ignore me? Send me back? Heavens, why not kill me?

"My court is so... cold." Gentle fingers brushed wet hair over my shoulder before they trailed down my back, making me arch away. "Shh... never evade my touch, mortal, or deny me your warmth."

His touch made heat creep underneath my skin, planting itself in the marrow of my bones, warming me from the inside. "What do you want with me?"

"You tell me. What could I want with the soft skin of a woman, her flesh warm and yielding?"

I shook my head.

"No?" His faint chuckle tingled down along my shoulder blade. "I'm tempted to tell you just how I will use this body, but let's not get ahead of ourselves and start with a simpler question. What's your name, little mortal?"

Mortal.

Was he... undying?

I swallowed hard. "Ada."

"Ada..." His voice emerged as little more than a whisper, almost like a caress to my name. "Your flesh is not untouched. That either makes you a whore or a woman with a husband."

A flare of heat let my chin rise. "My husband died two summers ago."

"Without ever giving you a child?"

A sudden emptiness hit my core. How could he know these things? "Life never blessed me with children."

Punishment for my failings as a woman.

No, not a woman.

An unwoman.

The King's command scraped over the nape of my neck. "Turn around and climb out."

Everything in me tensed.

I hadn't shown my body to any man but John, and only for the first two years of our marriage. "It's not decent."

His fingers wrapped around my throat from behind and his lips moved against my temple as he rasped, "There is no part of you I have not yet seen, sensed, or stirred. Whenever you consider disobeying me, know that I can make you. And nothing, *nothing*, bores me more than to make you."

I braced myself to face him. Life had stripped most of

my pride. Nobody would take the bit that was left, not even him.

I turned...

...and regretted it.

The King radiated hard-edged beauty that made me gasp, his tall physique sculpted into one of virility and strength. Dark lashes crowned gray eyes, something dark flickering in them as they slithered over where I hid my breasts. His roaming gaze left a trail of pebbled skin down my belly, lower, until he lifted his hand—

I sucked in a sharp breath.

His fingers settled on mine, luring my hand from my crotch, holding it up in support as I climbed out. "Who sent you?"

My throat tightened. "Nobody sent me."

"Do you think me a fool?"

I thought him a rude bastard. "My foot tangled in the mule's harness, and the beast dragged me from Hemdale. I swear by Helfa the Allfather—"

He gripped my hair, yanking my face so close to his that I could taste the bite of drink that clung to his breath. "Who?"

"Helfa..." I whispered through trembling lips. "The god we pray to."

"Mortals and their stories." Liquor mingled with the scent of ash and snow as he peeled back his lips enough to bare white teeth. "You betray the god you were given and burn him at the stake, then you conjure up one of your own? If you need to swear, mortal, swear it on me. Swear it by your skin, your sweat, your scars."

I nodded as much as his grip allowed, my scalp searing. "I swear it on all that."

"Mortals swear a great many things, but few prove true." He released his grip on my hair, only to let his fingers comb down along a strand. "Who do you think stands before you, little mortal?"

My chest curled when his thumb trailed along the swell of my breast. "The King of Flesh and Bone."

A loud chuckle burst from his lungs. "Ah... am I a king now? Prove it."

My eyes flicked up to him. "I don't under—"

"Bow before your king, my little mortal. How about a curtsy? Did the mortal kings banish them from their courts, or am I undeserving of such etiquette?"

My veins heated under the scrutiny of his stare as I curtsied for the first time in my life. Naked.

"How lackluster, even for a whore," he said, letting anger needle my skin. "How poor the state of your lands must be if you first run out of ale, then young virgins to lure me."

The sensible part of me urged to stay quiet.

Though my pride silenced it when I slapped his hand away. "I am no whore!"

"Kneel!" His shout softened my knees until they caved and hit the hard ground, not moving an inch, no matter how I pulled, shifted, fought. Why couldn't I move? "Shh, don't struggle against my command. There... calm your heart."

My muscles turned sluggish, as if disabled by some sort of magic, head lolling about as I strained my gaze to meet his. "Let me go."

"And have you tell the rest of your kind how you entered my kingdom?"

"My father's sick... maybe dying."

"Of course he is. As are all mortals." His cruel laugh matched the hard look in his eyes as he squatted to where I knelt like a slave. "For example, I could still carry you outside and snap your neck, but, ah... what a waste of a fine servant it would be. So young and beautiful, tormenting me with need for your warmth."

I frowned.

"Oh, you didn't know? Do not remember how I touched you like this..." He palmed my cheek, his lips taking on a lopsided smirk when I tried to pull away but... couldn't. "Every part of you, my little one, will serve me for eternity, starting with those lush lips. They will wrap around my length while I thrust against the back of your throat. And once you know the taste of my seed by heart, I will make every other orifice mine to play with. To fill and stretch until you quiver with need, begging me to allow you release."

Against the weakness of my muscles, I straightened. "You can do all those things to me, but you'll never hear me beg."

"No?" There was a terrible twitch of his upper lip before his eyes slipped between my legs. "Your hand, mortal. Already touching yourself, your flesh heated by all the promises of how I will use you." When my eyes dropped to where I quickly pulled my hand from my folds, shame gnawed at my core. Worse was how he chuckled, letting his thumb pad over my lower lip in play. "You *will* beg. And if you're a good little mortal, I shall spend my seed with your flesh clenching around me. Now, now, don't cry, Ada. You need yet more time to recover, for my hunger for your warmth is too great."

Was I... crying?

Yes, I was, because he wiped a tear from my cheek and

left. Each step of distance he brought between us returned strength to my muscles, yet I remained on my knees, listening to the quickening pound of my heart. Corpses in the corridors or not, I needed to get out of here.

I'd rather be a fool than his whore.

CHAPTER 4
ADA

I woke with my hands between my legs, three fingers wet to the second knuckle. They stroked at my swollen folds, pushed into my drenched center, and curled inside my channel until—

Mmm!

My lewd moan brought me to my senses, and I pulled my hand from my sex. God's bones, what was wrong with me? Why would I wake soaked like a harlot who'd heard the clank of coins, writhing and bucking against my palm?

Wiping my fingers on a fur, I rose and glanced about the room. I was trapped between four walls, the only source of light a magical glimmer emanating from the all-surrounding alabaster. Was it night? Day? How long had I—

I shuddered.

There was that noise again.

It had lulled me to sleep, the cacophony of never-ending groans resonating from the hallway. Behind those doors, brittle corpses grunted and wheezed, shedding limbs if they as much as bumped into each other. I'd seen it!

If I stepped through there now, they would snap their brown teeth and dig their fingers into the skin of my arms.

I knew.

Because I'd tried.

Twice.

My eyes went to the chemise Orlaigh must have laid out at the end of my bed—washed, starched, the tattered parts neatly stitched together. I slipped into it while my feet returned to the matted trail yesterday's pacing had left on the ground.

Back and forth I crossed the empty room, my gaze flicking to the door once, twice. Just how many corpses had I seen in the hallway? Five? Seven? Devil be damned, pacing would bring me no answers.

No answers, no escape.

Legs stiff underneath me, I stepped toward the doors. Each grunt rattling from behind shook my heart. Each shuffle of feet trembled those fingers I had reached toward the lever handle. How fast did corpses run, anyway?

I pressed the handle down.

A gap creaked open.

"Dinnea even think about running, lass," Orlaigh said with a swat of her hand where she stood at the door, surrounded by two corpses, three, five—

She squeezed in and shut the door.

Curse my poor timing! "Are you going to tattle on me?"

"Nay," she said like the friend I'd thought I might find in her, but what I needed was an ally. "Did ye get enough sleep?"

Enough? Too much?

I sighed, not bothering to ask just how long I'd slept—an hour or a day. "I heard your master say something about another gate. How many are there?"

"Four."

"And they lead where?"

"To the four realms of man, from the snow-tipped mountains behind the Nocten Gate, where I was born, to the rocky steppes behind the Solten Gate, and everything between." From where it hung draped over her arm, Orlaigh clasped a dress between her black-tipped fingers and let it fan out in all its shimmering beauty. "Look what me Master made for ye."

Again this word... *Made*.

I let my hand run over the dress's soft train, its hundreds of leaf-shaped pieces gently tingling against my palm. Almost like an intricate filigree of gold, the finest threads of silk veined together in a hundred shades of brown, forming a layer so thin it looked like paper.

When Orlaigh held it out before me with an encouraging nod, I climbed into the dress. "I've never seen something like this before. It's almost as though someone gathered leaves, rolled them, pressed them, and once dry, sewed them together."

She pursed her lips. "Master wants to see ye."

My breath caught on the boned bodice she strapped tight around my ribs, ends poking into my lungs until they burned with the foreboding flicker of dread.

Dread and determination.

Even if I had to face the King, this was my chance to stake out the Pale Court. Which way lay the Æfen Gate? When did the King take his meals? Where was his chamber, and when did he retreat there?

"Your skin is turning darker." I pointed at the smudges of black running along her nail bed. "What's the discoloration on your fingers?"

"It's rot, lass. The Pale Court wants to rest me body, but me Master makes it go away before we corpses crumble."

Up close, rot was... disgusting.

Even so, voicing it would be rude, so I nodded. "It's how you can go to nearby villages undetected for my food. Helfa knows no villager would trust a corpse who suddenly talks and requests stew."

"Nay, lass. I learned that when they found me out once, chopping me head off. What we fear most is what we don't understand."

Now I felt sorry for her. "The King said no age shall befall my warm body while in his service. What did he mean by that?"

"King of Flesh and Bone," she scoffed, and a soft smile lined her lips as she pulled a pair of silk slippers from the pockets of her dress, letting them fall to the ground with a *thud-thud.* "Aye, he had a good laugh when he came from yer room. See, lass, me Master commands all flesh and bone. Time wrinkles yer skin, and he straightens it."

That took me aback. "So, he controls the dead *and* the living?"

She nodded.

And it had to be true.

Why else had I kneeled at his command?

I slipped into the shoes made of soft leather adorned with white beads. "Why did he bind your soul and keep you as a servant?"

She competently tugged on the train, as if her fingers had once known how such silk had to fall. "Ach, lass, I stole from me Master."

"Stole what?"

Her lips pressed into a dark purple line for a moment.

"Something most precious to him; its loss so great, it drove the man insane."

Sounded about right.

"Some treasure?" The woman said nothing, but I kept pestering her for answers, nonetheless. "Is it the reason he cursed our lands? Made it so the dead won't rot in the ground?"

"It's no curse, lass." She reached up and brushed the tangles from my strands. "Me Master simply no longer leaves the Pale Court to ride about the lands and spread rot."

Ride to spread rot? I'd never heard of that before. But then again, the high priests had burned most books about the King—the stories about him nothing but distorted snippets and fading memories. If Orlaigh spoke the truth and I ran, would the King give chase and bring rot to Hemdale? To John?

One more reason to run.

"It must have been a long time since he left." Chances were he wouldn't even bother chasing me, and now I couldn't tell if that was good or bad. "The corpses outside are falling apart. One grabbed me and a finger fell off."

"They're old, so very old, and keeping the rot from them takes me Master great effort."

Or, in short, if I barraged through them with brute force, I might get away. "How many guard the hallway exactly?"

"Ach, lass, I only tell ye these things because ye will find out on yer own, anyway. Dinnae go making things harder on yerself, plotting yer escape."

"Don't blame me for trying to do something you once did. My father's sick, my husband likely trapped in some groanpit until the next full moon. The miller's wife from the next village over is pregnant with twins and needs care. Even if I fail, at least I can say that I tried."

She stared at me for a long moment, as if gauging my resolve, and something akin to pity came over her grandmotherly features. "Ye won't rest until ye tried, will ye?"

"No."

"Ten." That number hollowed my stomach, but only until she added, "Three come with me to carry water from the hot spring when yer bath needs filling."

I suddenly had the strong urge to wash. So... seven old, brittle, frail corpses while Orlaigh brought water for my bath. Could I get through them?

Only one way to find out.

"Ye're a bonny lass." Orlaigh fussed with my hair a moment longer until she finally smacked her tongue as if pleased with what she saw. "Come, me Master has to wonder what's taking so long."

On brittle legs, I followed the woman along a corridor that seemed to twist in itself. Floor became ceiling, then wall... floor... wall again. How was this possible? A glance over my shoulder and the door to my room shifted, right along with my stomach.

Focus.

Mark the way!

Corpses lined the walls behind us, staring at me, but at least they no longer snapped. I counted exactly ten. Each time we turned corners, I slowed, scratching marks over those edges where the odd stone was graying and more porous.

When we passed a large bridge shrouded in darkness, my steps faltered to a halt. Pillars stood crooked, the stone strewn with holes and dark patches of mildew. It chased a feverish chill up my spine, rising the fine hairs at the nape of my neck.

"What's this?"

"The Soltren Gate," Orlaigh said. "If ye ever run, dinnae go that way. Nothing lies behind it but grief and madness."

This entire kingdom was madness. "Which one is the Æfen Gate?"

After a subdued shake of her head, she jutted her chin toward where the bridge connected to a round platform. "To the left of his throne."

A throne that sat at the center of a low, circular dais, the King slouched with one leg draped over the armrest, the alabaster shaped like a web of tangles. Along the outline of its back, faces tooled into something like driftwood—

My steps faltered.

No, not driftwood.

The heads of two corpses sat in the frame, one to each side, their bodies and limbs almost braided into the throne. I'd seen hundreds of corpses, but none like this, their skin almost like dried leather ready to be peeled off in layers.

Breathe.

Nothing new.

Nothing but corpses.

I continued toward the throne. Our footsteps echoed from the surrounding stone, the massive chamber void of life, even in the loosest of terms. Where was everyone? More servants? Builders? Heavens, a seamstress?

Orlaigh stopped a few feet away from the lowest dais. "I brought the lass, as requested."

White shirt abandoned, dark breeches barely tied in the front, the King balanced a jug on his thigh and said nothing. First stubbles shadowed his face, powerful chest glistening with whatever dripped down his chin whenever he took a swallow.

What a mess this man was...

Orlaigh gripped my shoulder as if holding me back when the woman shifted her balance toward the bridge. "Bloody gomeral. Gone for a moment, and this is how I find the man? Drinking himself to a death he cannot die?"

Which would make him immortal. "Should I approach?"

"Nay, lass, back to yer chamber with ye. The Master's spiteful when he's sober, but he's terrible with his mind poisoned by drink."

I nodded, throat tying up as we backed away, eyes flitting about the chamber. Four bridges spanned a circle into black depths. Four corridors loomed between them. The bridge to the left of the throne was my way out of this nightmare. If I escaped the corpses somehow, I could follow the notches on the walls and—

"My little mortal." Deep, predatory, the King's voice cut through my next step, letting my foot stall mid-air. "Let's see how long it'll take you this time to kneel before your king."

CHAPTER 5
ADA

My pulse went wild.

"You may leave us, Orlaigh." The King dismissed her with a swat before he gestured me closer. "Approach."

My feet stumbled into motion...

...in the wrong direction.

They turned me around to face him, each step up the dais shrinking away the distance between us, no matter how hard I braced and fought. By Helfa, I wanted to be nowhere near him, yet I inched close. Closer. Closer yet.

An invisible force lifted my arm in time with the King's. Fingers connected, and he rose to guide me to his throne. When he slumped back down, he wrapped his arm around my middle. One pull, and he bodily hoisted me against him.

Shifting onto his lap like a doxy, I sensed the hard line of his shaft pressing against my thighs and wiggled. "No!"

"Shh." He brushed his lips over my earlobe where his breath tingled. "Remember, never evade my touch or refuse me your warmth, mortal."

I breathed against the dread in my chest. "I beg of you, let me go home."

"The Pale Court is your home now." The King grabbed the jug on the floor beside him and took a swallow as a corpse limped toward the dais with a new one. "And you, little one, are here for my entertainment. Being immortal can be dreadfully boring without the company of a warm body."

"Please, Your Grace, I have family—"

"Your Grace?" Another of his arrogant chuckles. "You can do better than that, can you not?"

My molars ground together for a moment, but pride would get me nowhere. "Master—"

"On second thought, *Your Grace* suits me, having been demoted to king." He stroked his knuckles over my cheek as something unreadable came over his eyes, like the faintest flicker of concern. "Master is the one thing you shall never call me, Ada."

"The women in my village need me."

"If I release you, more of your dreadful kind will follow." He sneered with such obvious disgust it made my nails dig into my palms. "They'll *bore* me with their demands, their offerings, their... threats."

Bore him?

Sudden fury surged through me. Fury and pain and a picture of John limping along the cobblestone with violets stuck to his unruly brown curls. Of the children turning in their graves. Of that sweet little boy who had pressed his damp head against my chest.

"When was the last time you left this place and saw what you're doing to us?" I choked as much on my words as on the lump forming at the back of my throat, but this much I would say. "The night I came here, a woman in my village gave birth to a child during the full moon, not knowing if it was truly alive or if it would be a stillbirth the next morning. How cruel are you to let a mother cradle and hush a babe already dead? The ones we love wander without rest, and our grief lasts forever."

"Hardly forever." My skin tightened when his lips trailed along the side of my neck. "It lasts until—blessed with mortality—it dies away with the last beat of your heart."

Cruel bastard. "Do you care nothing about our suffering?"

A pout on his lips. "No."

"Eee-nosh..."

My heart clanked against my throat.

That voice...

Laced with misery, it drove a shiver up my spine. From there, it spread along my limbs, faster when something shifted in my periphery. My eyes snapped to one of the faces protruding from the stone, its gray lips parting so slowly, sending a wave of bile up my throat.

Helfa, no!

The corpse's veiled gaze shifted to meet mine where he was embedded into the throne, hard features giving him away as a man, his voice as tortured as his body that snaked around the King's back. "Enooosh."

Enosh.

Not a grunt.

Not a wheeze.

A word.

"You're a monster." Disgusted by his brutality, I squirmed on his lap, trying to get away from this evil creature. "You had their souls bound like Orlaigh's, didn't you?"

"Now, now, stop struggling." My muscles slackened at

his command, dulled by this demon's spell. "There, that's a good mortal, all pliable in my hands. You want this as much as I do."

"I'll never want this." The scratch on my tone exposed too much fear, amplified by how I arched away from him. "Let go of me!"

"Mmm, so much fight in this mind where every fiber of your body has been starved for my attention. How long has it been since a man touched you like this?" A single finger ran down the train of my dress, only for his hand to clasp around my calf. "Did my new plaything get herself wet? When you touched yourself..." His hand brushed up along the inside of my thigh, leaving a trail of searing heat on my skin, then cupped where I grew needy and damp. "Here?"

My cheeks warmed at the humiliation. "Was it you?"

"Who else would inspire such a wanton act in his little mortal? Oh, how you dipped into your warm center, palmed your swollen sex, ground against your hand in search of relief but... ah, your king never granted it." The tip of his nose brushed over my temple with a deep inhale. "Mmm, and I sensed it all. Your hunger for my swollen cock laying claim to the back of your throat, your warm sheath, your tight ass that has yet to be subjugated to this kind of pleasure. Do you want me to show you?"

The way he circled my clit ripped an unbidden moan from me before I snarled, "You're debauched."

"Says the woman who's dripping with need." He chuckled, a dark sound like heavy chains dragging over hollow wood. "After she touched herself in this... *sinful* way, writhing in search of pleasure only I can give. In need of my length, the thickness that will spread you wide, the hardness of my body against your soft curves. Touch yourself for me."

No. No, I would never—

My hand shoved the silk aside. Betrayed by my body, I stroked between my legs with rhythmic movements that set my womb ablaze. I rolled my hips against the touch, sought it out like...

Like a whore.

That word pounded a flicker of wit back to life. I might have been many things—a scorned woman, a barren widow, a fool for thinking I'd had a plan here—but a whore... I was not and would never be!

I shoved my other palm against his chest, liquid rage tingling my fingers as I fought to lift them away from my folds. "You're the devil, just like they—"

"Ah, ah, ah! Your king didn't grant you permission to stop." Those colorless eyes regarded me with calculated coldness as my shaky hand dove back between my legs, swirling around my drenched hole until the blood in my veins thickened with lust that shouldn't have been there. "There, that's a good little... No, don't press your thighs together. Let me see how you play with what's mine. Mine to agonize with need; mine to torment with pleasure."

Pleasure set my body aflame with each corrupted thrust I bucked my hips against, no matter how my mind reeled, screamed, shouted that I didn't want this. Couldn't possibly enjoy this but, ah... Torturous heat slammed into me with such force, I arched my back, resonating the chamber with lewd sounds I barely recognized as my own. What was wrong with me?

"Yes..." The King thrust upward, grinding his hard length against my arse as he cupped my breast. "So long since I'd had a warm quim tighten around my cock and milk the seed from me. Do you deserve that, little one? My flesh pounding into yours until you come apart on my length? Hmm?"

No matter how I pressed my lips together, a moan forced them apart, followed by a mewled, "Yes."

"Have you been a good little mortal?"

"Yes," I cried like a madwoman.

"Are you sure?" *Crrk* made the silk, exposing my breast to the chill of the chamber before he roughly kneaded the flesh to aching, making my clit tingle with the onset of release. "You didn't try to escape me? Didn't mark my walls with notches?"

Smack.

My hand slapped against my sex, hard, shutting down my release so completely that my entire body shook with... with what? Disappointment? Had I gone insane? Even if he stirred my hands, how could I possibly want this?

"Mmm... you can't imagine, little mortal, how I ache to plunge into your warm flesh. To have you again and again until we're both so consumed with need, we will redefine the meaning of eternity." He took my hand and led my fingers to his mouth, groaning as he suckled the wet lust from each one with agonizing patience, letting his teeth scrape along my skin. "But you displeased me so, marking your way to a freedom you shall never have. Go now! Hurry back to your chamber before I come up with a punishment."

No. No punishment!

I quickly slipped off his lap.

"A change of heart." He grabbed my hand and spun me around. "Down on your knees." My knees hit the ground before he spoke the last word. "That's a good girl."

My eyes burned with anger as I looked up at him. "I refuse to be your whore, you bastard."

"With that insolent mouth of yours, you'd make a poor whore indeed." He sunk deeper into his throne and gave a suggestive thrust of his hips. "Undo my breeches and take my cock out."

I watched my eager fingers tug on the black straps, lust spiraling through me no matter how my mind reeled at the sight of flesh swelling beneath. Palms glided over soft, unscarred skin. They worked the leather down, revealing his thick length, even though he was only half aroused.

"Grip me tightly. Ah! Yes, like that, little one." Fed by thick, blueish veins, his shaft jerked inches away from my mouth. "Mmm... look how you're licking your lips."

My tongue strained to taste him, no matter how my thoughts revolted. My fingers wrapped around his girth, lust and loathing fighting at my core.

He clasped my chin, bringing my lips closer to his swollen flesh. "Run your tongue from base to crown. *Slowly*." His gray eyes clenched shut as I did, his groan mingling with how I hummed crooked delight. "Mmm, yes... how well this mouth of yours will serve me."

The faintest ember of hatred glowed to life at his words, yet I lapped a translucent bead from the slit of his crown, almost purring at the saltiness prickling my tongue. When his fingers tightened in my hair, guiding my head to take more of him, I did. My lips strained around his girth, tongue twirling around the wide flare of his crown. Each time traces of seed coated my tongue, my clit throbbed with need, almost like an echo to how his legs trembled the closer he came to release.

"Open. Let me fuck the back of your throat." Cupping my cheek, thumb stroking the corner of my lips, he thrust his cock into my mouth, filling it with his thick flesh while the muscles on his abdomen quivered. "Mmm... your mouth is skilled. Ah, Ada, bring my seed forth and you shall have a taste of me."

Strokes quickening, his moans shattered from the surrounding stone as he plundered my mouth until, with a raw shout, his hips first stalled, then jerked. Fingers tight in my hair, he held me still, releasing warm ropes of seed which splashed against my gums before they trickled down my throat.

"Swallow me down, my little one," he rasped. "Yes... ah, such a good girl. Spread it across your gums and learn the taste of my seed."

Swallow it down, I did.

And I hated myself for it.

Hated more how I smiled.

With a tug on my arm, he urged me to my feet. He gripped my waist and picked me up, sitting me back onto his lap, his erection still slightly hard beneath me. And with my mind dulled with this sense of humiliation, I let him.

"Now this... this deserves a reward." The King took the new jug from the dead footman standing idly beside us, took a sip, then reached it toward me. "Wine? No? Ah, where are my manners..." His other hand lifted toward the footman. "Of course, my woman shall have a goblet."

The corpse's skin first turned a speckled green, then blackened before it wrinkled, shrank. A nauseating stench cut through the air but faded a moment later as the flesh writhed and shifted, reducing to nothing but white powder. It dusted the air like a cloud of flour before it, twisting into a funnel, swirled toward the King's hand. There, on his palm, it shaped into a yellowish-white goblet, the stem embossed with motives of vines slinging around skulls.

Acid, rancid and sour, licked at the back of my throat. It swept onto my tongue, making me want to retch as my heart drummed in my ears. My hand reached for the goblet all on its own, nails digging into the material, forming a notch there as the King let wine gulp into it, seasoning the air with its macabre sweetness.

Not alabaster.

Not stone at all.

I'd walked on the dead, slept on them, had bathed surrounded by—

I swung a hand to my mouth, letting saliva pool underneath my tongue. One swallow. Even a drop of it running down my throat, and I would vomit onto the remnants of... people. Mothers, children, grandfathers, compacted into a bed, a tub...

...a goblet.

A goblet he prodded against my lips, demanding I drink from what had been a corpse only moments ago. "I made it just for you."

When he shrugged and sipped from it instead, my gaze fell to my dress, all blood leeching from my veins until my limbs numbed. "And what did you use to *make* my dress?"

Another swallow from the goblet. "Take a guess, mortal."

Skin.

Death covered me from my collarbone to my ankles, safe for where my breast had spilled from a rip in vulgar display. Everything around me spun, and I slipped off his lap, swaying for balance. Out. I needed out of this place.

I staggered down the dais. Blood rushed inside my ears with such force, it drowned out my steps as I hurried to the bridge. Only the King's laugh overwhelmed it. "Ah, yes, follow the notches back to the safety of your cage."

CHAPTER 6
ADA

Warm clothes.
Provisions.
Sturdy shoes.

I put on the slippers the King had *made* for me, perhaps from the hide of a cow, but it might as well have been someone's son. While far from sturdy, they would have to do. I could still pull some boots off a corpse outside, same with a thick coat to hide from the cold. Provisions, however, proved to be an issue.

Until the door opened and Orlaigh stepped into my cage, as the King had called it. "Breakfast, lass."

For once, good timing. "I want to bathe."

With a sigh, she closed the door using one hand while balancing a plate on the other. A plate made of bone—like everything in this crooked kingdom—loaded with slices of bread. It seasoned the air with yeast and the heartiness of butter, the scents strangely familiar in a place this rotten.

One I would escape once and for all.

She lowered it onto my bed, then hooked her hands onto her hips. "Ye dinnae look in need of one to me."

Yet I had never felt filthier in my life. "Where's your master?"

"Attending dead beasts."

Making my chances of escape all the better, no matter how slim it left them. I wouldn't stay in this kingdom built on death, ruled by a mad... whatever he was. In spite of his determination to keep me prisoner, how likely would he chase after me, leaving a place he hadn't stepped out of for over a hundred years? Small.

And if he followed...?

All the better.

He would bring rot to Hemdale—if I made it that far. That alone was worth whatever punishment he would come up with if he caught me. What was the worst he could do? Turn me into a chair? Weave me through his throne? He wanted me alive, that much he'd made clear—corpses presumably made poor whores.

I grabbed a slice of bread, since the walk to Hemdale would take at least a day if I avoided the roads, leaving me no time to beg for food at nearby farms. "Will you bring water for a bath?"

"Ach, lass—"

"Please help me. I'll try to run no matter what, but..." I set my pleading eyes on her, not knowing if I could trust this corpse, but I had no other options. "With your help, I'll stand a better chance."

After endless seconds, she cursed under her breath and walked toward the door. "Very well. If a bath is what ye want, I best hurry for water before it cools down."

I grabbed the bread and pushed it between my breasts for lack of better storage. My stomach hardened when I walked to the door, and not only because of the groans resonating behind the bone. If I told the priests how I'd entered the Pale Court, would they call me mad? Or would they come for the King, finally serving him the justice he deserved?

Three deep breaths bought me a sense of calm no matter how brittle. I reached for the handle, my muscles tensing, readying themselves to fight through seven corpses.

No... not seven.

Six.

One was a cup now.

I pulled the door open wide and jumped back, only to brace my soles against the ground. With a hard thrust of my legs, I let myself slam against the two corpses standing there.

A limb thudded to the ground.

Thud. And another.

Putrid and biting, the stench of what had to be rot crept into my nostrils, making me nauseous, but I wouldn't let that stop me. I elbowed my way through decrepit bodies, ignoring their groans, the snap of their teeth, those rough nails scratching along my arms, neck, calf until—

The corpse in front of me turned his head with such speed, his tongue slapped against his cheek like a dead snake, all because he had no lower jaw. "Ay-gaaah!"

The moment he reached for me, I ducked. One kick against his shin and the bone splintered, frayed edges cutting through his parchment-thin skin. He flailed his arms for balance, but hit the ground a moment later.

I didn't look back. Ignored the tremor in my knees, the blur in my vision, the unsteadiness of legs threatening to snap... and ran.

Straight along the hallway.

Left at the first notch.

Right at the two next.

"Ayyy-gaaah!"

My butchered name resonated the hallway, the agony on the corpses' tone blood-curdling.

Heavy footfalls sounded behind me.

Close. Closer.

My shoes slapped the bone bridge beneath me, eyes nervously flicking to the throne. Empty. My heart matched each beat with panic until...

No!

Sharp pikes of bone shot up from the ground around the dais. I skidded to a halt, the hem of my chemise catching on them, ripping with a *hrrk* as I turned to the next bridge. Was it the one to the Æfen Gate?

No matter.

Out! Just out!

"Going somewhere, my little mortal?" My heart stopped at the chuckle that followed. No, this couldn't be. Where was he? "What entertainment you've turned out to be."

The ground shook, lifting and thickening. I stumbled back and fell. Rolled. Rolled again until the chamber distorted into specks of light and dark.

I crawled, squirmed.

A hand grabbed my ankle.

I glanced back.

No, not a hand.

Gray and brittle, a bracelet of bone anchored me to the ground. I kicked it with the heel of my shoe. Once. Twice. The third kick shattered it, and I pushed myself back into a run, arms flailing for balance as I headed toward the bridge.

Any bridge.

More bone roped around my calves, but the force of my

thrusts shattered them all. To my left, the King strolled toward me, letting a sense of dread spread through my core. Worse was how he suddenly stopped, a cruel twitch coming over his upper lip.

"You'll never leave me, little one," he said as his smirk sobered into a grim line. "Now stop, or I'll have to make you."

He could try. "Never."

Another step.

Crack! Crack!

Pain shot into my legs.

I staggered for an excruciating step, and another, as if on bowlegged stilts someone had set aflame. I fell to the ground, palms sliding over the porous bone, chafing me raw. What had he done? I looked at my legs, feeling my lungs deflate and die in my chest. No, I would run nowhere.

Because he had broken my legs.

They gnarled behind the blur of tears covering my eyes, taking on the crooked shape of a dog's hind-legs, even as the pain slowly eased away. It shouldn't. With my legs this badly broken, shouldn't I scream in pain?

"There, there." Strong arms lifted me, pressing me against an even stronger chest. "Look what you made me do, little one. No king should chase his runaway servant, and certainly not into lands he hasn't stepped on for nearly two centuries."

I didn't want it to, but my face fell into the crook of his neck, letting tears run down his collarbone. "You broke my legs."

"Twisted," he corrected, as if it made a difference. He carried me over another bridge and from there, into a dark corridor. "Behave, and I'll straighten them."

"Where are you taking me?"

"To bathe, as my woman requested."

Gray bone turned into what appeared to be actual stone, dark like slate, which opened into some sort of cavern. Traces of mildew clung to the humid air the deeper we ventured until wafts of steam settled damp on my cheeks. They billowed from the surface of what had to be a hot spring, the water gently bubbling against the stone edge that surrounded it.

Beside it stood Orlaigh, her chin pressed to her chest, hands fumbling with the cotton of her dress as she mumbled, "Nothing good would've come of it, lass."

My head ached at my foolishness and a knot formed in my stomach for this betrayal. "So you ratted me out."

"Ach, lass, ye cannae ken—"

"Leave us," the King commanded as he lowered me to the ground, steadying me on my disfigured legs. "What a mess you made of yourself, little one."

I stared behind Orlaigh as she left, if only to keep my eyes from how the King let his breeches thud to the ground. My chemise went next, which he carefully tugged over my head as I swayed on unreliable legs, before he let the fabric pool between us.

Lifting me once more, he wiggled my crooked feet until the shoes slipped off, then he climbed into the water. "You'll never see the outside world again."

Oh, but I would. "Never is a long time."

Heat encapsulated me as he lowered us into the water, the way he gently wet my hair so unlike the beast who'd broken my legs. He let his hand run over my body with no restraint, washing me clean.

"You're mine, Ada." His dark whisper against my ear pebbled my skin. "My servant, my plaything, my woman. I'll never let you go."

No, he wouldn't, but I would escape him at some point. Had to get away from this devil who—

His tongue trailed over the side of my damp neck as his fingertips ventured between my legs. They circled, dipped, seduced until I whimpered with a need that bordered on pain.

A moan left my lips without consent. "Stop."

"Perhaps I was too harsh during our last encounter." His finger curled inside me, pressing against my walls, creating a sense of fullness. "Leaving you unsatisfied... *Tsk, tsk,* how rude of me."

Hands clasped around my waist, he lifted me from the water and sat me on the edge. I clenched my eyes shut when he prodded my knees apart, making me spread wide for him.

I jumped when his thumb circled my clit that throbbed with ungodly need. "I hate you."

"Only until I kiss you... right here." He pinched the little bud, making me squirm, yet I sensed myself arch into the rough touch. "Suckle your juices and fuck you with my tongue until you beg for my cock. Has a mortal man ever given you pleasure like this?"

The question shivered through me, robbing my voice, my breath, so I only shook my head.

"Allow me." He trailed kisses up the inside of my thigh toward my sex. Like velvet, his tongue stroked along over my entrance, higher, higher, until—

"Oh my god!"

His grin-hardened mouth covered my sex as he mumbled, "Quite so."

"Please..."

"I'll please you like no other can." He suckled on my folds before his broad tongue lapped at my center, tip circling my entrance, dipping in, working me to heights I hadn't known before. "Ah, my little mortal, how delicious you are."

"Please..." *Stop.* The word rested on my tongue, creeping toward shivering lips as they parted, but all that came out was, "Mmm!"

When I dug my hands into his raven strands, grabbing it by the fistful like a woman possessed, he groaned and buried his face deeper. He ravaged me so thoroughly, the word 'stop' faded out of existence against the pants and lewd sounds he teased from my lips. Every nerve in my body quaked, and I cried out as if in pain when my walls flexed, spasmed, until—

"Beg." He pulled back, lifted himself out of the water, and pinched my nipple until my peak died away. "Beg for forgiveness, little mortal, and I'll play with you some more."

"I don't want your forgiveness, if this is what it gets me." Anger rode me hard over what he'd done to me—what he *refused* to do—but I wouldn't give him this. "I'd rather have you sard all my holes than take pleasure from the mouth of the devil."

"Ah, why not say so sooner, mortal?" The ground softened and shifted underneath me, and the next moment, he flipped me around until my belly rested on hides. With his arm slung around my hips, he lifted me onto my knees, arse on outrageous display. "Uh-uh, no wiggling away. Remember? Good little mortals get their legs straightened. Given how much effort it takes me to make you kneel, I doubt you want to crawl about court. Do you? No. Now, little one, reach behind and spread your cheeks for me."

My arms reached back on their own accord, even as rage pumped through my veins. Fingers hooked into my cheeks, I spread myself wide, presenting myself like a bitch in heat. Whined like one, too, rolling my hips, arching my back as my womb flooded with lust that wasn't my own.

Couldn't be. Would never.

But it was there now, making me hurt for him to push his length inside me. "What are you doing to me?"

"Oh, little one, have you forgotten who I am? You called me the King of Flesh and Bone." He nudged his crown at my slick entrance as his fingers buried into my waist. "I am the heat between your legs, the throbbing in your cunt, the moan in your throat, the tremble in your bones, and the ache inside your belly, hungering to make me sate it."

I moaned, relishing how he dipped into me ever so slightly, stretching me, only to pull out and let his flesh pound my entrance with wet *smack-smack-smacks* to complete my eager humiliation. "You're the devil."

"On more than one occasion, mankind has called me the devil." He pushed down between my shoulder blades until my arms gave out. "Let me show you pleasure like only the devil can."

A devil who let his crown slip higher.

Too high.

"Pleas— Ah!"

He thrust up into my darkest place, past untrained muscle that wanted to clench against the sudden invasion. A painful one that strangled all air from my lungs, making me dig my fingers into the hide as he forced himself deeper inside me.

"Shh, I need you to be still while I use this hole." He shoved his length inside my arse, making it sting and burn in a million places. "You'll learn to love this, my mortal. Will come apart from pleasure with your ass tight around my cock. Yes, you want that, my little plaything... So good with how you open up for me."

My muscles slackened at his praise.

"Ah!" His masculine groan vibrated deep in my flesh, letting the burn around my hole morph into a warm tingle. "Yes, my woman likes this. Look how nicely you're spreading your cheeks wider, taking me so deep. So good." He stroked into me with quickening thrusts, spreading my hole wide, letting a second pulse pound around my clit. "Mmm, come apart on my cock. Let your ass clench around my length. Yes, like that. I'll leave a nice load of seed deep in your belly."

Gradually, the hunger at my core roared into something ravenous—as did my disgust, mostly for myself. No, I couldn't possibly enjoy the demon's cock up my arse.

Yet I arched my back, bracing the hides each time he pumped into me, his voice ragged around each satisfied sound forming at the back of his throat. Heavens, the need in those hands that gripped me with bruising strength, the unrestrained way he pounded into me, the shifting of the muscles on his stomach when I glanced back—

A tingle crested toward my clit. "No..."

"Yes, little one. Come with my length deep inside you." The faster I shook my head, the faster he fucked me until, pushing to the hilt, he set me ablaze. "Now! Do it! Yes... how nicely you're gripping me. Ah, take my seed, little mortal. Mmm, yes, this needy hole wants it all."

Heat seared through my limbs, blazing along my spine, engulfing me so completely until, with the last fading flickers, it consumed all of me. Charred me to the shame in my bones, the confusion in my mind, and the gleaming embers of rage.

What had I done?

What had he made me do?

"What creature are you?" I asked, my voice strained.

"I am your god." The blasphemous statement didn't register nearly as much as how he pulled out from my arse, letting a trickle of seed run down my leg. "As old as time, born from nothing, I came into existence with one purpose: to rule and rot the flesh and bone of all that lives, so I may cleanse the Earth of its remnants and command over them. Theres's no place, my little one, where you could hide from me. Not forever."

A curse cast by an enraged god.

What if those old tales held more truth than the priests let on? Why else would they have burned the books, eradicating any and all written proof of this god, and let time sweep away the rest?

I struggled a swallow down my throat. "So you're no king."

"What a predicament in terms of proper address." He lay down next to me, pulling me against his chest as if... as if we were lovers. "Considering what just transpired between us, I believe we are beyond formalities. You may call me Enosh."

Like the corpses in the throne. "Enosh? What does it mean?"

"Form. Some may call it appearance." A kiss against my temple. "It is my true name."

CHAPTER 7
ENOSH

"Snap the lass' neck and have yer brother bind her soul." Orlaigh lowered a tray onto a stool beside the bed, filling the room with the sweetest warm apple scent. "Ye're even crueler if ye hold her here forever alive."

I glanced down at the mortal sleeping beside me, muscles soaking up her warmth like a seed after an age of frost. How long since I'd last touched a woman? Nearly two centuries.

"Bound corpses make poor bedmates." Tried it once, didn't care for it. "I much prefer her alive and warm."

"Already the lass sleeps at the first yawn, even if she just woke. Keep her body from decaying as time ought to and ye will slowly drive her insane."

I combed my fingers through Ada's blonde tresses. If my little mortal woke now, she would blink up at me with bright blue eyes. Finger stiff from an old fracture, skin scattered with scars of various sizes, and a heart that beat strong albeit with a concerning irregularity... for a god formed to perfection, her imperfections fascinated me the most.

Safe for her inherent depravity.

She'd tried to run from me.

Remnants of anger surged through my core at the memory. Fingers itched to break her neck with little more than a thought and bind her soul to her body. The dead had little interest in leaving the Pale Court. Even if they wandered, they always returned to their master.

I was Ada's master.

Her body was bound to serve me...

... in death, yes, but who was there to judge?

I shifted closer to her, veins surging with that deep-rooted yearning to rut between her legs until bone shattered around us, setting her ablaze at her core—and myself right along with it—burning so hot together that eternity would lose its dreadful meaning.

That... proved an issue.

The dead obeyed.

The living warmed.

I could not have both.

Such a frail, unpredictable thing this... mortality. Oh, how I envied man for his ability to die. Come to think, hadn't I been created to mirror mankind? Was made of flesh and flaw?

It was only right that Ada now sated the desires of my flesh and suffered the crimes of my flaw—utter possessiveness.

My little mortal had come to me.

And I would keep her.

For eternity.

If it came at the cost of her sanity, then so be it. Nothing the God of Whispers couldn't ease in exchange for me to keep his harem of corpses smelling fresh.

"She shows no fear toward the dead." Not like Njala

had, ever so displeased with the Pale Court, no matter how I'd shaped it to her wishes. "No disgust."

"It's the world ye created with yer absence." Orlaigh glanced back at where I tugged a fur higher over my little one. "She's a bonnie lass. Has her wits about her for the most part. And we both ken she'll run from ye, and I dinnae blame her."

And she might succeed.

Ada had marked the bone from chamber to throne room, had taken detailed assessments of the gates, and had quickly discovered the miserable state of my corpses. Over the span of eternity, opportunities for escape would abound.

The thought alone filled my veins with anguish that clenched my teeth. It coursed through me so rapidly, already her neck offered itself to break. Until she inhaled and a handful of breasts pressed against me, their warmth coercing me into a state of... calmness.

No, I very much wanted her alive.

But how to keep her from running?

The word *promise* echoed, but I quickly banished it from my mind. A mind so stuffed with memories of pacts, vows, and pledges sworn by mortals—most broken within the first decade. What good would it do to offer Ada certain freedoms for her promise to remain by my side, ever so faithful?

Nothing.

Oh yes, my little mortal would pledge her loyalty and love, swear an oath from the sweetest of lips, and then she would break it. She would run from me. Abandon me to eternity, my wicked, wayward mortal.

The past had taught me no different.

"I could keep age from her flesh and break her legs in

three places." An acceptable compromise, buying me ample time to chase her down should she ever escape my kingdom.

Orlaigh shook her head and laid out the dress I'd made for my woman, braided from the softest of hairs. "If ye want the lass to hate ye even more, breaking her other bones is the way to go about it."

Whatever else would I want?

Love?

My breathing hitched at the thought and panic clawed my chest when it no longer expanded with Ada's inhale, robbing me of her warmth. Of all the things existence had cursed me with, my ability to love was the worst torture—second only to my inability to die.

No, the vicious sentiment of mankind was neither needed nor desired, for I would claim all parts of her form, again and again, until we were so consumed with each other that love paled in comparison.

Besides... "Twisted. I merely *twisted* them."

"Ye hurt her."

My muscles tensed. I despised pain, but my woman had left me no choice. That mankind had apparently demoted me from god to king beyond the Æfen Gate didn't bode well, and so, I'd had to make a point.

"She's waking." This close to her, I sensed it so strongly: heart beating slightly faster, ears twitching at the sound of my voice, body temperature rising. "Did you bring enough honeyed milk for the both of us?"

Orlaigh raised a brow. "Ye want... milk?"

I offered her a stare that invited no further remark, thumb stroking over Ada's side to rouse her quicker, no matter how I envied her for this mortal need. "How blessed she is in her ability to sleep away half of eternity."

I took the warm cup Orlaigh handed me before I sent her for more milk, then watched my mortal waken. The way she stretched sinews and muscles sent a tingle through my limbs.

It extinguished when blue eyes narrowed at me with contempt. "Why are you here?"

"I have no reason to be elsewhere," I said. "My kingdom has become so dreadfully dull ever since I denied your dead entry, the bit of effort it takes to rest the beasts is negligible."

She shifted away from me underneath the furs, but no further than my arm hooking around her waist allowed. "Did you sleep beside me all night?"

"My form requires little of it." Sleep only ever came to me in those rare moments of calm and completion, which had last been over two hundred years ago, my mind weary beyond exhaustion. "But I watched you throughout, yes."

I had stroked hard flesh that hadn't known touch in just as long, shaft jerking with the desire to spill my seed deep into her womb. So long since I'd bedded a woman. Still, I understood she required her sleep and so, I hadn't disturbed her.

I allowed my mortal enough freedom to prop herself up onto her elbow before I handed her the cup. "Warm milk with honey. Orlaigh also brought us fried apples, buttered bread, and cured ham."

"Us?" She hesitantly took the cup, sweetening lips that had been so skilled around my cock. "Do I have to eat breakfast with you?"

"Whyever not? Even if my form doesn't require it, I enjoy good food like any mortal." I broke off a piece of bread and held it to her lips. "Eat. We both know you're hungry."

A frightened woman would have refused with an

excuse. A docile woman would have eaten from my fingers with a thank you on her lips. And a naïve woman would have slapped the bread from my fingers with a snarl.

But not Ada.

Snarl, my little mortal did.

But then she reached for the entire platter of bread, draped ham over one slice, loaded the edges with fried apple, and started eating even before she lowered it to her lap.

Too proud to accept food from my fingers.

Too smart to refuse it altogether.

After all, escape required strength.

It didn't displease me as much as it should have; no, it charmed me more than was rational or sane. A dull companion slowed time only further. What an intriguing creature this mortal was. How could this woman hold my gaze with her chin held high, while guilt brittled her bones and shame soured her flesh?

I devoured the piece of bread, moaning at the smoothness of freshly-churned butter coating my gums after such long a time. "How did your husband die?"

Her gaze immediately dropped, going adrift somewhere in the furs. "Climbed the falls over at the Fork of Almach searching for pinweedle moss. The rock was wet and he slipped. A fisherman found him at the bottom of the falls, his body trapped between rocks. Said he drowned, but I think he died the moment he hit the rock. Took a chunk of his head out."

An accident, yet I sensed how guilt infested the marrow in her bones. "You're blaming yourself for his death. Why?"

Her head sunk, along with her voice. "Because I sent him up there."

Neither flesh nor bone were free of failure. Why blame

herself for the slick on the rock, the cutting breeze along the fall, or the misstep of a limb? She did to such a degree that the weight of it cumbered even my shoulders.

"Had you love for your husband?"

"What I had was a roof over my head, food in my belly, and my own garden." She grabbed another slice of bread, eyeing me warily, observing, thinking... scheming. "Even without love, I had it better than most. Only took his belt a dozen or so times."

"And what offenses deemed pain an appropriate punishment?"

She shrugged. "Talked back in front of the townsfolk, mostly."

Yes, she was a mouthy little thing, but I quite liked it. It made for excellent entertainment. "Have you not been quiet and obedient?"

My little one shoved the bread around in her mouth as she spoke, lacking all the graces of nobility, but they'd started to bore me a good while ago, anyway. "I've sometimes been quiet. Now and then, obedient. I've certainly never been both at the same time."

"And did the punishment correct your... defiance? Should I fashion a belt from the next beast coming to the Pale Court? Maybe it'll cure your desire to escape."

"Nothing cured in our home but the salted ham hanging from the rafters."

My chest ached as neglected muscle pushed a faint laugh from my lungs. "So outspoken, your loyalty to a man this rotten confuses me greatly."

"John was a good man."

"So good, he only took a belt to you a dozen times? I despise pain, Ada. But not as much as I despise those who inflict it without mercy."

"Because you have a right to speak of mercy?" Shaking her head, she tossed what was left of her bread onto the platter, the blood in her veins thickening with dismay. "Yes, my husband whipped me, as do all others. But he never kept me under lock and key, never forced himself—"

"Calm your heart."

"—on me, even when he swayed home drunk from port, and he certainly didn't push his length up my... my burning arse..."

Her voice trailed off as I slowed her compromised heart, tampering her anger into the faintest tingle beneath her skin. Ah, my little one hadn't liked it when I took that hole. A little too roughly, too, since she'd torn but, oh, how tight that untried muscle had been around my aching cock.

"You did that." She pressed a hand against her chest, but only until her blazing eyes snapped to mine. "So, it's not enough to take the last bit of pride from me, but now you have to steal my rage?"

"A good little mortal gets my mouth on her cunt." I cupped her cheek, relishing how the weight of her head pressed into my palm because I made it so. "A bad little mortal who runs from me gets my cock up her ass before I pull out and spend my seed all over her face. Or perhaps, welts on her hide after all?"

"Take a belt to me if you have to, but it'll achieve nothing."

Or I might just chain her to my throne. "Will you run from me again?"

Lips trembling, she braved my gaze. "Yes. I'll hide in the back of beyond until my hair's gray."

Her honesty pinched me somewhere. "You should have lied."

"No point in making myself a liar if we both know you won't believe me, anyway."

Eternity already scraped its claws over my mind, the thought of losing her chilling the blood in my veins. Perhaps I needed to break her neck after all? But then she would be cold...

Against my better judgment, I caved to the desperation manifesting in my core. "What will it take to make you stay?"

A swallow dragged down her throat as her brow lifted, undoubtedly judging my sincerity. "Spread rot and let the dead in."

"I won't break my oath to see yours spoken."

And I better remember it.

She tortured her upper lip long enough, I wanted to suck it between mine to make her stop. "Then rot my husband's body."

The bones of a bastard who'd beaten this woman, and even now, who burdened her with the false responsibility of his death? For him, she would give herself away like a fool?

I had only known this mortal for a short while, but I could tell she was no fool. That made her a liar after all, whispering promises from the most tempting of lips, only to ensure her escape. Had I hoped differently for a moment?

"I won't rot your husband's bones, little one." I rolled out of bed. "How can I make my home more comfortable for you? Should I send Orlaigh to gather books? Paints, maybe?"

The mortal's posture stiffened, the innocence in her eyes not matching the deceit in her voice. "Can we leave the Pale Court? If only for an hour so I can... see the sky—"

"The sky."

"—and birds, and trees—"

Did I look so easily fooled? "You'll get books and paints."

And a bone collar.

Yes, that should do.

"The most vibrant blues." I turned and strolled toward the doors, letting the surrounding room dissolve as I refashioned walls into chains. "You want to see the sky, little one? Then paint it onto the ceiling, for you'll never see it again."

CHAPTER 8
ADA

Decorated with hundreds of fangs and the spindly bones of rodents, the bodice of my dress fanned out at the waist, letting an endless amount of white feathers cascade down the dais. When it came to my attire, Enosh spared no effort to make me look like a queen.

Aside from my collar.

That made me look like a prisoner, no matter how he'd tooled the thick ring of bone around my neck with images of birds he promised I would never see again.

Brush in hand, I dipped the fine bristles into a small jar of paint made from green pigment and, based on the nutty smell of it, linseed. Trailing it along the edge of the dais, I added another vine to the motive, winding all the way to—

Clank.

"Devil be damned, I'll never reach the right side with how short he keeps my chain." A tug on the collar to let some air to my skin, then I scooted back until the tense string of bone rings *clonked* to the ground. "Here. Take the brush and finish the vine."

"Ach, lass, me fingers are too rotten to even clasp it well," Orlaigh said, her hands a speckled green whereas her lips had gone a dark purple.

"One would think you deserve for him to freshen you up, given how you tattled on me."

"Stopped ye from trying to run again and get us both into trouble," she mumbled. "I had no other choice, lass."

No, she hadn't.

Orlaigh was nothing but a prisoner of a different kind. Whereas Enosh had chained me to his throne for my attempted escape, Orlaigh's help very well could have earned the old woman to become the collar around my neck.

Or another face on the throne...

I looked up at the corpse woven into the bone. He looked back, his eyes milky-white, yet I sensed his chilling stare on me. As silent as the Pale Court, he observed me but never made a sound.

Probably because Enosh had removed the mouth of both, leaving nothing but the shift of a tongue behind dry, brown skin. Every now and then, he restored the corpses, only to let me watch them rot away again in what had to be eternal agony.

I tossed the brush onto the bed Enosh had made for me, like a roundish nest of bone beside his throne, the inside fluffed with fox pelts and feathers. "Who is he?"

Orlaigh glanced up from where she sat on the dais with a book on her lap. "Lord Tarnem."

"What did he do?"

"Lured me Master into a trap. A valley surrounded by mountains, the ground so frozen, no bone made it to the surface to help him fight off the ambush. They cut down the few corpses he had with him for protection and captured him."

Yet another tale proving to be too true for comfort, scraping away my thinning doubt of Enosh's divinity. "Was fire involved?"

"Ach, lass, the flames could be seen from five towns away. Kept 'em chained to a pillar where they burned me Master for a fortnight." A slow shake of her head. "Terrible thing, death by fire. But death never came for him while he screamed in pain; skin growing back one moment, only to char black again the next."

"I had no idea he could feel pain."

A discovery that should please me or, at the very least, give me a sense of comfort. Instead, my skin broke out in gooseflesh, my mind drifting to the distinct smell that followed Enosh around—like ash sprinkled over snow.

"Gods are not so different from us, lass," she said. "Me Master suffers like any mortal, be it a battered head or a broken heart."

"A broken heart?" That lured a scoff from me. "As if he has one."

Orlaigh looked at me from a tilted head. "Is it so hard to believe that he loves and lusts like any man?"

"Oh, I believe the lust part." Still felt its sting in my backside, too. "It's the love part I cannot comprehend."

She only shrugged.

I jutted my chin toward the other man, who never as much as blinked, his thin strands of brown wisps snaking around the porous bone. "And the other?"

A sneer came over her features, showing off a row of graying teeth. "Commander Joah Mertok."

"What did he do?" When she struggled with the page of her book to make it turn under her unreliable fingers, I leaned over and turned it for her. "Has Enosh always been this cruel?"

"Crueler. For a time. The dead and the living forget, lass, taking their sorrows to the grave." She looked up from her book, letting her black-veined eyes lock with mine. "Gods do not, and rage on."

Dread weighed down my shoulders, and I looked over at the crumbling bridge. What had happened to Enosh that made him abandon his duty, sequestering himself in this empty, dull place? On more than one occasion, he'd called us mortals wicked. Aside from feeding him to the fire for weeks, what other cruelties had he endured?

Should I care?

As if my thoughts had conjured him, the man strolled over a bridge and walked up the dais, once more dressed in black breeches and a white shirt. With a gesture of his hand, he dismissed Orlaigh and lowered himself onto his throne.

"Come to me." Two taps against his thigh as if I was his dog. "Kneel before your god."

"You lack a great deal of divinity for a god and do a poor job at fulfilling your duty."

He smiled as if my snarky remarks amused him.

Then he let a wave of weakness gnaw on my knees until they caved in. A death weight followed, pushing against my shoulders until my palms hit the bone.

He made me crawl to him, feathers catching on the edge of the dais until some ripped off, wafting around me like snow as teeth and bones clanked on my bodice. "I'm not an animal."

"No, animals get scraps, whereas I make certain you receive the best meals from beyond the gates, the softest pelts for your bed, the best paints gold can buy. You've been pulling on your collar again." Hooking a finger under my chin, he guided my head to rest on his lap and gently stroked the sore skin beneath the bone ring. "I'm afraid in regard to your chain, I had to choose thickness over length."

"Because you don't have enough bone to maintain the Pale Court." The reason why I'd been able to break his shackles and one bridge had holes the size of a wolf. "Your kingdom is falling apart around you. Why? Because Lord Tarnem burned you at the stake?"

"He also disemboweled me... twice." His fingers combed through my hair like he often did, a digit slowly tracing along the shell of my ear. "My little treasure is tired."

"I'm always tired." My senses dulled from hours of doing nothing but pace and paint. "Is it night? Day? Nobody ever sleeps. It's... confusing."

As if I were a little child in need of a nap, he plucked me from the ground and cradled me to his chest, my bone chain clanking against his throne. "Paints. An entire kingdom as your canvas. The finest dresses I can create. Berries with nearly every meal. What else does my woman need to be content?"

"You're making me sound like a spoiled brat, not a prisoner."

"A spoiled prisoner, then," he said, as if a cage wasn't a cage, no matter how pretty. "More books, perhaps?"

"I can't read."

His eyes went to the stack of leather-bound books beside my bed, jaws clenching as if he scolded himself for not noticing sooner. "Then I shall teach you."

Ah, great. What a fool I was, earning even more of his attention.

"There aren't many books left to read ever since the

high priests outlawed all writings but those the temples provided."

"Praising your false god, no doubt."

"Why would they do that?"

"You're not listening, little one." Another pitying stroke through my hair. "Mortals are wicked creatures, always striving for more power than they can handle. If the masses pray to a god who doesn't exist, then the mortal who speaks for said god amasses great power. Riches too, I would assume."

My mind went to the tithe the priests collected twice a year. "The temples have gold-plated signs."

"I have little bone at my disposal, it is true. The price I pay for an oath given." With a flick of his hand, he reshaped my collar, widening it enough that a calming chill settled on my skin. "The stiffness in your muscles over your discontent is cumbersome."

"If it's so bad, how about you take me outside for a walk?"

"No." A kiss against my temple. "But... I'm ever so tempted to send Orlaigh for fresh flowers whenever you please me."

My skin heated beneath my collar, driving out his soothing chill until it itched again. "I don't want damn flowers."

Fuck the violets on John's grave, too! I wanted to get out of here, drag three millstones onto my husband's grave, then run from Enosh until my skin wrinkled and my hair grayed.

But the god only sighed, as if my mortal moods bored him. "Careful with that mouth of yours or I'll find something to stuff it."

As if to make a point, I watched my hand lift to knead

over the significant bulge behind his leather breeches. *Only trickery.* "If the idea of my escape vexes you so, then why won't you rot my husband's bones like I asked?"

"You want me to leave my court—after two hundred years, no less—to rot the body of a wife-beating man?"

I'd rather be beaten than collared and raped. "I won't expect a god who abandoned his purpose to understand the meaning of duty."

"Duty?"

"Of a wife."

"Something you seem to take very seriously." His gaze intensified, eyes slipping to my lips for a second. "How come?"

"I gave my vows."

"Vows," he repeated slowly, as if tasting the word. "No mortal will find rest within my court, little one."

"I'm not asking you to rest his bones at the Pale Court. You'll just turn him into a cup and make me drink from it."

"There's an idea that makes this worthwhile." Of course, he chuckled, ever so amused. "Now, lift your skirts and show me how wet you are."

Only trickery.

Regardless of how Enosh stirred my flesh, I didn't truly lust for the god. As long as I remembered it, recited it like a prayer, then my body wouldn't betray me again.

I shook my head, ignoring the heat climbing my inner thighs. "I won't."

"Very well. Touch me, then."

That... was unexpected.

He leaned back and stared at me, amusement sitting in the depths of his turbulent gray eyes. One corner of his lips carried a slight uptick. It hiked into a lopsided smirk as I reached my damned hands for his chest.

Leisurely, I palmed the vast plains of hard muscle before I let my fingertips curve down along the dips and valleys of his abdomen. A bastard like him shouldn't be this perfectly built. I balled the hem of his shirt in my fists and pulled it over his head, his scent wafting off him like flames licking the wet chill of a winter night.

His chest rose and fell easily with each breath, the shoulders above wide, with strong muscles tying into the trunk of a broad neck. He was so beautifully sculpted, every inch shaped to divine perfection that hid the depravity in his heart. Enosh was so terribly cold, so terribly cruel, just… so terrible with how he folded his arms behind his head.

"Yes, just like that," he praised, striking a long-neglected chord deep within me until it hummed. "Touch me, my little one."

The soft lilt coming from his lips only deepened my utter humiliation, and how I cupped his cheeks with a lover's touch. I stroked the sharp line of his jaw, dug my fingers into his long, black strands, and thumbed his bottom lip in nothing short of worship.

Only trickery.

My folds didn't truly grow wet when I reached his breeches, frantically undoing the laces to release his hard flesh.

My insides didn't truly heat when I brushed my skirts aside and mounted him, knees braced against the bone of his throne.

And my body didn't truly tremble when I reached between us, lining his crown up with my sex before I impaled myself on his thick—

"Oh my god!"

"No need for such formalities." His arms remained folded behind his head, no matter how I rocked against him, rubbing my clit over his hard body. "Call me by my name."

"Arrogant jerk."

"Stubborn, insolent, beautiful woman," he rasped. "Take your pleasure from me, Ada. A reward for my good little mortal, and how stunning she looks, collared and chained."

A ripple of anger tensed my muscles as lust and loathing fought within my core. No, this was no reward; this was mockery. A blatant display of his power over me as he watched... and did nothing.

Enosh neither forced nor restrained.

Instead, he agonized my flesh with unwanted hunger, letting its fangs bite so deep into my heated center, lust won—and flesh answered the call of its master. I bucked against him, seeking pleasure while my mind echoed with the fading lifeline of my prayer: *only trickery, only... trickery, only—*

"Kiss me!"

Already my weight shifted toward him, tongue wetting my lips. His breath tingled over my mouth, the warmth of his proximity seeping deeper, deeper, until—

I pulled back on a mumble, "Only trickery."

"Only trickery, hmm? What makes you so certain?" Deep and lustful, his groan purred across the skin of my neck as he reached for the bodice of my dress. "How can you tell where your obedience ends and your cravings begin?"

He undid the laces of my bodice, exposing my breasts to his greedy lips. They suckled a nipple into his mouth, tongue teasing the little bud until it grew painfully hard. He did the same with the other, warm hands kneading the flesh, weighing it.

I moaned, relishing the time he took to fondle my breasts, giving them attention they hadn't known in so, so long. "None of this is real."

"You feel painfully real to me, little one. Now kiss me." When I did nothing, he gripped the bone chain near my collar. "Kiss me!"

A hard pull and he hauled my face closer before he slanted his mouth over mine. Confident lips brushed the corner, kissing me with ravenous need before his tongue stroked my lips apart.

The hunger in his kiss, his unforgiving grip on my chain, the absurd tenderness of his hand as he cupped the back of my head... it sparked a need I had no control over.

Fingers trembling with defiance stroked over the arch of his brows, down the slant of his cheekbones, only for my arms to wrap around his neck. I hated myself for it, but that didn't keep me from rolling my hips each time he thrust upward, working his thick cock deep into me.

He gripped my chin in the vise of his hand and something desperate fleeted over his gray eyes. "Say my name. My *true* name."

"Enosh..."

He answered with a grunt and guided me along his rock-hard length, filling my sex with pleasure it hadn't known in years. Oh, the thickness of his flesh, the bliss of how he filled me so completely, the obscenity of all this. It was... was...

"Not real."

A cloud of feathers puffed up around me. *Clank, clank, clank* went teeth and bone as my bodice fell into just as many pieces, skipping down the dais, leaving me naked.

Enosh rose, slipped me off him, and spun me to face the corpses in his throne all in one movement, his snarl predatory. "It's realer than you'd ever confess to yourself, so let me help you."

He gave another yank on the chain until my collar pulled against my throat. "Your flesh has been deprived of touch for so long that it blooms beneath my hands. It calls for me, longs for me."

When a burning sensation spread across an arse still sore, my hands grabbled for hold, finding it on the bone of his throne. "No. No, please... not there."

"Not there," he repeated as he slipped lower and thrust into my cunt, seating himself completely before he pulled back, then snapped his hips forward again. "Ah, you're gripping me so tightly all on your own. You want this. You like this."

Hard thrusts turned to aggressive pounding as he panted, fucking me so hard that the porous bone I held on to chaffed my palms. My body heated as I arched my back and, Helfa forgive me, I braced against him so I could take him deeper.

"So good. So wet and eager for me, no matter how you snarl." His next hard push set me aflame. "Yes... say my name. Do it!"

A scream slipped from my lips without permission. "Enosh!"

"Ada," he groaned in response. "So warm around my cock..." A deep stroke pinned me between glorious hips and the judging stare of two corpses. Ropes of hot seed filled my womb while Enosh's trembling fingers stroked through my hair. "Mmm... there's your reward, little one. Feel how I spend my seed inside you. Ah, it's all yours. Only yours."

When the height of pleasure ebbed away, nothing remained but bleakness. There was no fighting this; there was neither escaping this pleasure nor the shame that tortured my conscience.

Clenching my eyes shut, I said, "Guess I ended up at the whorehouse after all."

Still seated deep within me, he leaned over and ardently kissed between my shoulder blades. "Flesh of my flesh, bone of my bone. Never my whore, forever my woman."

CHAPTER 9
ADA

I was dead.

I had to be.

Time meant nothing to the dead.

Time meant nothing to me.

It no longer passed in hours, minutes, or even seconds, but instead, time passed in pieces of my soul chipping away one moan at a time.

"Enosh..." *Clink.* Dignity, gone.

"Enosh..." *Clink.* Duty, gone.

"Enosh..." *Clink.* Hope of escape?

Gone.

Whenever I was awake, the god worshipped my body in ways I hadn't known existed, from feasting on my sex to rutting me from behind while he pinned me against his throne—sometimes the dais—strokes so violent, bonemeal dusted my breasts after.

He brought me pleasure so many times, it overwhelmed and exhausted me into compliancy. The kind where I often fell to sleep rolled up in my nest, or worse, sitting on his lap as he nuzzled my temple.

When I was his good little mortal—screaming his name across the Pale Court—he brought me flowers. He turned the dais into a garden of pink roses, fragrant lavender, and stunning lilies—all plucked from fields I would never walk again, placed into a cage of bone so I could watch them wilt.

And I wilted alongside them.

Limbs heavy and senses dull, I kneeled on the ground before Enosh, where he sat on his throne, and yawned. "I'm tired."

"You only just slept, my little one." He twirled a strand of my hair around his finger, once, twice, then draped it over my bone collar. "Your body shouldn't be so tired, its weariness burdens even my senses."

Had I just slept? "Is it night or day?"

"It is both and everything in-between."

"I don't understand."

"No, of course not." Scooping me up from the floor, he rose and took that one step into my nest, letting me sink into the warm bed of pelts and feathers. "Would you like to paint?"

As if I had any canvas left. The surrounding dais was covered in paintings of roses and ravens. "You could take me outside."

"Or I could bring outside to the court." He showed me his hand, palm up, and let bone dust form into the skeleton of a bird. Shortly after, gray flesh covered it and black feathers appeared around it. Its wings soon flapped, lifting into the air, only for tiny feet to wrap around the edge of my hand. "You can play with it."

"I'm not a child." A hard-to-defend statement considering how I clung to his neck as he cradled me. "How can you not get bored in here?"

"I assume immortality cured me of that." His fingers slipped underneath my skirts, stroking my inner thigh. "What happens when my little mortal is irritable?"

"That depends."

A snarky remark? His cock down my throat. Pretending that I felt nothing? So many orgasms, it left me sore. Refusing to moan his name? His fingers pinching my clit. Snarling at him, calling him a bastard, and cursing him to drop dead? His cock up my arse...

"I'm unclean," I said after a while and, when wrinkles formed between his brows, I clarified, "My bleeding arrived when I woke."

"I know. Why does my mortal woman think I had Orlaigh provide cloth and braise for it?" Something I might have called considerate if I wasn't the prisoner of a lusty god. "How curious of you to call yourself unclean for something so... natural."

"Helfa forbids a man to lie with his wife while she's impure."

I flinched at my words.

I shouldn't have said that. Enosh hated few things more than talk about another taking his place beyond the Æfen Gate. On a much more serious note, I also shouldn't have said it because I wasn't his damn wife.

"*I* am your god." Where I expected rage in his voice, I only found the slightly elevated pitch of a smile, as if he were so very pleased with how I'd called myself his wife. "And I see nothing impure about you or the act we share as man and woman while you bleed." He leaned over and pressed a kiss to my cheek. "Very well. I'll give you this one concession, my little wife."

My pulse thudded faster.

Did he truly spare me the indignity?

Because I'd called myself his wife?

That... scared me.

I rubbed at my tired eyes. "I'm not your wife."

"Indeed, you never gave me your vow."

A sudden heaviness settled on my shoulder, followed by a voice I'd almost forgotten. Almost.

"Flesh and scar and skin and bone, feed her body to the throne," the voice sing-songed into my left ear before it shifted to the other, curdling the blood in my veins. *"Sweat and breath and soul and flaw, my brother surely... fucked... you... raw."*

My skin crawled wherever muscles tightened. I was mad, mentally unwell. My mind drained from the dullness and monotony of this place; why else would I now hear voices?

At the very first shiver gripping my arms, Enosh cupped my cheek, bringing my eyes to meet his. "Why is your heart racing?"

My shoulders hiked toward my ears, but it did nothing to ward off the cacophony of whispers hushing through my skull. *"Heart and blood and veins and death, the third will come and steal your breath."*

"What's this voice?"

"Voice?" Enosh took my face between his hands, thumb stroking over trembling lips. "What does it say, little one?"

"Terrible things..."

With one quick move, Enosh slung his arms around me as though to shield me. "Get out of her head."

"But it is... so..." The whisper turned into moist breath, breaking against my cheek. *"Fun in there."*

A man took form beside us, his face inches from mine until he shifted back. He perfumed the air with sandalwood, staring at me with grass-green eyes. He straightened to an impressive height and skipped down the dais; long, auburn hair shifting on a brown felt jacket elaborately embroidered with golden leaves.

"Did John escape his grave? Who will take care of Pa?" Voice mockingly high-pitched, the man fanned himself as though he was close to a fainting spell, feeding my veins with liquid anger even as my mind struggled to understand what was happening. "Had I done my duty as a wife, my poor John wouldn't have a—"

"Enough!" Enosh barked.

"—hole in his skull. His death is on my conscience. I am worthless. An unwoman." The man clapped his hands. "Oh, what delicious agony houses behind those blue eyes of hers, matching your misery, Enosh, so per—"

The man choked on his words before a swell of blood pushed from his mouth. Thick and dark, it ran down his chin, dripping onto a spike of bone now protruding from his neck. The air turned heavy with the taint of metal. Glancing down at it, he wrapped both hands around the spike and dragged it out under gargling wheezes.

My stomach convulsed at the sight, my mind spinning so wildly that I hugged myself, unconsciously shifting closer to Enosh. "You killed him."

"I wish." With a sigh, Enosh wiped a palm down his face, which he then dismissively waved at the man who fell to his knees, chin sinking to his chest. "Ada, meet my brother, Yarin."

Brother.

The word stabbed my temple.

As if Enosh wasn't bad enough already...

A wet chuckle drooled from Yarin's lips. "She doesn't think well of you, brother. I dare say she hates your guts."

Did Enosh just flinch?

I must have imagined it as he curled his fingers into my waist with a possessive grip. "How long have you been hiding between her thoughts?"

Yarin rose—the hole in his neck gone—and brushed his fingers over the blood staining his jacket. "I only had this tailored a fortnight ago. Now look what you've done. It took a great deal of traveling to find felt of such quality and craftsmanship."

"How long?"

"Ever since you cheated Eilam and kept her from dying." Yarin slowly spun, head shaking repeatedly as he glanced about the chamber, then his eyes settled on Enosh once more. "You're notorious for taking what isn't yours to take, Enosh, and it vexes him so."

My gaze bounced back and forth between the men. "Who is Eilam?"

"Our brother."

When Yarin winked at me, my head swung to Enosh. "You have two brothers?"

Enosh's hold on me tightened. "Stop whispering into her mind before I needle your bitter flesh with bone!"

"You've always been so quick to threaten physical punishment. And no, Ada, we're not brothers in the mortal sense." Yarin's eyes held mine captive. *Adorable, how he stashes you away like his little secret. And look, he set a blue gemstone into your collar.* "We're purely bound by this brotherly love between us. Isn't that so, Enosh?"

"You're making her nervous," Enosh grunted. "Stop muddling her thoughts, or I'll have my corpses drag you outside and toss you onto a pile."

"Her thoughts are muddled already. Mortals do poorly if deprived of light and stimulation. I tried it. She slit her wrists." A powerful set of teeth sunk into an apple Yarin had pulled from a pocket, ripping a bite with a wet *crk* before a sly grin formed on his mouth. "Anyway, given the poor state of your court, your threats leave much to be desired, and... um..." Yarin raked a lazy hand through his strands. "My, my, would you look at this shithole. No servants, no feasts, no music. Only the Pale Court stripped to its bare bones, so to speak, and my brother drowning in self-pity and the cunt sitting on his lap." Green eyes snapped to me. "What pleasant company your mouthiness would have provided at my court."

I straightened. "What court?"

"The Court Between Thoughts," Enosh said on a groan. "Believe me, little one, you don't want to go there."

"Oh no, you don't, Ada," Yarin added. "It's dreadful. All my entourage and I do all day is fuck and sing and drink... and fuck. On a more serious note, brother, I can tell you two converse little beyond the beastly grunts you exchange when you bed her." Yarin lowered himself to the dais, one leg folding over the other. "See, Ada, Enosh rules over the bodily remnants of everything that once breathed. Your soul, however, belongs in my keep. And then there's your life breath, of course, which was supposed to go to Eilam. Unfortunately for you, mostly, my brother here is so smitten with you."

"Guard your thoughts or he'll twist them," Enosh whispered into my ear, lulling my muscles into a state of lethargy with calculated strokes along my spine.

"Oh, you don't want me to twist them for you, brother?" Yarin's eyes locked with mine, and whispers infiltrated my head in never-ending echoes.

"I've never been worth anything to John while Enosh locks me away like a treasure. When was the last time a man wanted me? Lusted for me? Does the god not tend to my needs? Kisses me

so gently? How much longer can I deny there's true pleasure in his touch, and—"

Yarin groaned.

Another sharp piece of bone protruded from his neck, this one shaped like a dagger, but he quickly pulled it out with yet another chuckle.

Pain bloomed around my temples. No, those thoughts hadn't been mine. Never would be.

"If only you wouldn't have done that, Enosh," Yarin said. "She might have loved you on her next breath."

Everything on Enosh stilled, and even his breathing suspended for an overlong moment before he said, "You're testing my patience, Yarin. Why are you here?"

"Can you truly not tell?"

Enosh sunk his head into his palm, his dismay so obvious he almost appeared... mortal. "You came to demand the corpses."

"Quite so. Three souls I once bound to their bodies for you."

I perked up at that. That could only be Orlaigh, Lord Tarnem, and the commander.

"Precisely, Ada." Yarin's comment triggered a flinch. Between Enosh's ability to control my body and his brother's power to meddle in my thoughts, which one of these gods was worse? *"We're all equally terrible,"* he whispered into my mind. "Now, I demand you supply my court with those four new corpses you owe me in return. The ones I have are starting to stink up my bed."

"Three corpses."

"Four. With interest." Yarin smacked his tongue. "Or did you believe two hundred years wouldn't come at a premium?"

"What a curious time to show yourself—a month after

she arrived—when you've remained blissfully absent for over a century."

"What can I say...? Eilam sought me out, lamenting about how you pushed the borders of your prerogative once again, keeping something from him that was..." Yarin sighed. "And so on and so forth. In any case, I expect you near the town of Airensty in ten days. Rumor has it the Tybosts will lay siege to it. Battering rams. Siege towers. Oh, what a spectacle it'll be! You know full well how battles excite me."

Enosh tapped a thumb against his chin, his voice a mumble. "Airensty..."

I breathed against the quickening beat of my heart, struggling it into a state of calm. Had Enosh noticed? Airensty lay several days' travel on horseback from Hemdale. If I could convince him to take me with him—

"Surely there has to be another battle in another direction," Enosh said. "Mortals quarrel all the time, and certainly not only beyond the Æfen Gate."

Yarin tilted his head, lifting his chin in an almost taunting manner. "Ah, yes, the Soltren Gate then. Who wants to see oil poured over those men pushing the battering ram then set aflame, if we can instead... Oh, I just remembered... because you killed everyone beyond that gate."

My fingers numbed.

Killed everyone?

No. Calm. I had to stay calm.

I didn't even dare to lift my brow while the two brothers stared at each other, air tainted with aggression. After almost a month, I couldn't afford more of Enosh's suspicion. One way or another, I needed him out of the Pale Court to have a chance at escape, no matter how slim.

"You could always try to lure him toward the edge of the bone and push him down." Yarin's stare remained on Enosh, but something sinister played around his lips. *"Maybe you can get rid of him like that."*

My eyes went to the ring of darkness surrounding the throne chamber. A gaping ravine of never-ending blackness that swallowed the glimmer of bone and the echoes of the Pale Court. What if Enosh's immortality ended at the bottom of it? Could he be killed like this?

"He cannot, but you can always throw yourself down during an onslaught of madness." Yarin scoffed a bitter laugh. "Now I'm certain she hates you. I suppose it offers cause for entertainment and... Whatever do you do all day, Enosh? You bury yourself in her womb and then what...? Stare? Drink? I say it is time for fresh— Orlaigh!"

The moment Orlaigh spotted Yarin, she gave him a dismissive wave, though a smile tugged on the corners of her lips. "Ach, as if yer brother dinnae trouble me enough already, now ye came to shush me about court?"

"Old Orlaigh, as plucky as ever. When was the last time my brother led you across the bone in a ceilidh, huh?" Yarin shot up, hurrying over to take Orlaigh's hands. "Let us dance and remind my bore of a brother how lively the Pale Court had once been."

"Nay, leave me old bones—"

"Nonsense!" Yarin wrapped his arms around the barrel-bellied woman, lifted her, and swung her around the chamber in circles. "Ada, won't you join us? How could my brother resist a plea from lips I'm certain he had sucking his—"

"I refuse," Enosh shouted, seething beside me, veins along his arms swelling with what had to be rage.

"Now, now, brother. You might want to reconsider,

given the likelihood of you needing another soul chained in the future." His eyes flicked to me for the fraction of a breath, but long enough to raise the hairs on my arms. "Did you forget what happened to your last woman? Poor Njala, bleeding out from her throat."

A dark pit formed at the bottom of my stomach. His last woman? What had happened to her?

As though Enosh had noticed my unease—which, he probably had—he placed a kiss against my shoulder. "Airentsy. In ten days. Now leave my court."

Yarin lowered a giggling Orlaigh back down before he bowed. "Madam, I thank you for the honor of this dance."

She pressed a hand to her sternum. No doubt she would have blushed had her blood not gone black such a long time ago.

Even as Yarin straightened, green eyes searching mine, the god faded until nothing was left but the dull chamber.

That, and a final whisper. *"Such a joy to be in your head. And Njala...? Well, he killed her dead."*

My blood cooled. "Who was Njala?"

Enosh regarded me, his cool demeanor crumbling with each frown forming between his brows, showing me a glimpse of something behind his arrogant wall of indifference I couldn't name. "If I take you with me, little one, will you promise not to run?"

"If I promise, will you rot my husband's bones?"

"I will not."

I promise.

The lie brushed over my lips, but I licked it away and swallowed it whole. Enosh had already made me a whore, but I wouldn't allow him make me a liar.

"Then I'll promise no such thing."

CHAPTER 10
ADA

"A, n, d." Letter for letter, I put the sounds together like Enosh had taught me, finger trailing over black ink on yellowed paper. "A, an, and the g, o, d... g, go, god, and the god r... ra— Curses!" With a groan, I let my face sink into the copper pelts of my nest. "It'll take me hundreds of years to read this damn book."

Worse yet, I would still be alive, stuttering around stories where one letter looked like the next. If the tail went up from the circle on the left side, it made *buh*. From the right side crossing to the left? *Duh.* If the tail went down, it made *puh*, but on which side? Left? Right? What fool came up with the idea of creating a letter and tipping it around in books?

"Patience, my little treasure." Enosh folded an arm under one side of his head where he rested inches from me in my nest and tugged a strand behind my ear. "You did well."

I hated when he praised me.

Loathed how something inside me soaked it up like the cracked ground did when rain came after a drought. *'You did well'* sounded so much better than *'You failed to conceive yet again.'*

My finger went to the gemstone set into my collar, trailing around the smoothed edges that came together in the shape of a teardrop. "What's this stone?"

"A diamond."

When I glanced down hard enough, until chin hit chest, I could see it sparkling a deep, vivid blue from the bottom edge of my vision. "Where did you get it?"

"From the royal house of Nazameh. They're long gone, decimated during one of the many quarrels about lands, wealth... power."

"Is it precious?"

"To me, it's something of beauty that matches the color of your eyes—a blue like the sea between the Kilafa mountains before the land split apart and drowned some thousand years ago." His hand stroked over the sway of my hip and the thousands of black feathers that covered me as he rose. "But yes, mortals consider it precious."

I'd never worn anything precious. Never held much value to anyone except Pa, even though a widowed daughter made for an expensive burden. Husbands were generous with their seed when it came to making babies, but stingy once the midwife came knocking. That some worried my fruitlessness might be contagious didn't help matters...

Enosh let a high-collared jacket of black leather form around his torso, the bone buttons carved with skulls. "It's time."

My gaze drifted to the cloud of bone dust swirling at the bottom of the dais. It formed the distinct shape of a horse, coming together in sturdy bones as my chain dissolved where it rested on the steps. Hide soon followed, covering the creature in brittle skin before dull hairs arranged in a black coat.

I rose, brushing down the black feathers of my dress. "What's this?"

"Yarin is waiting for us."

My stomach bottomed out. "*Us?* You're... you're taking me with you?"

"I'd rather have you by my side where I can see you than return home to find your collar broken and the few corpses I left scattered in pieces across the court." He walked up to me, his black hair framing his regal features so perfectly, and took me into his embrace before he whispered, "This will only hurt for a moment, my little one."

My heart stumbled over a beat before it hit the back of my throat. "No, please, Enosh. Don't do this—"

"Shh..." Warmth swathed me, coaxing my stiff muscles into a false state of ease. "Once we return, I'll mend your bones."

Crk-crk-crk.

Bone crackled beneath me.

Pain shot up and down my shins. It seared my flesh, pushing me toward unconsciousness. I heaved, wheezed in air, choking on my own saliva until—

"There, there. I'm already dulling the pain away." Enosh caught me at my first sway, carried me down the dais, and propped me on the horse's back.

I pulled on the train of my dress, sour bile sweeping up my throat at the sight of bone spurs stretching the skin along my shins so taut it yellowed. "I should've expected no different from you, you fucking bastard."

His chuckle echoed from the surrounding bone as he gracefully swung himself onto the horse behind me, his voice a purr across the side of my neck. "If my woman wants my prick up her ass, she only needs to say so, and I shall oblige."

Nothing but a quiet threat, all while he caressed me into a state of dull acceptance, slowing my heart until it beat evenly. I didn't hate him nearly as much for breaking my legs as I did for calming the rage pumping through my veins into a mere tingle.

And a comforting one at that.

Bastard.

Enosh wrapped his arm around my middle, anchoring me to him, which was a good thing considering I'd never been one for riding sidesaddle—and there was no saddle at all. "We'll ride over those hayfields you claim to miss so dearly."

"And see the sky you promised I would never see again."

He grunted.

In that, I took some small comfort.

After Orlaigh gave me a satchel with bread and dried meat, we left through the Æfen Gate. Hooves clopped over stone and up the incline, back through the passage Augustine had dragged me through. At the surface, I clenched my eyes shut against a sun suddenly too bright for eyes accustomed to the dim glimmer of the Pale Court.

Enosh's chest hardened behind me, his entire body rigid while the cracking of bones and squishing of flesh drove out the faint chirping of birds. "Keep your eyes closed for another moment."

"Oh please, as if a carpet of smashed corpses is worse than how one of your decrepit servants dropped his jaws into my soup during the last meal." When he made a gruntled sound at the back of his throat, I casually asked, "Will rot follow you to Airensty?"

"No. It is something I purposely do, going so far I can

even distinguish between which body rots and which will not." So I'd achieved *nothing*. "Open your eyes. See your sky and your birds."

I kept them closed for another five breaths, sucking in the moisture of the dew beneath us, the waft of soil climbing into my nostrils, and the first traces of winter berries lingering in the air. My lungs expanded until the leather bindings of my bodice moaned, sun and shadow playing over my face in a caress of warmth and cool.

My eyes blinked open and my heart ached at the sight of a crow circling the pink-streaked horizon. "It's beautiful."

Enosh glanced down at me, brushing one of my strands tousled by the breeze off my shoulder. "Indeed. So captivatingly beautiful."

Did we speak of the same thing? My head turned to glance back at him, but I stopped myself. If it had been flattery, it meant nothing coming from his lips.

"Don't you enjoy this?"

"Very much. But what I enjoy even more is the lightness coming over your chest after you've been so sluggish as of late," he said, as if it came as a surprise to him that chaining a woman to a throne in a dim chamber might have this result.

His fingers stroked over my belly as if ensuring himself I was, indeed, still here, infusing my body with... nothing.

No prickle.

No pleasure.

So I wasn't going insane after all.

Which could only mean one thing... "You have no control over my flesh out here, do you?"

"Only over the dead scattered across these lands." As though he despised admitting it, his voice hardened. "Make no mistake, my little one, I have an endless amount of bone at my disposal to make certain you remain by my side."

As if he needed such drastic measures. "You broke my legs."

"*Twisted*," he corrected with a sigh of annoyance. "A necessary precaution, because even gods are not all-powerful. The living are wicked, the lands we ride dangerous from what little you told me. I can't satisfy my brother's demand, keep you from running, and avoid danger all at the same time."

"Danger? You can't die."

"No, but you can."

"My god, are we riding *into* battle?"

When he kicked the horse into an unnatural speed, I shifted out of balance, but he quickly steadied me against him, saving me from a fall. "Mortals are wayward creatures."

"Toward the god who's abandoned them."

His low chuckle vibrated against my spine, but it held no humor. "Do you believe this is the first time mortals would rebel against a god? The living have chased me since the beginning of time like the waves chase across the seas, ever so predictable in their hither and tither with ebbs of worship and floods of them doubting my divinity."

My stomach clenched, my mind going back to what Orlaigh had told me. Was this the life of a god? To be chased and chained, disemboweled and burned?

"Why?"

"Because I require flesh and bone to maintain the Pale Court," he said. "Something mortals aren't always willing to give up. The higher they are in station, the more they treasure the bone of their kin, as though it makes a difference to me if I drink from a baron or a beggar."

Neither would I want Pa to span a bridge. "But the dead walk toward the Pale Court on a full moon on their own, anyway."

"Only because I deny them to rot in the ground. I have no control over it. Naturally, the dead seek my closeness because I am their master."

"Is it true corpses once burned?"

"The only curse I cast about the lands." He nodded and pressed his lips into a grim line, a gesture so human, it looked out of place on the face of a god. "Of all the deaths I didn't die, my little mortal, the one where they burned me at the stake for a fortnight was the worst. To this day, the stench of ash follows me, as if my skin somehow trapped it when it returned."

The hairs rose on my arms as I thought back on the witch the priests had burned last winter, her high-pitched screams forever branded into my memory. Hemdale had reeked of singed hair for days, bitter and biting. Imagining Enosh screaming like she had...? For a fortnight?

Bile licked my throat.

"I'm sorry." I didn't want to be, but the apology slipped from my lips without consent. "Why did Lord Tarnem capture you? Because you wanted his wife's bones or something?"

His deep inhale pressed against my back. "He sought me out nearly two centuries ago. Asked me to raise an army of dead for him so he could fight off a group of barbarians invading his lands. Gods ought not to meddle in the affairs of mankind, but... what he offered in exchange..."

I turned back to look at him once more. "Offered what?"

"His daughter Njala." It wasn't so much the name that offered me another puzzle piece to a picture I struggled to grasp, but how old traces of pain roughened his tone. "She was supposed to be my companion for eternity."

Something pinched beneath my ribs, then again when I took in the features of a god gone ashen. "Did you love her?"

His features hardened, brow taking on an audacious curve. "Your question suggests that you think me capable of love, little one."

At first, I hadn't, but the longer I looked at him, the more I had my doubts. More than just his general smugness shone in his eyes, like little flickers of agony hidden behind an immaculate mask of cold-blooded ruthlessness.

It had cracks.

Nothing but fine veins weaving through it, scratching away at his usually arrogant demeanor, his divine superiority. Did I dare find out what was behind that mask? If he'd loved her, why would he have killed her? Perhaps Yarin had said it to twist my head?

When my temples ached from all the wondering, I looked forward again. "Orlaigh once told me you love and lust like any mortal."

"Love is a painful curse," he said. "Now I only lust, slaking it in the tight holes of my little treasure."

I flinched.

Was that a blessing... or a curse?

I'd never wanted his lust.

Cared even less about his love.

"Did she have love for you?"

His fingers curled where his other hand rested on my hip. "Take a guess. I long to hear your judgment on this matter. Could a woman love this cruel bastard?"

My attention lifted to his shiver-inducing eyes, the smooth cheeks beneath without a single whisker, and the soft curvature of his lips framed by inky strands. Enosh was magnificent to behold, no mistake, a perfectly constructed trap to catch the silly hearts of young, unknowing girls.

The way he kissed me often, combed my hair with his fingers, and read me stories too difficult for me to decipher... There was a gentler side to him whenever he wasn't busy breaking my legs. If Njala had seen more of it, had not been a plaything but a companion, might she have loved him?

I gave my nod of approval. "I think she might have."

A muscle jumped in his jaw, quickly hidden beneath the sly curve of a self-satisfied smile. "You think me worthy of love?"

"No," I said, watching the grin slip off his lips like molasses in winter. "Some two hundred years ago, perhaps, before you turned your back on your duty."

The sun retreated behind clouds, casting his face in terrifying shadows, but he said nothing.

When he slowed to a walk by the edge of a dense forest, I asked, "Why are we stopping?"

"There is little bone in these woods. We'll have to ride around it. Follow the trail of the dead so I can call on them should mortals be foolish enough to corner us."

"Corner *you*," I corrected. "You cursed their loved ones to wander, not me."

"If the King of Flesh and Bone rides these lands after nearly two centuries, tell me, Ada, what might be the worth of the woman he holds in his arms? If they took her from him, what would the King be willing to do to get her back?" The more I thought about the question, the more I tortured my lips, but I didn't break skin until he added, "From the moment we left the Pale Court, you were hunted."

My stomach convulsed, dread seeping into my core,

where it clashed with bile. "Is that why you took me with you? To put another shackle on me once I understood that even escape would bring me no freedom?"

That bastard patted my thigh as if rewarding me for a lesson learned. Priests all over the realm called on people to capture Enosh. High Priest Dekalon wouldn't want a god to ride the lands again, undermining his power and authority. Once word spread of Enosh's presence, there would be no safety from my own kind... for both of us.

Except at the Pale Court.

That realization sunk in.

Sunk in and festered.

I blinked back useless tears. They neither untwisted bone nor changed how he'd tricked me. "Did you lock her up, too?"

"Njala came and left as she pleased until wicked mortals stole her from me in their never-ending pursuit of power." A kiss to my head. "You will remain by my side for eternity."

I stole from me Master.

My fingertips numbed, so I stroked them through the horse's mane. "That's why you condemned Orlaigh to your service... She's the one who stole her?"

"In a lapse of judgment only; otherwise, she would grace my throne like those responsible for Njala's death."

Her death.

The more I learned of all this, the less sense it made, mostly because everyone told me something different. What did Orlaigh have to say about this? She once told me that mortals feared what they didn't understand, and I had no inclination to spend eternity in fear. Who was this creature who held me captive?

A god with no conscience?

A man with a grudge?

His next words came calm, but concise. "Heed my words, little one, you have no friends out here, not anymore. Word will spread of the woman who rides with me, eats with me, beds down with me. The wicked might go to great lengths to get me to remove this... curse, as you call it, stealing you away to use as bait."

Bait.

My mouth turned dry.

I truly was doomed, wasn't I?

My voice came out a mere whisper, vocal cords thin. "And how far would you go to see me returned?"

Did I have any value anywhere?

His answer came as the click of his tongue. The horse galloped over the land, hooves thundering so loudly underneath, it almost distracted from the deafening rush of blood in my ears.

Never my whore, forever my woman.

Those words had meant something to me when he'd spoken them, if only for the bit of dignity they'd returned.

His silence stripped it away once more.

CHAPTER 11
ENOSH

"Why did you refuse me your promise not to run?"

After hours of silence, the question startled my woman enough that she hissed under the ache of her sore muscles. "Lying's a sin, and I've piled up enough of those in the last month."

"Had you given it, I may not have twisted your legs, little one. Maybe you could have escaped."

For a while.

She shifted from one seat bone to the other. Hours on horseback had taken its toll on her flesh, but not once did she so much as whimper, as though leaving the Pale Court was worth the pain.

Feet wiggling whenever long strands of grass brushed along her ankles, lungs expanding wide when we passed fragrant flowers, a gentle smile lining her lips whenever a breeze wafted around us. When had her mortal body ever felt this light, this warm and alive in my arms?

Never.

Perhaps Orlaigh was right. I couldn't lock her away

between bone inside a kingdom as quiet and cold as death. It hadn't always been like this. Winding staircases adorned with the most intricate motives, bridges spanned over statues so detailed you could see the veins of the animals they depicted, rooms appointed with the finest furniture... Ah, the Pale Court was a shadow of its former glory.

Because I'd made it so.

I had given an oath never to receive mankind's bones again and look what it got me. My woman's chain had been so short, a good part of the dais around my throne remained unpainted. How fine the other part looked with her vines and those delicate roses shedding their petals.

"You wouldn't believe me anyway," she said after a while. "If I have to be a whore, then at least I want to be an honest one."

"I don't recall ever paying you." She shifted again, her muscles souring with shame, her bones growing heavy with guilt I failed to make sense of. "Why so much distress over a word?"

She shrugged, her gaze drifting toward a waterwheel that spun along a creek, the wings of the mill cutting the air. "A man is free to divorce his wife after three years of fruitlessness. Can even sell her to the whorehouse. John never did."

I shifted sideways, clasping her chin to bring her gaze to mine. "Fruitlessness?"

"I never gave him a son, as is a woman's purpose." Her voice was so strangely thin compared to that bite she often carried. "To make it worse, I was the one who sent him for pinweedle moss. Healers say it cures a barren womb, you know. So up the falls he went to where it grows, only to hit his head and die. It's my fault."

Her fault?

Oh, my little naïve mortal. Her womb was neither cursed nor barren. Perhaps the only thing I would have rectified, no matter how I adored her imperfections, for she would carry my child, painting eternity with life and laughter. Giving me the purpose of a man instead of the ungrateful duty of a god.

But a babe in such a bare place...?

Oh, what a predicament.

"Is that why you're so desperate to rest his bones, little one?"

She nodded. "It's the least I owe him."

"So devoted to a man who never claimed your heart?"

"It's not the man I'm devoted to, but the promises I made before—" She stopped herself right then. "Well, you know. I swore an oath before a priest, vowing to be a good wife, and I intend to see it through in death, for I didn't in life."

"An oath before a false god." All forgiven because she worshipped me so nicely when she kneeled by my feet, dozing off with her head on my lap while I stroked her soft hair. "And a pathetic act of guilt."

She spun around, her blue eyes narrowed. "An act of duty and commitment. Not that I expect a god who abandoned his duty to understand its meaning."

Ah, there was that bite again.

Adorable.

I rewarded it with a kiss to her temple. "Duty. Vow. Oath."

She used those words often.

All things she remained faithful to over a husband tossing in the ground with each full moon. And all it had taken was a ridiculous vow before a priest who worshipped a god who didn't exist? For all the things I understood of Ada's flesh, her soul eluded me, as was my nature.

My woman cared little for dresses finer than those of any queen, the rich food I provided for her sustenance, or the diamond set into her collar. How refreshingly honest this midwife was compared to the titled stock of lords and ladies who painted their lips as though it would hide the lies they spoke. As Njala had...

But not my Ada.

No, my little one marked the bone, barraged through my corpses, tried to escape my kingdom, and snarled at me whenever her lips didn't tremble with a moan. She pledged nothing but her hatred; she swore nothing but her escape. And now she even refused to make me promises she knew she wouldn't keep?

That made a promise from her mouth valuable, indeed.

So trustworthy, I longed to kiss one from her lips. I wanted to taste her commitment to remain by my side. How blessed that bastard of a husband was to have a woman who, even in death, honored her vows. And what if I wanted her to make such a vow to me? Ought I to take her as my wife?

Mmm. Lots of temples between here and the Pale Court...

I stroked over her belly that would swell with my child soon enough. "Your flesh is perfectly imperfect."

And I longed for it almost as passionately as I ached for the devotion and dutifulness she'd stood by all this time. For the wrong reasons, yes, but with admirable resolve, nonetheless. What did a husband do with a wife, anyway? So many customs in so many places, all equally confusing.

"People are staring." Her neck shortened as she curled herself against me in a poor attempt at hiding her face.

"Devil be damned, you had to ride in on a dead horse with white eyes and give me a damn feather dress, right?"

I willed my mare up an incline, avoiding the farmers and merchants who moved grains and goods along the road. Their mumbles followed us as long as their stares, sparking restlessness in my core.

"Hold on," I said, once more spurring my mare into a canter, eager to return to the safety of the Pale Court, but there was the issue with my woman's exhausted flesh.

We didn't slow until the first bellows drifted on the wind, along with the bitter fumes of burnt oil. Each time metal clashed against metal, my little mortal retreated deeper into my arms.

I quite liked it.

Then the bellows turned to screams. Screams to deafening battle roars that manifested in nothing short of bloodlust, which swept through the lines of soldiers like a flood of rage. Axes hacked into flesh and crushed bones, pikes scratched along metal until they found their way into guts.

Wounded scattered the ground, screaming in pain, some dragging themselves over the dirt toward their severed limb. Oh, mortals and their frail bodies... fighting over creeks, riches, titles, only to end up as food for the crows.

Flames crackled where they'd lit the ground on fire, smoke rising in raven-black billows. On instinct, I steered away from it, but the stench of my charred flesh already crept into my nostrils.

"This is awful," Ada mumbled when, far ahead of us, a soldier thrust a sword into another's belly.

When I spotted Yarin, clad in leather armor with a sword in his hand, I rode up to him. "Blending in?"

"I don't have corpses to come to my defense, should I need it." The God of Whispers winked at my woman in that certainty he had around females, knowing their every thought. "I'm afraid you missed the part where they set the oil-soaked ground on fire and burned hundreds, brother. A coincidence... or immaculate planning?"

"Mortal needs slowed our travel. Mark the corpses you want raised."

"You've only just arrived." Yarin sheathed his sword. "Maybe a stroll along the nearby creek, Ada?"

"Your brother broke my legs."

"*Twisted*," I corrected, but Ada stiffened against me as he undoubtedly poisoned her mind with his whispers. "You won't blend in anymore if I raise the dead and send them after you faster than you can shift into your realm."

"I only said that I'm surprised you didn't snap her neck yet." At the pinching of my lips, Yarin's curled into a smirk. "The dead never run from you, and you seem oh-so desperate to keep her."

"Point out the four bodies."

"Raise five more for me." A growl formed at the back of my throat, but only until he added, "Do this for me, and I'll make your woman love you."

A shift beneath my ribs.

Love me.

Whatever that weasel saw on my face brought a self-satisfied smirk to his. "She'll adore you, brother."

My heart quickened.

Adore me.

"She'll be tormented by such ardor that she would never leave your side," he said. "Never."

Never leave.

Always stay.

Everything inside me demanded that I comply, even more fervently when Ada cut my brother a poisonous glare. No matter how deep my power reached into her flesh and bone, answering the desperate call of her neglected body, her rebelling soul sat behind a barrier not even I could breech. How long had it been since I roused her lust?

Longer than she would accept.

Let alone confess to herself...

Should that bother me?

No, but it did with such alarming intensity, I was tempted to agree. To have my mortal reach for me at her own choosing, pledging herself to me like only my enamored woman would.

Or my wife.

"Mark the bodies," I bit out.

"Suit yourself." Yarin gazed over the field. "Let me see... mmm, which ones to keep?"

"Are you jesting? You haven't even bound them yet?"

"Weighty choices shouldn't be rushed." Yarin tapped his lips and shrugged, glancing over the stone block walls surrounding Airensty. "One must choose the men and women he surrounds himself with wisely. Ah! This one will make for fine entertainment."

I let my mare follow him toward a dead soldier, pressing my mouth against Ada's ear. "Listen to him and he'll drive you mad. It is his nature."

Ada nodded. "Is he doing it to you as well?"

Driving me mad, for certain. "None of us have power over the other. We don't sense each other's presence, which makes Yarin, in particular, quite a nuisance."

Ada watched with rapt attention when Yarin reached his hand over the dead body, binding the man's soul to its flesh. "What happens if he doesn't chain it?"

"Souls detach from their mortal bodies after a while, slower if death came suddenly, and you cling to it longer. Once it leaves, it becomes part of his realm, a loud place between the gruesome thoughts of mankind."

When Yarin arched a brow at me, I focused on the corpse, commanding it to rise. Leather armor groaned as the man first twitched, then stood, glancing around disoriented.

The soldier pressed a hand to the gaping wound on his belly, fingers shaky when he pulled a dagger from his guts under whimpers. "Wh-what happened?"

"He feels pain?" Ada asked.

"Or so he believes," I clarified. "Raised corpses with their souls bound don't understand what they are... at least, not at first."

"So, he thinks he's still alive."

"Ah, Enosh..." Yarin swatted toward the wound. "Please do fix this. Otherwise, he'll just bleed on my rugs, not to mention how ghastly it looks."

All it took was a thought, and the wound closed beneath the leather while the corpse grew frantic. Such was their plight as their minds were too simple to grasp what lay beyond their mortal realms.

Whatever Yarin whispered into his mind calmed him, and my brother strolled over to a woman who wept over the body of a man—presumably, her husband.

He stroked his fingers through her matted brown hair, then grinned up at me. "Under all that filth, I daresay she's beautiful."

"Also, alive."

"Nothing that can't be fixed."

Ada's heart beat faster, stumbling over its irregularity

as Yarin pulled a knife from its sheath. "He can't just kill her."

"He won't." Not in her sense. Eilam loved to preach about how there needed to be a balance between the three of us, throwing a fit whenever one of us ended a life. "Close your eyes, little one."

She didn't.

Of course she didn't.

My little mortal watched as Yarin leaned over the woman, placing the knife in her lap and his mouth to her ear. "First, little Henry taken by yellow fever, and now Thomas... What's there left to live for? *Nothing*. Why not put an end to this misery?" Without a single tremble, the woman took the knife and pressed the glinting blade to her neck. "Do it. You know you want to. Can't stand the thought of continuing like this. Do it now. Cut!"

One slice, deep enough that dark red blood sprayed from the woman's neck with each dying beat of her heart, raining down on her husband's corpse, soaking the front of her dress.

I tasted bile.

Not mine.

My little mortal leaned away from me before she retched onto the ground. She emptied her stomach of her breakfast as all strength leeched from her muscles. I would need to find her food and, if possible, a bed so she may rest.

"Shh..." I pressed a hand to the back of her sweat-covered neck, sensing how the exhaustion of the day finally overpowered her. "See, my little one? Your plight could be worse. You could have ended in the arms of my brother instead."

"I didn't think this through," Yarin yapped as he bound the soul. "That's on you, Enosh. Always rushing me. Now look how she bled out, her skin all pale and sickly. At least fix the wound or it'll make odd slapping sounds each time I thrust into her. Who wants that?"

With a sigh, I closed the wound, then let the woman rise. "Two more. Hurry up. My little one is tired and in pain."

"That one over there, with the spear stuck in the head. Oh, don't cry, sweet thing." Yarin stroked tears from the woman's face that would dry out soon enough on their own. "There will be no more hunger, no sorrows. I'll take care of you now, yes?"

The woman nodded. "Yes. You'll take care of me."

"That's right, my love. You're mine now, and I'll have you in any way I want."

"Any way you want," she crooned and pressed her hips flush against him. "I love you."

"Of course you do." Yarin's eyes snapped to mine as my veins heated, but they ignited when he grinned and asked, "Jealous?"

CHAPTER 12
ADA

"We shall bed down at the tavern," Enosh said, steering toward the glinting lights of the town ahead. "You need a warm meal, a bed, and rest. Something I should have taken into consideration, but... I haven't had to care for a mortal in a long time."

He said it as though he wanted to apologize for starving me half a day but didn't quite know how. "Thank you."

The tips of his fingers slowly raked over my scalp, which he did often, seemingly content with the monotone motion. "How come you never remarried?"

"Probably because proposals are sparse around barren women who got their husbands killed." Beyond tired, I let myself sink back against his chest. "Eternity will feel twice as long if I keep wondering so... will you tell me how Njala died?"

There was a long beat of silence until he finally cleared his throat. "There was an argument between Lord Tarnem and me when he demanded more corpses than we'd agreed upon. Against my telling her not to get involved, Njala left the Pale Court without my knowledge to speak to her father."

"Orlaigh helped her sneak away?"

His chin brushed along the side of my head as he nodded, first stubbles catching on my strands. "He kept her from me, sending her across the land with Commander Mertok, trying to force my hand by keeping her out of my reach. When he refused to come to his senses, I marched thousands of corpses to his hold. He offered a parley then, stating a misunderstanding, saying that he himself had fallen victim to a betrayal. He lured me into a frozen valley."

"And trapped you."

"Ah, my little one, a moment of utter folly on my part, but gods are not free of failure, and I was desperate. Eventually, I freed myself and leveled his kingdom to the ground. I chased across the lands beyond the Soltren Gate in search of my companion. But by the time I reached Njala, months later, Commander Mertok slit her throat as... as an act of revenge."

My ears pricked at the hesitation. "You didn't chain her soul?"

"It departed quicker than I could act."

Quicker than he could act.

An unexpected hollowness formed in my core. When I turned to look at him, I shuddered beneath his unguarded stare and how those hairline cracks in his icy mask opened into gaping craters. Shadows played around his face in the setting darkness, as though wanting to hide what I discovered behind the fractured facade of the cruel god.

For the first time since Enosh had taken me captive, I saw the man beneath the immortal, heartbroken and vulnerable, the reasons for his undying rage clearer the more he shared with me. For us mortals, grief ended with death, but his lasted for an eternity, spent as what had to be a lonely existence.

I straightened and looked forward once more, not liking how all this softened me toward him. "If you killed those responsible for your loss, then why condemn the rest of us?"

"Because the depravity at the mortals' core is to blame for all this, their never-ending hunger for power, which is not for them to have."

"If we're all so bad at the core, then why keep me? I'm one of them."

"Mmm, yet you carry the least of it, a precious particularity about you I failed to recognize when you first came to me."

There was that word again.

Precious.

My core expanded at the sheer sound of it, my ears utterly unaccustomed to the word. How twisted my life had become, where I tried to escape the man who refused to let me go, only to get back to the man who'd once wanted rid of me.

I rubbed at my itchy eyes. "One step out of your court and you could've cut one of those virgins down some idiots had sacrificed off a trunk two hundred years ago."

"Lift your chin. Higher!" His fingers wrapped around my throat, tilting my head back until he had access to kiss along the side of my neck where he whispered, "For as much as I torment you with need, you do the same to me, mortal, or I would have tossed you outside to let you die among the corpses. Servant, plaything, treasure... above all, you are *my* woman."

I shuddered.

Not an unwoman.

Not a woman.

His woman.

He held no power over my body out here, but his words infiltrated me just the same, sending gooseflesh across my skin. The ardor in his tone even over a word such as *plaything*, the possessiveness of his grip where another had once threatened to discard me... The urgency with which he wanted me roused a faithless flutter in my belly.

I ignored it. "Maybe—"

"There he is!"

My gaze swung around.

My fingers numbed.

A handful of villagers hesitantly approached from a dark orchard, carrying limp corpses or wheeling them on handcarts, the moonlight breaking against the blades strapped to the three men among them.

Enosh hissed at the sight of the torches they carried, the horse dancing underneath us as if it sensed its master's fear.

He *feared* fire.

Why else would the feathers grow damp against my skin where he dug his fingers into my belly, pulling me against him as he shouted, "Return to your hearths!"

They didn't turn but at least they stopped, exchanging glances, shrugs, and mumbles. Of course, gossip about a man riding a dead horse had spread.

"M'Lord..." A woman stepped forward, the girl draped over her arms a pale blue even against the orange flickers of fire, old sores speckling her cheeks. "This is Anna, my only child. The pox took her three winters ago." Her eyes shifted to me for a breath before the woman lowered her head. "My husband and I will give you all we have if only y-you... merciful Lord, please let her rest. For days, she battled the fever. All I w-want is for my daughter to rest in peace. Y-you have this power, do you not?"

My throat shrank to suffocating tightness as I glanced over my shoulder at Enosh. His jaws clenched; eyes so fixed on the flames licking the moist evening air that he spared the girl not even a glance. The girl wasn't mine but, had I been blessed with a child, wouldn't I beg the same as this woman did?

Yes, I would.

Only when I pressed my hand to Enosh's chest did he look down at where I touched him, then his eyes met mine as his deep voice verged a predatory growl. "Little one, the answer is *no*."

I swallowed against the grip of heartache and hatred. "She's just a child."

The one I never had, yet I felt her mother's agony bone-deep. Whatever had happened to Enosh, these people had nothing to do with it. Least of all this little girl, her brown hair neatly braided, the end tied with a purple ribbon.

"Enosh," I whispered. "Can you do this for me? Just this once? Please? Rest them, and they'll be on their way."

At that, the muscles in his jaws jumped, but he neither barked nor grunted. Was he considering it? He had to be. Oh, please, please, he had to give me this one thing.

But he shook his head ever so faintly, letting my heart sink as he looked back at the woman. "I have no use for your earthly possessions. Go home."

"But Lord!" The woman ran up before me, her little girl's lifeless limbs tossing about, but it was the hiss of fire following behind her that straightened Enosh's spine. "I am your humble subject. Whatever you wish of me, I will..." Her voice trailed off, eyes going to me once more before she rearranged the lifeless body of the spindly girl. Then, head lowered, she pushed the threadbare cotton of her dress down, exposing a breast. "If you wish to lie with— Augh!"

The man beside her fisted her hair and yanked her about with brute strength, but still, she didn't let go of her daughter as arms flopped about. "How dare you whore yourself out in front of everyone?"

"She's doing it!" The woman stabbed a finger at me, voice tight with grief and anger. "He can sard me forward and backward, plunder all my holes—"

Smack.

Her husband's palm hit her hard enough that the woman spun, then sunk to her knees on a groan. "Shut your mouth before I beat you close to death. Harlot!"

A cry lodged from my throat. "Enosh, please—"

"Be quiet," he snarled, then turned to let the strength of his voice shatter through the night. "This is my only warning. Leave, before I let the corpses open the ground and swallow you whole."

I trembled at his roar.

No, the ground did.

It shifted beneath us, letting some people stagger sideways while a wooden wheel vibrated off its axis. The handcart broke down, letting two beaten corpses roll off and splay out in the dirt. A woman cried out.

"Enosh, the ground is shaking..." My words drowned beneath the villager's screams. "Wh-what is happening? Oh my god, oh my god, oh my— Are you doing this?"

The corpses twitched.

Their death-veiled eyes blinked open.

They jerked to their feet.

Except for the girl.

Still resting in loving arms, Anna wrapped her small hands around her mother's neck, then clasped tightly. She choked her mother harder with each violent snap of her jaws. Little teeth dug into the woman's neck, cutting through skin and ripping flesh until her mother screamed. Yet the woman didn't let go, clasping her daughter tighter as she scrambled to her feet and ran.

It was too terrible.

Too painful to breathe through.

"Stop it!" I shouted, hands pressing to my mouth as I watched the dead chase the living. Whatever rage my voice carried, in the end, it distorted into a long wail of helplessness. "She's just a little girl…"

Enosh held me tighter. "Be still!"

He let the horse thrust into a canter, passing town after town until my arse burned nearly as much as my tear-filled eyes. The wind made it only worse as we thundered along a dirt trail that eventually changed into the *ca-lop-ca-lop* of iron clashing cobblestone, lights illuminating windows from afar. I twisted and dug my face into Enosh's shirt, dampening it with my tears.

This late in the evening, villagers paid us no mind. Not until a man spotted the horse's white eyes, starting that first mumble, which soon hushed across the village like the foreboding breeze of a storm. They all came together—some wearing their nightcaps—while sleepy-eyed children hid behind skirts as they took in our dead steed.

After Enosh passed the scorching waft of heat from a quiet forge, he rode the horse up to the tavern and dismounted. "I sense the tension in your muscles and the sickness roiling in your belly." He pulled me down, immediately steadying me on my gnarled legs. "Dare run, mortal, and I shall have the most decrepit corpses the ground has to offer drag you back."

Sickness wasn't nearly strong enough a word to

describe all the nasty things I wanted to spit at him. After a month at the Pale Court, I'd nearly forgotten how the world outside suffered, fathers feeding their dead children to the wolves just to keep them from wandering.

I pushed his chest. "Right now, I'd crawl through the shit in the streets to get away from you."

He gripped my arms with bruising strength and shook me. "You want to leave me?"

"How could I not want to leave you? Any woman in her right mind would!"

Something ignited in his eyes. "Then my brother shall give you a wrong mind!"

"I hate you." I lifted my chin high and met his stormy gaze. "I hate you so much that not even your brother is powerful enough to change that."

His head jerked back as if I'd struck him. It lasted for the fraction of a breath before his gray eyes darkened with... I wasn't sure.

He picked me up, carried me up the steps to the tavern, and kicked the door open. "Oh, little one, how you'll scream my name within the next hour."

"The fuck I will."

Behind the door, the three-story tavern lay empty—aside from the town's drunkard leaning crooked against a wall of wattle and daub. The stench of ale soured between the cracks of rough-hewn tables and benches. Beside them, the tavern keeper stared at us from underneath her plain, cotton wimple.

She blinked wide eyes at Enosh, her hands fumbling with her brown skirts as she curtsied. "I think... I think I know who you are. Heard stories as a wee lass."

"Then you'll know it best to be quiet about it."

She nodded. "Does the King need a boy to lead his horse to the stables?"

Enosh frowned. "My horse is in need of nothing, but I require your best room. You will bring us fresh meats, warm bread, and berries if you can find them. I also expect a tub to be brought to our room filled with clean, warm water and a rag."

She stared at me for a moment until, with a start, she worked herself out of her daze. "Yes, Your Grace. Gretchen!" Fingers snapped toward the narrow archway behind her. "Come to heel, girl! We have a guest, none less than the King of Flesh and Bone himself. Go prepare the large room. Take the driest kindle—"

"No fire." Enosh rummaged through the pocket of his breeches, letting a handful of gold coins clink into the woman's meaty palm. "Will this cover the night?"

"Your Grace is too generous," she said, reaching the coins back to him. "After a life full of nothing but tales about you from some stinky old priests... I don't want your gold."

"My woman is weary. Let this be clear, I will not tolerate your begging at my door. Take the coin, for none of your kin will find rest with me."

The woman chuckled, a hearty sound that shook her entire belly. "I have no children. All kin abandoned me when I was a young lass. All I have are three dead husbands who broke my heart and my purse. I beg of you, do not let them rot."

"I can tell we'll be good friends." Enosh turned toward the stairs, following a pale Gretchen, pressing me tighter against his chest as he whispered, "I shall raise corpses outside for protection. Nobody leaves this town... least of all, you."

CHAPTER 13

ADA

I sat in the small tub Gretchen had brought, posture stiffening whenever Enosh rubbed a soaked rag over my back. Even though steam billowed on the surface, his touch brought chills to my skin. What sort of monster would stir up a child's corpse? And let Anna's little teeth cut into her mother's neck, with the little ribbon bouncing—

I pressed my hand onto my mouth to stifle a sob, a sick feeling twisting my gut. "She was a little girl, Enosh... probably not even four when she died."

Behind me, a low growl trembled his chest. "We will not speak of it."

"Can you imagine the desperation of a mother if she offers her warm body to the god who cursed her only child with eternal cold? To let him fuck her in the most ungodly ways—"

"By nature, I fuck in godly ways," he scoffed, tossing the rag into the tub with a splash. "Luring nothing but the sweetest moans and gasps from your skilled lips."

Only trickery. "You'll stir neither lust nor longing out here."

Because there was none.

Because there never would be.

"My woman is particularly contentious this night." He hauled me up by my arms until my face met his icy stare, water splashing around calves that wanted to snap. "Shall I tell you how many times you came apart with your quim tight around my cock at your own inclination? Will the rebellion of your mind ease or worsen for knowing?"

My pulse sped up.

Not true.

"However much of a god you might be at the Pale Court... out here, you can't disguise loathing as lust or pain as pleasure."

He lifted me out of the tub, his whisper against my ear like metal scraping over rock. "Oh, my little one, that suits me just fine, because neither can you disguise the opposite."

Fragrant straw crunched beneath my shoulders as he lowered me onto the bed, the air perfumed with dried lavender hanging from the rafters. Standing at the end of the bed, Enosh peeled off his clothes, watching me like a predator might its prey.

When he climbed onto the bed, naked and hard, I kicked my useless legs, shifting back for distance. "Stay away from me."

"Shh... remember?" His hand clasped around my foot, bringing it to his face before he placed a kiss on my ankle. "Never deny me your warmth or I shall withhold my touch."

A gasp parted my lips as he trailed his tongue along the inside of my calf. "I don't want your touch."

"No? Your body doesn't prickle when I do this?" The back of his hand stroked up along the inside of my thigh as he inched between my parted legs, letting my skin tingle. "Your bones tremble for my attention, little one. Your flesh screams for my touch. It speaks to me, its master, and I answer it fluently—a language perfected over the course of a month. Listen!" His fingertips ghosted over the curls between my legs, barely touching, driving up the anxious beat of my heart. "Mmm, your breathing becomes quicker as your veins swell with blood, urging me to touch right... here." He pinned my clit beneath his thumb, sending pulsations into it that morphed into heat rippling over my sex. "Yes, that is how my woman likes it best, the little gem restrained until... Ah, ah! Stop wiggling."

He climbed over my crooked leg as he continued to torture my clit. He lay down beside me, one arm angled to support his head as he whispered, "My poor woman came to me so deprived of touch, shunned by her husband, isn't it true?"

Familiar pain announced itself in the cracks of my heart, amplified by the deafening beat of the organ as his finger rounded my opening. What if he was right? What if I'd been so starved of the strong set of a man's arms that I'd taken refuge in the embrace of the devil?

His finger entered me. Pulled out. Pushed in again. "But I worship your body, can't you feel it? How I circle, push, and dip... bringing you the sweetest pleasures?"

My breathing hitched.

No. Not true.

Not true, not true, not true.

I turned my head away, disgusted with myself over how his finger penetrated me easily, pressing my inner walls in that way of his that made my spine arch. "Try all night if you must, but you'll achieve nothing."

"Mmm, I am a flawed god, but nobody can accuse me of

impatience." His smile-hardened lips brushed along a tendon on the side of my neck, his breath warm against my earlobe. "Do I not stroke and pet and dote on you for hours, little one? Tease this little bud until it peeks from its hood, hard and needy? Like this. Mmm, yes. Slow. Gentle. That's how my woman loves it."

My lungs stalled, putting a crack in my voice. "I feel nothing."

"Is that so?" My lie earned me a thrust of his finger before he curled it inside me, letting delicious pressure expand there. "You're not holding your breath right now? You're not clinging to that exhale as if it will help you ignore how my finger spreads you? Fills you? Almost makes you moan but— Ah... you need the thickness of my cock. Do you feel it?"

I shook my head.

"I do," he whispered, twirling a blonde strand around his finger. "I feel the tingle on your scalp, the stiffness in your right toe as you arch it, the tension in this muscle right here." His fingers slipped behind my neck, rubbing a sore knot at the left base of my skull while his other hand added a second finger inside me. "I feel every cell in your body and how it longs for me, aches for my touch after years of scorn and neglect. Oh, my little one, let me worship your body the way your man ought to."

I simmered in a confusing mix of disgust and desire as I breathed into his touch. "It's not real."

It couldn't be.

I wouldn't let it!

But... oh, his skilled hand.

"Stop denying and give in to me." His fingers abandoned me as he slowly brought them between our faces, before he stroked them into my mouth, hooking them behind my teeth, letting the cream of my arousal spread tart across my gums. "Mmm, my little one got herself all wet again, making such a needy mess between her legs that I shall tend to. Let me have a taste of my woman's cunt." Slanting his mouth over mine, he drove his tongue to part my lips, moaning at the taste he found there. "Oh, flesh of my flesh, bone of my bone, you desire this as much as I do. You crave the undivided attention of my touch, how I listen to your muscle's every whim, answering your body's every plea."

My vision speckled.

"Little one," he whispered, "you're holding your breath again. Your lungs are burning. Breathe. Breathe! There... that's my good mortal."

Air rushed into my lungs, and I blamed it for how my nipples hardened. A sense of emptiness filled me where his fingers had been only moments ago, aching to be filled after years of abstention. It hurt, letting moisture gather on my forehead—and more between my legs in maddening waves of aching need.

"Shh, I know where you need me." Two fingers trailed down between the valley of my breasts, along my belly, and through my curls until they thrust inside me. "Mmm, I left you wanting once, but never again, my precious woman." A scoff. "How the blood buzzes around your heart whenever I say that word. *Precious.*" My chest turned weightless for a breath, and another as his lips brushed along the shell of my ear where he whispered, "*Precious.*"

The word crawled into my veins, spreading right through me with torturous heat. My body fevered, pelvis shifting toward the hypnotic rhythm of his fingers stroking me, the large palm that rested against my clit, indulging it with constant pressure.

At the first cautioning tingle around my clit, I sucked in a sharp breath. "I hate you."

"Shh, do not disguise your lust as loathing," he crooned inches from my ear, curling his fingers inside me, promising wicked pleasure with how he palmed my tender nub. "Give in to me. You know you want to. Want me to drown you in pleasure until you resurface and bloom. Ah, you are so close, my little one." His breathing came faster, harsher, panting against my neck with each thrust of his fingers. "Mmm, such heat around your pulsing gem. Release it. Let go."

I cried out at the torrential wave of pleasure as a riptide surged through me, lifting me to the highest high before it dropped me into the shameful gorge of defeat. Something fractured inside me with my next inhale—perhaps my sanity, though likelier, my self-respect.

"Good girl." Enosh's purr broke against my forehead, where he nuzzled the fine wisps along my hairline. "Mmm, do you believe it now, little one? That you long for my touch?"

My ragged breathing soon hiccupped into a pathetic sob. How many times had I succumbed to this man and how easily he weaved pleasure through me? Had I truly been so deprived of touch, of attention, of the feeling to be *wanted* that I enjoyed this depravity?

His finger stroked through the middle of my forehead and down to the tip of my nose. "Why would you want to escape such pleasure?"

Reality crept back into me one strained inhale at a time. Perhaps I was mad, or lonely, or debauched—God's bones, maybe I was all three at once. Nothing but a mere mortal with a beating heart, pitted against the devastating whims of a virile god.

He could have my body.

But never my soul.

Never its surrender.

Braving his sly grin, I shifted away from his touch. "No pleasure in this world could make me want to stay around your corrupted character."

Something cracked in the abyss of his gray eyes. For a grin-dropping second, it appeared as though his mask broke in too many places all at once. Unable to sustain his air of superiority, the age-old face behind the decaying veneer contorted in... yes, anger.

It screamed around a god enraged, barely contained by his mortal form. The room shook in much the same way the ground had earlier, and the glass in the window clattered. Did he do this? Because he was mad? Mercy god, what angered him so? Escape was but a dream already faded.

His hand went to my throat, right above my collar, not choking me but clasping hard enough as if to let me know that he could. "I hold you for hours after we coupled, feeding you from one hand while the other strokes your hair until all tension leaves your muscles. The little skin I have left at my disposal, I weave into the finest dresses, and the softest pelts line your bed." His forehead lowered against mine, and his eyes closed as he shifted his mouth against my lips. "Kiss me." He slammed his mouth to mine, kissing, suckling, and when my lips remained stiff and still, he nipped me. "Kiss me!"

His roar stilled my breathing, but I found a sliver of confidence in how his hand slipped off my throat to the sound of dust raining from the crossbeams. "Make me."

A breath barreled out of him.

A second passed.

Two. Three.

At his next inhale, the room stilled, and his cold mask repaired itself with a new layer of ice that chilled the blood in my veins. "My little mortal is still disquieted over the girl I refused to rot, even though she's begged and pleaded so nicely."

No matter the disdain dripping from his voice, his eyes and the slight frown between them somehow didn't match it. I didn't know what to do with that—or how his lips curved into a new smile promising nothing good.

Carefully, so very carefully, I parted my lips. "Sometimes I told myself it was a good thing I never had a baby, especially when I heard of the ones still in their cradles the morning after a full moon. I don't know. Maybe... maybe gods just don't understand the agony of losing a child."

"You don't know the extent of my agony," he said as a tremble hushed across his lips, but it was gone with my next blink, his mask solidly frozen in place. "If I rot this child for you, what will you give me in exchange?"

Internally, I scoffed. What a ridiculous question. What did I have left to give? What else did he want that he couldn't simply take?

"What do you want?"

He cupped my cheek. "Become my wife. Give your vow before a priest and god—*any* fucking god—and take me as your husband."

The shocking question stuttered my breath. "W-what?"

"I want your commitment, your devotion, your vow to remain by my side. To return to it, should anything ever separate us."

I snapped my mouth shut and draped an arm over my breasts, the room suddenly cooler. What a piss-poor proposal was this? He wanted me as his wife? But... why?

"You've gone mad."

His stare on me didn't waver. "Do this, and I shall rot the girl."

Brittle silence stretched between us.

My mind wandered to Anna. To the little boy born on a full moon. Every child I'd ever held, pressing them against me as if they were my own, even if only for the first seconds of their lives.

I was doomed to serve Enosh for eternity, no matter what. The god wanted my damn vow? What difference would it make to me? Was my pride worth more than gaining rest for even one child? No, but I couldn't help but wonder just how much this vow was worth to a god.

Three deep breaths bought me the resemblance of the boldness it took to negotiate with one. "And if I agree to become your wife, will you also rot John?"

"However much your determination to see the vow to your husband fulfilled pleases me... I won't." Whatever firmness his voice had held at first, in the end, it frayed like threadbare cloth. "I made a vow."

"So did I. Sounds like a predicament to me. An impasse."

Where I expected another shout, the muscles in his jaws merely hardened. A strange energy coursed through me, one reserved for the women who held their husband's attention, instead of being threatened with the whorehouse. The fact that Enosh thought on my words gave me a sense of... of value? What was this god willing to do to secure my vow? God's bones, was it truly possible I held sway over him?

"It's a terrible deal." I held his stare. "One child for a vow until death do us part to a man undying?"

Enosh gave a weak scoff. "Are you negotiating with a god?"

"I'm negotiating my bride price with the man who wants to marry me." A breath of courage. "No more collars and chains."

"The chain goes, the collar stays. You look stunning with it."

Oh, whatever. "No chains. You'll never twist my legs again. I want a decent room."

"You'll have it. All of it."

My heart stumbled over the next beat, upper body drawing away as I stared at him in mute shock. That... was easier than I'd anticipated.

Clearly, I hadn't demanded enough.

"That's not all," I continued, emboldened by this reckless sense of having value to someone, even if it was the damn devil. "You'll rot John. In addition, I want to leave the Pale Court once a day at least for a little—"

"Absolutely not."

"The first or the latter?"

"Latter. Now that I've been sighted, people will gossip, plan, and scheme. That I have been demoted from god to king beyond one gate doesn't bode well for the others."

He had a point there. "Every other week—"

"Once every fortnight for a brief time, and only in my presence."

"Fair enough." I could give him that, but not without adjusting my own demand. "Also, you told me on our way here that you can distinguish between people when you spread rot. I want you to do it for the children. Any corpse under the age of twelve beyond the Æfen Gate."

"Out of the question!"

"But—"

"I do not rest the wicked!"

I flinched.

None of us spoke for long moments.

That was it.

That was where my sway ended.

Still, it reached further than I'd imagined.

"Children aren't wicked," I said and reached my hand to his, surprised by the way he immediately let them intertwine as though he feared I might otherwise slip away. "Even you have to know that."

"Oh, little one, if you believe this will go unpunished, then you are mistaken." He stared at our interwoven fingers. "Very well, I shall ride the lands and rot the children once gossip has calmed. I'll rot John then, too, if only so I won't have to hear his name from my wife's lips ever again. But there is something else you will give me in exchange." He shifted on the bed, flame of the candle driving out the gray coldness of his eyes, replacing it with something less cutting. "On a moment of my choosing, you will come to me. You will not be allowed to refuse me, and you shall kiss me until your lips are benumbed. You will commence the act we share as man and woman, and see it through until we are both spent, not once denying its pleasure. Deal?"

With a nod, I made a deal with the devil.

Because to him, I had value.

That realization cracked through years of condemnation. As much as I had been worthless to John, what if my value never lay with the man in the first place? What if my purpose had always been to bring rot to those children I'd never been blessed with?

And if the woman who rode with the King of Flesh and Bone had negotiated this much out of him, whatever else might his wife achieve?

CHAPTER 14
ADA

After a few hours of restless sleep, Enosh woke me by stroking a finger down the length of my nose as he whispered, "I sense how tired you still are, but we cannot stay much longer."

Head still fogged, muscles weak with exhaustion, I nodded and sat up. "They formed a mob?"

"Nothing but a handful of fools rallied together by the town's priest."

"You saw them?"

He rose and extended his hand to help me to my feet and toward the chamber pot. "Through the eyes of the dead that I've posted around the area to keep word from spreading."

"Good, or every follower of Helfa will be after you, trying to capture you and drag you before the high priest. Every king, every lord, every duke... High Priest Dekalon has their fealty."

Something I'd once considered justice now proved quite the inconvenience. I couldn't have others meddle in my plan to get the god to return to his duty. Something I'd considered laughable last night—until I remembered I had all of eternity to get it done.

"Mankind rebelling against a god..." Enosh thumbed the stubble on his chin. "A nasty habit of your kind that springs up every couple of centuries or so, doubting themselves, doubting their beliefs, doubting me."

I limped over to the washbasin on a table in the corner. "We best avoid the roads."

"We still need a priest to wed us. Quietly."

"What does it matter? You have my vow."

He slipped on his shirt and let his black jacket form around him. "I am indifferent either way—mortal customs or a promise given before a false god—as long as I receive the exact same vow you gave once before."

I swallowed my sigh and turned to him. "I believe there's a small temple hidden in the forest not far from here. My father once brought crates of salted fish there."

"Very well."

Not even a finger twitched on him as he let thin chips of bone form around me. Row upon alabaster row encapsulated me like fish scales, though matched the flow of fabric, its collar snug and high.

I lifted a brow at him. "Armor?"

Unable to walk down the stairs on my own, he once again picked me up. "A precaution. Such a terrible inconvenience at times, mortality."

The mumbles grew louder with each descending step. Once downstairs, we faced a room where at least twenty people gathered. They stared at us from unwashed faces, but the scrutiny in their eyes landed heaviest on me.

"Your Grace," the keeper said, hands nervously pinning graying hair back underneath her wimple. "They came unbidden, no matter how I told them to stay away."

Pulling me tighter against him, Enosh stepped through the parting crowd. Whispers, pleas, wails, and promises—he ignored them all and walked outside.

Wax from the candlemaker scented the air, the sky above us still gray. A small group of men stood gathered beside our horse, all armed with daggers and the occasional sword. Except for the priest, who clutched the Tome of Helfa to his robed chest as though it would help him.

He made the sign of Helfa—two fingers tapping his forehead before he lifted them heavenward. "In the name of Helfa the Allfather, I hereby demand you surrender yourself to His holy judgment. High Priest Dekalon has long ordered your arrest, so you may stand trial for your crimes committed against this realm."

Unimpressed, Enosh only lifted me onto the horse's back. "Leave, and you shall escape with your life."

Metal hissed when a man unsheathed his sword, giving pause to my next inhale. Clueless idiots, all of them, though I could hardly blame them for their ignorance.

My eyes flicked nervously to those few villagers hiding between merchant stands and hides stretched on frames. Being among this many people with the god was uncharted territory for me—there was just no telling if he would spare them... or kill them all.

Fearing the latter, I addressed the townsfolk, "Listen to his warning, or he'll—"

"Capture him!" the priest shouted. "And take the woman."

Fool!

While most men scattered to surround Enosh, one made the mistake of setting his eyes on me. "Aren't you ashamed of yourself, wretch?"

With one quick leap, Enosh dug his fingers into the

man's greasy brown hair and yanked him before the gasping crowd. One moment, the god's other hand was empty and the next, his fingers wrapped around the handle of an alabaster blade.

He stabbed it into the man's throat.

Bile rose behind my tongue.

The man clasped his hands to his neck. Blood sprayed from the gaps between his fingers with each beat of his heart, forceful at first, but then quickly slowed into trickles. His knees hit the blood-splattered ground with a *thud* before he collapsed to the side and twitched.

Frozen in shock, everyone stared at Enosh as he held his hand over the corpse and said, "Watch. Watch and see what happens when you cross me." When the man's body had only just stilled, Enosh's voice verged a dark growl. "Rise!"

The man stood in an instant and turned toward Enosh, struggling to lift his head where the blade must have injured sinew and muscle, yet he snarled, "What've y-you done?"

"Witchcraft..." the word mumbled from many mouths at once. "Dark magic!"

Enosh tossed the bone blade to the man—who caught it with ease—before he gazed over the crowd. "Seek me out, mortals, and you shall end like him."

No sooner had Enosh spoken the words did the man thrust the blade into his belly. He stared down at himself, screaming frantically, stabbing himself so many times the air soon reeked of shit. His tattered cotton trews darkened as urine trickled down his legs, pooling by one foot.

Screams, prayers, curses... Chaos descended upon the town as its inhabitants fled into their homes—as did the remaining men, leaving the priest stammering a prayer.

I pressed a finger against my trembling lips as Enosh mounted behind me, my stomach convulsing in a never-ending cramp. I was no whimpering thing who fainted at the sight of blood, but I'd had about enough for one day.

At the horse's first step, bone chips fell away from around me. They piled on the ground in a cacophony of *clinks* and *clanks*, like snow crystals hitting a frozen lake in the depth of winter. What remained was another dress of feathers, a soft yellow this time.

"I sense your unease," Enosh said.

If he expected me to tell him that caging those men behind bone would have ensured our escape just the same, then he underestimated my resolve to see *all* people rot in the ground.

I wasn't a fool.

Over time, more such incidents would follow once Enosh rode the lands again, undoubtedly running into religious fanatics and the soldiers sworn to defend their cause. I'd rather him kill them than see the god captured again, sparking such a rage inside him it would take another two centuries to abate, ruining all my efforts.

I might have all of eternity to get Enosh to do his damn job again, but I'd prefer another month, maybe two. Whoever he killed during that time would serve a higher purpose, right? He had warned them; Enosh didn't kill indiscriminately.

No, he didn't.

"Just tired," I said when he left town and followed a prattling creek toward an old mill. "I know I should probably have asked this last night but... once you rot John, can you give my father a message? Only that I'm well and that I don't want him to worry."

"You are correct, little one. You should have negotiated it last night."

My shoulders slouched, but I could hardly blame him for my own stupidity. "How powerful are you, truly?"

"How do you mean?"

"You can spread rot and remove it, dull pain, alter flesh, and command bone. Sometimes the ground shakes. It did last night, twice, and the windows clattered at the tavern."

"You have not even seen a glimpse of my power, mortal."

What a terrifying thought. "Have you ever altered anything on me?"

"I have mended you, have I not?"

"Beyond that."

He glanced down at me. "You have ten and two scars on your body, and I trace them while you sleep. Your heart does not beat as it ought to—it's like a symphony to my ears that I could single out over the span of towns."

"My mother died giving birth to me because of her weak heart." Or so Pa had told me. "Where are we going?"

"To Anna."

My fingers clenched at the unexpected answer. He remembered her name?

The horse hadn't come to a stop when Enosh dismounted near the mill and pulled me down. "This will be quick."

He announced himself with a kick against the door. Rusty hinges howled as it swung open, the stench of filth behind it nauseating.

Shrouded in dimness, figures shuffled, wood moaned, and a woman shrieked. It took my eyes a while to adjust. Anna's father stood leaning with his hands on the table, something unreadable coming over a face wrinkled by hardship.

His hand slowly wandered to a knife protruding from a chunk of dried meat. "What is it you want with us?"

Enosh glanced around, his fingers digging into the feathers of my dress as his eyes landed on the musty corner. There, on a mat of straw, cowered the man's wife, one eye swollen to little more than a red slit, the wounds on her neck glinting red against the sparse light from the dying embers in the hearth.

Anna leaned with her back against the wall, still again, neck and torso tied to the brick with filthy ropes. They stood in stark contrast to the new bow she wore atop her immaculate braid, red like the ribbon on her fresh dress.

Something inside me broke at the sight.

Enosh must have noticed because his thumb brushed along my arm as he carried me over to them, lowering me between a corpse and a woman only slightly more alive. Her jaw, the side of her neck, her collarbone... God's bones, she carried more bite marks than I wanted to count.

"How blessed man is in his ability to surround himself with family," Enosh said, reaching for the woman's face but pulled back as she flinched. "You didn't lie when you threatened to beat her close to death."

"Turn her around if her ugly mug irks you," the man sneered. "Sorn her arsehole all you want, then begone. We don't want you here and that... black magic of—"

He choked on the rest at the sight of a corpse stepping into his home. Not just any corpse, but the man Enosh had killed earlier, his gaze now abandoned, his soul gone.

"Make a wrong move, mortal, and my servant will eat you alive." Enosh broke the ropes around Anna with one finger and picked her up. "I'll return for you in a moment."

I dragged myself over the floor behind him, crooked legs kicking to propel me forward. "Where are you taking her?"

"What is he doing to my Anna?" Her mother helped me to my feet and, together, we left the musty home.

Shaky arms and unreliable legs carried me toward the ancient oak beside the creek, where Enosh stood with Anna lifeless on the ground beside him.

The woman wept, sinking to the ground, and tearing me down alongside her, but the noise faded under the *shk-shk* of a bone spade shoveling soil. My mouth turned dry.

Was he...?

Something moved beneath my sternum at how Enosh lifted out a grave, the very act of it going against everything I thought I'd known about this man. No grave was needed for him to rot Anna... but still, he dug it anyway.

Once the hole was deep enough, he lowered Anna into her grave and covered her with dirt. Then, a moment later, *poof*, the soil collapsed.

Beside me, her mother whimpered, "What happened?"

"It's rot," I explained from the little I've seen of it. "She's at rest now."

"Thank y-you," the woman whispered, her filth-crusted face rubbing over my feathers, streaking them brown.

We left her by the grave and rode off, a whirlwind of emotions raging at my core as I glanced back at Enosh. "Why did you do this? Why make a grave?"

Seconds ticked into eternity as he remained silent until, after a heavy swallow, he said, "Because I *do* know the sorrow and agony of losing a child."

CHAPTER 15
ADA

My heart shriveled inside my chest. "You had a child?"

"Not truly." Enosh's gaze went adrift somewhere in the distance. "I only got to enjoy the cadence of her heartbeat for a little while before Mertok took her away. My daughter died in Njala's belly when the commander slit her throat."

There was that pity again, shifting beneath my ribs as if it rearranged them right along with my perception of this man. More than just the loss of a child lingered in his tone. I heard the agonizing loneliness of his existence, the monotony of an eternal life committed to duty, and the lament this had caused him.

As someone who'd prayed for a child many times, I understood the gnawing ache of its absence. If someone took my child from me, chances were, I'd call them wicked, too.

Or worse... vow revenge.

I glanced up at Enosh, the stubble on his usually pristine face so unlike the chiseled perfection he'd maintained for over a month. "I didn't think gods could sire children. Why was your daughter not like you? Immortal?"

"Who can say?" He shrugged too stiffly to carry his usual aloofness. "Among mortals, not all children inherit their father's curses, do they?"

My ears twitched at the dismay in the undertone of his voice. "So you consider your immortality a curse?"

"Ever since I stood over the body of my dead child..." His eyes took mine captive with their unguarded openness, as though he allowed me a rare glimpse of the man behind the mask. "Wanting to follow her, but duty-bound to remain here for eternity, left with nothing but the memory of her heart's cadence."

Everything stilled inside me, giving resonance to his words and the pain they held, almost like an echo of my own. "As far back as I can think, I've always wanted a child."

"Yes, your love for children is evident. I have no doubt you will be with child before long."

That took me aback. "But I'm barren."

"Your womb is healthy and hale."

Cautious excitement coursed through me. "Because you untwisted it."

"Oh, my little one, you have never been barren," he said. "Has it never occurred to you that the fault was with John?"

My blood chilled.

No. Never.

Every man knew the woman was to blame. But then again, no man knew Enosh was a god, so maybe men knew nothing at all. If the god who ruled over flesh and bone said I'd never been barren, then why would I doubt him? Enosh could be cold and cruel, but he was as honest in his threats as in his promises.

My next breath suspended itself at the idea and all that it implied. Had I truly blamed myself all those years for no reason, shouldering John's disappointment and the gossip of Hemdale?

Unwoman.

Subtle anger weaved through me at the memory of the word, the hushed whispers that had followed me from village to village. How some had warned women away from me as if I carried a disease. What if I fell pregnant with Enosh's child?

Heavens, my heart beat too quickly for all the wrong reasons. A child was what I'd wanted for so long; the thought of cradling my own, feeding it from my breast, kissing it—

But I couldn't want it with him.

I didn't.

I paced my breathing, which helped clear those thoughts that would only drive me into useless hysteria. "Thank you for rotting Anna."

He offered a low grunt. "Don't ask it of me again beyond our agreement."

Oh, but I would.

I might have forever failed at escaping Enosh, but that was a small price to pay in exchange for children to find rest and peace. Smaller yet for what I set out to do during my eternal life—to open the Pale Court to the dead. But how?

Once we returned, Orlaigh and I needed to have a chat.

"You should have negotiated for my silence if you didn't want me to ask it of you again," I said. "I might have settled for less."

"I might have offered more."

A genuine smile curved his lips, offering a strange sight with how it smoothed away the edges of his usually severe face. Had he been like this before the loss of his unborn child? Could he be like this again?

As if he'd seen the question in my eyes, his features hardened, shutting me out, as though he decided I'd seen enough of him. "This search for the temple is starting to bore me."

"Over there." Untangling myself from his grip, I pointed left toward the sunstar peeking from the treetops of scattered pines. "Guess I can no longer call myself your whore since I'll be your wife."

He clicked the horse into a faster pace toward the temple. "You're about to wed the King of Flesh and Bone. Correct me if I am mistaken, but that, my little one, makes you a queen."

That shut me up until we reached the temple grounds, which turned out to be nothing but a shrine inside a small building of whitewashed brick. Few graves scattered to one side, most weighted down with boulders. To the other side, a small cottage lay quiet, although a candle flickered in one of the small windows.

Enosh rode up to the door, giving it two hearty kicks with the heel of his boot. "We are in urgent need of a priest!"

Inside, furniture moaned and plates clanked.

The door swung open and a moment later, a man poked his gnarly nose out. "Who dares disturb my silence during such ungodly an—" Stumbling back, the man made the sign of Helfa as he blinked at us from underneath thick, white brows. "This cannot be..."

"Are you what they call a priest?"

"A priest is what you seek..." The old man scrutinized Enosh for long seconds. "Father Leofric is my name. A priest I am, yes."

"Prove it." Enosh dismounted, seashells crunching underneath the impact before he pulled me down and draped me over his arms. "You shall wed us before your... god as we take our vows as husband and wife."

Father Leofric stood mute for a moment, his eyes flicking between us and the stack of books on the table beside the door. As much as he recognized Enosh, word of his presence might not have spread to this quaint place in the woods yet.

"You are the evil that plagues these lands, as depicted in the holiest of books," Leofric said, his voice thin and shaky. "I cannot possibly wed you before the eyes of Helfa."

"You will either see to our wedding or I will see to your funeral, mortal." The threat in Enosh's voice had the man's neck shorten by an inch. "Choose, Father Leofric."

A faint wail escaped the old man before he stumbled for his Tome of Helfa, which rested on a wooden holder on a shelf. "Vows, yes, yes, yes. The King wishes to be wed... Where is my... ah—"

Father Leofric haphazardly draped a gold-embroidered stole over his shoulders and slipped into his brown, hooded cape before he grabbed the holy book. Then he stopped and eyed my dress. "Does your bride not wish to don her blue?"

I looked at Enosh. "The bride has to wear blue, the color of innocence."

"If a blue gown is what she requires, then she will have it," Enosh said. "Lead me to the place of this... ceremony."

"Right this way, if you will." Father Leofric dipped his head, waving toward the shrine. "It's small indeed, erected almost one hundred years—"

"Inside then."

Enosh carried me through the wooden archway, the building only big enough to hold two short pews and a small pedestal before a simple sun made of metal, nailed to the brick behind.

And as he carried me, plumes of smoke danced around me. They brushed my skin, tingled my neck until, surging toward me, they manifested as feathers in all shades of blue. Traces of green weaved through them, almost like in the shape of eyes, depending on how the low-hanging sun filtered in.

It was... beautiful beyond words.

When my feet reached the ground, Enosh clasped my waist tightly to keep me from falling. "You will begin now."

Father Leofric hurried up the pedestal, his eyes flicking between the gown and Enosh, the word *witchcraft* on his trembling lips, but he kept it to himself. "Kneel before Helfa."

"I kneel before no mortal," Enosh scoffed, "and certainly not before the faithless figments of man's feeble mind. And my wife cannot kneel for I twisted her legs. Begin the ceremony!"

Father Leofric's face wrinkled up, but he spared me no more but a sideways glance before he nodded. "Very well. Your names?"

My throat tightened. "Adelaide."

"Enosh."

"Enosh," the old man mumbled as his shaky fingers clasped a nearby quill, pulling it from the inkwell before he scribbled into the book of bindings. "We will recite the vows before God. Adelaide, speak after me."

But I knew the vow by heart. "I, Adelaide, take thee, Enosh, to be my wedded husband, to serve and to obey from this day forward, for better for worse, for richer for poorer, in sickness and in health, to love and to cherish, for eternity, and thereto, I plight thee my troth."

Everything stilled around us as I gave away my vow, and with it, myself in every sense of the word—my body for him to have, my life for him to hold for eternity.

Father Leofric gave a curt nod. "Now you, Enosh."

Hands clasped around my waist, the god repeated the vow with no hesitation. "I, Enosh, take thee, Adelaide, to be my wedded wife, to command and to protect from this day forward, for better for worse, for richer for poorer, in sickness and in health, to... to..."

When Enosh stalled, Father Leofric cleared his throat and repeated the last part, "To love and to cherish, for eternity, and thereto, I plight thee my troth."

A whirlwind of emotions swirled in the depths of Enosh's gray eyes as he cupped my cheek. "I shall cherish you for eternity and give you all of what I have. Except for my heart, for we both know I have none to give."

My stupid stomach sunk slightly as though I could possibly feel rejected by a man I didn't want. Perhaps because Enosh had a heart, as much as it disturbed me to admit it—one filled with rage and grief, but not as black and hateful as I'd first accused.

Father Leofric stood flabbergasted for a moment, but eventually nodded. "Very well. In the name of Helfa the Allfather, I hereby pronounce you husband and wife."

Enosh went out of his way and dipped his head ever so slightly. "Mmm, priest, what a dreadful circumstance for you that I have just vowed to protect my wife."

Warm droplets splattered my face.

My eyes clenched shut on instinct, but I didn't need to see to know that Father Leofric was no more. I wiped a hand over my face, pressing my lips together to seal away the taste of iron. When I blinked my eyes open again, the old man bled out by my feet from a bone spike in his throat, his mouth gaping like a fish out of water.

As I stared down at the dying man, a question pounded to life at the back of my mind. If Enosh had decimated an entire realm for his companion, what would become of the world if something ever happened to his wife?

CHAPTER 16
ADA

A day later, I woke in Enosh's arms. Not an uncommon occurrence, except for the fact that the god himself was asleep.

Dark fans of his lashes lowered, chest rising and falling at an even pace, lips slightly parted... During all my time at the Pale Court, not once had I witnessed him asleep.

Why now?

Propping myself onto my elbow, I let my finger stroke a raven strand from the god's face. My *husband's* face. I'd touched him many times, but had I ever truly felt him? How his hair refused to part a certain way as I stroked through it? How soft it was toward the ends, which spread out over his brawny chest? How his skin pebbled beneath my touch, tiny bumps spreading across—

His fingers wrapped around my wrist just as his eyes sprung open. "What are you doing, little one?"

Yes, just what was I doing? "Touching you."

"Do more of it." He took my hand, guiding it to survey the sway of his dark brows, down the fullness of black lashes, and along the perfect curvature of his sensuous lips, all while he held my stare with ardent concentration. "What say you? Does it meet my wife's approval? Am I not shaped to divine perfection?"

"An age-old soul hiding beneath the beauty of a young man."

"Quite so."

I wasn't sure what reaction I'd expected next, but it certainly wasn't something so mundane as the man letting go of my hand in favor of a good stretch. He extended corded arms that could break my spine and took a deep breath, taking his time as if he hadn't done so in ages—and perhaps he hadn't.

"How long since you last slept?"

"Two centuries." His sleep-roughened voice prickled across my shoulder as he turned to face me, letting my head slip into the cradle of his arm. "When I do sleep, it is often for days, months even, and so deeply that little can rouse me."

"Why now?"

He thumbed my brow, slowly following its sway with a tenderness he displayed more and more often. "Mmm, my wife is curious." His voice faded against the side of my neck where he kissed me, then he trailed his lips along my collarbone and down the fullness of my breast as he maneuvered himself on top of me. "Because if I sleep now, I trust I shall wake with you waiting by my side." He sucked my nipple into his mouth and swirled his tongue around it, followed by a careful rake of his teeth. "Your kiss, *wife*."

A kiss he came to collect as he shifted on top of me, wedging his legs between my knees so I would spread for him. His mouth covered mine as he rocked his hard shaft against the junction of my legs, pressing down until my clit pulsated. Enosh suckled my lips, drinking them in before he parted them with a stroke of his tongue. It came together with mine in play as he moaned into my mouth, a hungry sound that heated the blood in my veins—likely without his involvement, and I wouldn't bother pretending otherwise.

My hands wandered to his back, sensing the shift of his muscles beneath my palm, the hard bone running along his shoulder blade, the—

He pinned my arms over my head. "Oh, my little wife," he whispered against my lips, "I still owe you a punishment for defying your god and trying to refuse him your warmth."

Even as he sat back on his haunches to smirk at me, my arms remained restrained over my head, the bone wrapped around my wrists shackling me to the bed he'd made for us.

"What are you doing?" I thrashed once, twice. "You said no chains."

"No, no chains. They would allow for movement, and you shall have none of... Ah-ah-ah, stop struggling against your bonds." He pulled on my ankles, spreading my legs apart, only for bone to wrap around them and tie me down. "Mmm, my little mortal vexed me so at the tavern. Let me show you, wife, how much it hurts when I deny you my touch."

Said hurt shot into my sex, torturing me with such need that my hips bucked in search of friction... but found none. I rolled my pelvis against air, only for my stomach to convulse when nothing offered relief from this violent need around my cunt. Fire raged at my core, sending waves of heat through my body that scorched me from the inside, only for it to break against the coldness of an absent touch. My nipples rose, hard and needy for attention, for someone to pull them, suckle them, pinch them.

They went ignored.

"Terrible, isn't it? When you are so consumed with lust but have nothing to share it with, not even something as simple as a hand." He lay beside my shackled body, reached between my legs, and pressed his palm against where I hurt, soothing it into ripples of bliss. "Friction. It's in your nature to move, buck, and rub in search of it. But remove it..." Another cramp of pleasure shot into me just as he retreated his hand, making me toss and mewl, the sensation strange and painful in its intensity. "Deny touch when you succumb to such pleasure, and it hurts."

Pain and pleasure roped around me, winding my body so tight I couldn't tell them apart as I shuddered, tossing between the constraints of my shackles as I reached my peak. One that shattered me into a million pieces, only to put me back together again, feeling empty and dissatisfied.

"Never again deny me your warmth," Enosh whispered against my ear as he played with the curls around my sex and the manacles retreated. "Now turn onto your belly."

My hackles rose and I stared up at him. Nothing good ever came of it when he wanted me in that way, with my arse on display and for the taking. How did I deserve this? Hadn't he just punished me?

"Remember, my woman forever, to serve and obey." He retreated and sat back on his haunches, his hair tousled from sleep, but it made his presence no less commanding. "Turn onto your belly. Now."

My muscles tightened with dread, but I slowly turned under the scrutiny of his stare, unsure as to what had been worse—him making me or knowing that I was likely doing it all by myself.

"That's my good wife." His dark voice rasped over my shoulder blade as his weight settled onto my back, his hip rocking against me in circular movements, each roll letting his crown inch toward my darkest hole. "Shh... no need to grow tense. Do not mistake me, my treasure. Your ass is mine and I'll use it whenever I wish, but it is not what I want right now."

At that, his lips ghosted down along my spine, from where it spread into gooseflesh as his mouth went to my—

Dear God, he couldn't possibly... Oh!

The tip of his tongue burrowed between my cheeks, tunneling toward a hole he'd used many times, but never like this. Digging his fingers into my arse, he spread me wider before he greedily lapped at me, circling the tip of his tongue around the ring of muscle.

"I ought to cherish my wife... every part of her, even this little hole." As if to make a point, he lapped slower, letting it tingle in the most delicious way. "Next time I take you here, I might ease you into it with this. Make it wet and needy until it begs me to stretch it so nicely."

He made my back arch, or perhaps I arched it as I moaned, "Oh my god..."

His obligatory snicker followed as he dipped inside, wiggling the hardened tip of his tongue in a way that sent surges of need through me. My hand slipped beneath my hips, venturing toward my cunt, where I played with my hard bud—

His *tsk* stilled my fingers. "What a poor husband would I be if I left you to chase behind your pleasure, hmm?"

His weight pressed down on me once more.

I braced for a violent thrust.

Instead, Enosh entered my cunt slowly, stretching me wide, one agonizing inch after another. "Ah, you are so deliciously ripe, your womb flourishing between the rush of blood."

I moaned when he seated himself fully inside me and stilled for a moment, for once allowing me time to adjust. "Ripe?"

"Ripe for a load of my seed." His suggestive stroke from my waist to my belly sent a shiver across my skin. "I will give you what no other has. And what is that, my little one? Tell me."

I shook my head.

He retaliated by drawing back, only to snap his hips forward again. "Still stubborn."

"Still arrogant."

"Rightfully so." His hand slipped beneath my belly, only for his fingers to wander lower. He pressed against my clit, pinning it until it grew a second pulse. "I will sire a son or a daughter on you. Your belly will grow heavy with the child of a god. Our child."

A moan escaped me unbidden.

His words infused my blood with liquid desire, and for once, I had no doubt it was my own. It stoked a flame deep in my core, burning me with a longing I'd carried for years. Years!

"Yes, I will fill you with my seed, again and again, until it catches in your womb." His pace quickened and his breathing altered, masculine groans mingling with the *slap-slap-slap* of skin against skin as he snapped his hips in quick pulsations. "Mmm, I am so close. Five more strokes. Four. Three. Ah, yes, you want this perhaps even more than I do. Show me how nicely my wife can clench around me, milking the seed from me to the last... precious... drop."

I bore down against the workings of his hand, pressing my lips together against the scream building at the back of my throat. It dislodged anyway, mingling with his throaty groan as we both reached our acme of pleasure. The intense throbbing of his shaft joined the violent flickers around my clit until his hips lost their rhythm, and Enosh's deafening roar shattered from the bony walls.

With a sense of utter exhaustion, as though all energy had left me in one spark, my body turned sluggish. Enosh wrapped his shaky arm around my belly, lifting my hips as his weight retreated, allowing me to inhale deeply. But only until he pushed between my shoulder blades, pressing my chest into the furs.

"Stay like this," he commanded as he gingerly withdrew, all while steadying my hips, keeping my arse raised high. "Do not spill a single drop of my seed, or I'll have to repeat this sooner than you can recover. *Tsk-tsk...* my love, did I not tell you not to spill?" His blunt crown swiped up along my folds, slowly, until he nudged my entrance once more. The sudden invasion of his cock made me gasp as he pushed deep, then he slowly retreated, and suddenly collapsed onto the bed beside me, grinning at me. "I put it back in."

I wasn't sure what to do with this, or the unexpected thrill beneath my sternum for that matter, and only stared at him, not even daring to shift my balance. "Even hale women take time to conceive."

"Ah, but I quite enjoy the effort, my treasured wife." One arm propped underneath his cheek, he raked his fingers through my tousled strands, brushing them over my shoulder. "We have all of eternity to make children."

Children.

As in, more than one.

A gentle buzzing started beneath my skin, like little pulsations of excitement I couldn't condone—or fully condemn. "Let's hope a plow horse comes in before then, so you can have a cradle of bone ready by the time I give birth."

He gave a long exhale as he took in the room he'd formed for me, pupils going from bed to stool to bookshelf—and that was it. No tub, no table, no trundle. Only four thin alabaster walls forming a small square room, as bare and boring as the rest of the Pale Court.

It bothered him.

I could tell by how his lips pressed into a white slash, and he briefly rubbed two fingers over his temple as if warding off a headache. It quickened the pulse in my veins because I could use this to my advantage.

But he only sighed and said, "Mmm, but there is always wood from beyond the gates."

Blast it to hell, I made no progress here. "I'm hungry."

His brows knitted together, probably because I wasn't hungry at all and he knew it, but I needed the man out of the room and Orlaigh here in his stead. "Very well. I will have Orlaigh bring you food and take the opportunity to assess the bridges."

"Thank you. Can I... can I move now?"

Reluctantly, he nodded. "I shall have you again once you have eaten."

I sat up and, unable to help myself, stared behind his firm buttocks as he left. When the doors closed, my gaze went to the stool and the clay pitcher of water that rested inside a bone basin.

The longer I looked at it, the more my skin itched. I should wash his seed out of me, shouldn't I? What woman would want a child with Enosh? But if I was hale, how long could I escape that fate? And if it might help me get him to open the gates to the dead...? Wasn't I allowed then?

I swallowed.

Looked forward to it, even?

Orlaigh cut my internal ramblings short when she stepped through the door, balancing a platter with bread and, from the sweetness of it, steamed pears. "Ach, lass, have a look." Platter placed on my bed, she lifted her hands and wiggled ten immaculate fingers. "Not a speck of rot on me old bones. Whatever ye did to me Master, do more."

I sensed my forehead wrinkle. "That's an issue because I have no idea what I did, exactly."

A hearty chuckle shook her chest. "Only taken the man as yer wedded husband."

I quickly rose to wash between my legs, then slipped into my chemise, and took a warm slice of pear. "And gave a vow he doesn't need. Enosh would've kept me locked here for eternity in any case, so what's the difference?"

She placed her hand onto my shoulder, the touch cold but the gesture warm. "The difference, lass, is that me Master couldn't make ye give a vow."

Nothing bores me more than to make you.

One of his first words to me.

Well, he hadn't looked all too bored when he'd made me swallow his seed or viciously fucked my arse. What difference did it make to him if I came at my own choosing, given how little effort it took him to make me? None. Not unless he actually cared about my opinion of him.

Or my feelings...

My stomach tumbled as I thought back on his brother's offer. *I will make her love you,* he'd said. *She'll adore you.* Enosh had responded with silence. Something I'd dismissed as arrogant indifference then, but what if it had been hesitation? If he had the very human desire of a mate and a child, what if he also desired to be loved?

My mouth turned dry.

Could I ever find affection for the heartless god?

No... not heartless.

Saying Enosh had neither heart nor compassion would have been a lie. The grave he'd dug for Anna, the pain in his eyes over a daughter lost, that he'd agreed to at least rot the children...

It worked on me.

Scraped away my hate one small kindness at a time, uncovering compassion for his pain and an understanding for how the curse damning our lands had come at the hands of mortals. Still, sympathy was a long way from love.

I devoured the slice of pear and turned to Orlaigh. "Tell me about Njala."

She eyed me for as long as it took the old woman to shake the furs covering the bed. "Aye, I was there when the little lady came to this world. Nursed her moments later, then watched her grow. Bonny lass. The first proposal for marriage came when she was only thirteen summers old. Dinnae let me catch me breath either, shushing me about even as a wee thing."

"Did she go with Enosh willingly?"

Orlaigh pursed her lips and lowered herself onto the edge of the bed, eyes going adrift on bone before she turned her head and gave me a smile too tense to be sincere. "Ach, lass, as willingly as any daughter of any lord may go with any stranger he sees fit. A young thing, sixteen summers old, with her reputation stained because of how they found the lass in the stables with that bloody—" A thick swallow struggled down the rest before she rose, shaking the same furs yet again. "Years, a decade, centuries... dinnae even remember the lad's name anymore. Ach, how the little lady cried when me Master brought us here."

So she'd been forced, as was the lot for most girls, regardless of station. "Was he cruel to her?"

"Lass, if anything, me Master wasn't cruel enough," she said on a sigh. "Ach, the little lords and ladies with their starched bottoms, never content with what they had. The room too cold, the footmen too dead, the sight of corpses too ghastly."

"She didn't like the Pale Court."

"Nay, lass, no matter how me Master shaped it whichever way her mood swayed, so taken was he with the foolish thing."

The only thing he'd ever shaped for me with enthusiasm was my collar. A fact that, somehow, twinged between my ribs.

"He truly loved her."

Another twinge.

Did he love her still?

"Mm-hmm, he loved her..." The shadows beneath her wrinkles darkened before she mumbled, "Loved her to death."

I wrapped my arms around my middle, warding off a sudden chill. "What do you mean? Someone slit her throat, correct?"

"Aye, Commander Mertok," she said, matching Enosh's version of this closely enough. "For three days, me Master hid himself away with her corpse, keeping the rot from her in a frenzy. Oh, how the Pale Court shook, bridges cracking right through the pillars."

Given how he'd made a tavern shake in anger, I didn't have the courage to picture how he must have been when Njala and the baby died. "Did she... return his love?"

She tilted her head and lifted a brow. "As sincerely as they teach any lady of good breeding."

So... she hadn't loved him.

Why not?

Enosh had a loving, attentive side to him. By the sound of it, Njala had seen more of it than I ever would. In a time when the god had done his duty, could it have been so impossible to fall in love with such an annoyingly handsome man? Had Enosh known she hadn't loved him?

"It's hard for me to imagine how he must have been before she died," I said. "I only know him as an enraged god with a grudge."

"Ach, lass, the lands beyond the Soltren Gate are no more, all over quarrels of the heart." Her hands stalled on the furs and her pale green eyes bore into me. "Worse than a god in rage is a god in love."

CHAPTER 17
ENOSH

Throughout my existence, I had stood in valleys now covered in water and climbed mountains now crumbled. I had conversations with kings surrounded by riches and beggars rotting in rags. I had seen the sky on fire and the seas turn to endless ice.

Decades. Centuries. Eons.

Never before had I had a wife.

A mortal so selfless and true, she'd negotiated with a god to gain rot for those children she'd never birthed. Little over a month with Ada, and she conflicted everything that had been true to me for two hundred years.

It did nothing to cure my obsession.

I lounged on my throne, one leg perched over its armrest, watching my wife with utter fascination. How she gingerly trailed the hairs of the brush over a young blossom, the lack of a chain allowing her to turn the throne room into a garden of thorns and roses. More curious was how she grabbed the next brush from Orlaigh's rot-speckled hands with not a trace of disgust stalling the movement.

The strangest flutter came to my chest, touching me in a place where I ought to be numb. Ah, my little one called me heartless, the world I had created cruel; yet it had produced a woman so at ease around the remnants of death, she had begged me for rot instead of fainting at the sight of it.

A most perfect mate.

My woman, my wife.

My queen?

"You may leave us, Orlaigh." I rose and descended the dais, only to sit beside Ada and glimpse into the depleting oils. "My little one is running out of paints."

Her eyes remained fixed on the sway of yet another vine, but it didn't escape me how her blue eyes flicked to me for a fraction of a moment. "Don't bother sending the old woman for more. I'll run out of canvas even sooner."

Ah, my mouthy wife and her snarky remarks, pointing out the lack of bone at any opportunity that presented itself. Whatever her simple upbringing, when it came to convincing me to open my gates, she lacked no ambition.

I hooked a finger underneath her chin, bringing her mouth close enough to mine that I sensed the heat of our lips merge. "There are always the bridges."

"And leave our child with nothing to paint on once he's old enough? Whatever will he do all day?"

"Perhaps I will take pity on a corpse outside and turn it into a doll."

"Bone cradle, skin tunics... heavens, an arm to play stick and hoop, and someone's skull for a rattle. That has to take at least three." Her eyes ensnared mine with stomach-fluttering intensity. "Taking pity on one simply won't be enough."

An unexpected laugh escaped me, no matter the

somber truth of her words. "Ah, I am gaining the sense that my wife will not stop pestering me."

"A husband's lot until he dies." She shrugged, chewing down a self-satisfied grin. "Or in your case, for eternity."

Mmm, such was the ignorance of her mortal mind. She didn't understand that I favored an eternity plagued by her ambition over a single stroke of time without her by my side.

I raked my fingers along the back of her neck and into the warm weight of her tresses to cup her head. "Ought we to negotiate anew? Your silence on the matter in exchange for three corpses?"

"You haven't been around a lot of women if you think a woman's silence comes so cheap."

"I have not." I brushed my lips along the corner of her mouth. "You are only the second living woman I have touched, yet you are second to none."

Her heart gave a single, out-of-rhythm beat as she blinked up at me. "Sometimes you say the nicest things when you're not busy threatening to throw me onto a pile of corpses."

"My pleasure."

There was a faint scoff. "I'm not sure I have anything left to offer."

"Start with a kiss."

Her lips tingled so nicely as she wet them in anticipation. Her mouth brushed over mine, letting my pulse quicken alongside hers. I shared in this sense of weakness claiming our muscles as our faces drifted together. Breaths mingled. Lips connected. Parted. I kissed her, deep and drinking, enjoying how she offered no reluctance, no fight, no pretense. And yet...

And yet...

A single muscle tensed at the back of her neck as it often did whenever we touched, refusing to ease on its own, no matter how I stroked, caressed, thumbed—no, it remained stiff and stubborn, a manifestation of her unyielding mind, turning our kiss stale against my tongue.

My thoughts wandered back to how she'd pushed me away at the tavern; her beautiful eyes filthed with the promise that she will never have affection for me. Something utterly inconsequential to a god, and it shouldn't bother me so.

So why did it?

We'd come to an arrangement, hadn't we? My little one had given me her vow to remain by my side, to always return to it. With loneliness banished, what else was there to want?

Nothing.

No, nothing.

Except, perhaps... her mouth straining on the thickness of my flesh, while my cock fucked the back of her throat until that cursed muscle gave.

"Open your mouth, little one." Fist curling in her hair, I pushed her head down while taking myself out with the other hand. "Take me between your lips and suck. Mmm, yes... like that."

Oh, what a dutiful little wife she proved to be, running her lips down my quickly hardening length, even as she shuffled for balance and arranged her limbs. Such a beautiful creature, the gulps and wet suckles coming from her lips nothing short of mesmerizing.

"Yes, ah, you do this so well, my precious wife," I moaned, caressing her hair and the shell of her ear in the way that never failed to soften her. "Take me deeper. Mmm, so perfect."

She swallowed my cock in greedy gulps, letting her lips run over the thick veins feeding my shaft, only for a new rush of blood to swell them further. My crown imprinted itself at the very end of her, a mere finger-width from a muscle that... would... not... give.

The way I gripped her hair tighter barely eased the heated itch around my knuckles as I pushed her head down, feeding her thrust after thrust of my hips. Little coughs tingled around my crown—more intense when her throat clenched—letting my testicles rise with my approaching release.

Gripping myself at the base, I pulled her mouth off me, watching how rope after rope of seed splattered onto her face. It caught on her lashes, painted her pink lips, and dripped down from the tip of her nose as I held her still.

Ada glanced up at me from glistening eyes. The harder her cunt throbbed, the more her diaphragm tightened. Nothing but a spreading extension of that knot in her neck, refusing her complete surrender to us. And what was it to me, a god? Was my wife not mine, married and oh-so perfectly marked with my seed?

"You did well." A knuckle cracked as I eased my hand from her hair and pulled her up for a kiss, tasting myself on her lips. "Go to your room and clean yourself up. Choose a book while I wash in the spring, and I shall bring you release upon my return, then I shall read to you. Go!"

As she stumbled to her feet and then down the dais, I willed the muscle in her neck to surrender. I made what she failed to do on her own, what I could not inspire, the act leaving me dull and tired.

I shucked off my shirt, letting it drop to the dais as the leather around my legs turned to the finest powder waiting on my command, then headed toward the spring.

The moment I entered the cave, warm moisture settled on my cheeks, the air woven with traces of salt and minerals from the mountain in which the Pale Court sat. A welcome change to the staleness of ash clinging to my skin, which faded as I sunk into the hot water. It would return soon—it always did; a constant reminder of the pain I'd endured.

Sudden coldness gripped the surrounding stone as a familiar voice whispered, "Enosh..."

I might have been immortal, but even I shuddered when Eilam loomed over my shoulder. "Yarin had an excuse but, if I remember correctly, I owe you nothing."

"Aside from an apology." Eilam stripped from a threadbare tunic that must have been centuries old, slipped into the water, and tilted his head back to soak his eerily white hair. "You stole the mortal woman from underneath me, turning her final breath into one of many more to come."

My muscles tightened. "What is it to you?"

"There ought to be—"

"Balance!" Yarin emerged from the corridor with the gutted corpse of a man shuffling beside him, wedging a sigh from me. "How blessed I am to arrive at such time where I can listen to Eilam's awe-inspiring lecture on balance. On my word, it gets more exciting with each century he repeats... Oh, are we bathing? I love to bathe!"

My temples already ached at his grinding chatter, but they pounded when he slipped out of his boots. "I do not recall inviting either of you."

Eilam stared at how pearls of water ran down his arm, my brother so wholly unaccustomed to his form, something so simple as water running down his skin eluded him. "Continue to tip the balance, Enosh, and I shall not be so lenient a second time."

My molars ground together. "Are you threatening my wife?"

"Enosh!" Yarin gave an exasperated gasp. "I believe he just threatened your *wife*."

"Death threatens your wife." Eilam gave a lazy shrug. "She is only mortal, after all. Nothing but flesh and thought and breath. Insignificant."

I gripped his hair and pushed his head underwater, letting the splash of droplets mingle with Yarin's chortle. Bracing against the way Eilam struggled and fought, I hooked a leg around his, ripping him off balance, only to watch my brother drown. As equal as we were in strength, Eilam had the dexterous development of a child.

Only when he expelled his final breath and drifted seemingly lifeless on the surface did I let go. "Why are you here? Again?"

Yarin huffed. "Is that a way to welcome your favorite brother?"

"A thoroughly high-handed statement."

"Considering that Eilam is currently drifting on the water, thinking he's dead where he cannot die, I presume, gives me some leeway for said statement." He slipped into the water uninvited, but at least he gestured for the corpse to stay back. "In any case, look what happened to my new toy."

I didn't so much see the man's guts dangling from a gaping wound in his belly, but sense how it bounced and twisted with every shift in his balance. "You broke it."

"I broke it," he said, his tone void of any culpability over it. "Luckily, I happen to have a brother who can fix—"

"No."

"—and I happen to know that I am his favorite, so he would never deny me this small favor."

"No."

"Your wife is quite right... What a bastard you are," he said and leaned his head back against the edge, expelling a breath toward the gray stalactites looming above. "Let me tell you, Enosh, I am no man of casual infatuations, but I have grown quite fond of this one ever since Airensty."

The corpse bowed, letting his bowels smack against his naked kneecaps. "Thank you, Master."

"Yes, yes, yes, now hush your mouth and let the gods talk." Yarin swatted the air until the man stepped back. "Please make him pretty again."

I glanced over my shoulder at the corpse, naked aside from the thin gold chains decorating his cock. "Whatever do you want with this man?"

Yarin chuckled. "Brother, a god ought to have a preference, and mine is... none. I have no preference. You should try it some—"

Eilam kicked his legs and flailed his arms, heaving in a breath as he wiped his hair from his face, his pitch-black eyes boring into me. "You dare do this to my form?"

"Rude." Yarin *tsked*. "Everyone keeps interrupting."

"Mortals call this drowning," I said. "One of the better ways to die from my experience, since I am the one bound to my form and all the pain it can endure. Come near my wife, and I shall call upon every bone in the ground until the earth shakes and the land cracks once more, raising an army that will raze kingdoms, continents, the entire world... killing *everything* that breathes."

Eilam coughed up a final swell of water, his arms shaky from centuries of avoiding his form. "My brothers' fondness for mortal bodies confounds me greatly."

"Ah, yes, spoken like a true virgin who doesn't know where to put his cock, mostly because he has yet to figure out just where it hangs." Yarin tapped my shoulder, guiding my attention back to the corpse. "Here is a fantastic proposal from your favorite brother... na, na, na! Hear me out! Fix him, and I shall make your wife love you."

My molars ground together until my jaws ached. "Why would I want that?"

"Because you're half enamored with her already," he whispered, letting my spine adopt the stiffness of the rock behind me. "So unpredictable. Love. If you do not stir it one way, it may just stumble another. Ah, how Njala's soul called out his name when it came to me... *Joah. Joah! Oh, where is my beloved Joah?*"

The name pounded inside my skull like a never-ending echo, heating the blood in my veins until sweat dampened my forehead. "Do you have a wish to drown as well?"

"Who would have thought that the very man who stole her away from you would gain her heart and affection during those months you searched for her? Chased her into her death, really. So unwilling was she to return to you, the father of the child growing in her belly, she instead chose to die at Joah's blade. Tragic. Oh, so... tragic."

I pushed down the rage, the bone-deep fury that caused the stalactites above to vibrate. Yes, a tragedy, how my companion had sworn me her love from the sweetest of lips... wicked, wayward mortal turning a god into a fool.

But it would not happen a second time.

I shook my head. "I have no need for more illusions."

"You are so difficult to negotiate with," Yarin said. "Very well, no illusions. New offer. Fix him, and I will *not* make your wife love you. Instead, I shall give you... let's say... fifteen words."

"Fifteen words?"

"To relay to your wife, forged to penetrate her in a place

that might take you centuries to reach, if ever. Do not send a spike of bone through me for saying this, beloved brother, but your understanding of a woman's heart equals Eilam's ability to find his genitals."

His offer roused a flutter around my organs. Hmm, fifteen words to reach into her soul, stoking affection for me. She would adore me; she would love me.

That damn muscle would give.

Against the hairs rising along my arm, I fixed the corpse with a mere thought. "Fifteen words."

"Plus, one of advice, because you are truly my favorite of brothers," Yarin said. "Deliver those words during an act of kindness, giving her something she desires. It will touch her so deeply. And if it fails...? Well, you can always slit her throat and replace her with another mortal, like you have done before."

I turned my head and stared at him. "The mortal Joah Mertok slit Njala's throat."

"Oh, yes, I know," he said with a chuckle. "I just never figured out if he was alive when he did it, or if he was already dead."

CHAPTER 18
ADA

T he polished fangs adorning the bodice of my dress clanked with each step as I headed across the bridge toward an empty throne. Enosh had left through the Æfen Gate earlier, undoubtedly assessing if soldiers lined the Blighted Fields in an attempt to cap—

"...keep yer rotten mouth quiet." Orlaigh's hushed mumble invaded my thoughts, putting a hitch into my next step.

She glared up at the throne from the bottom of the dais, one hand clasping Enosh's shirts in need of washing, the other shaking a scolding finger at... at one of the corpses?

A shudder lifted the hairs at the nape of my neck. Had they groaned again? They did that sometimes, their muffled nocturne almost forming words; wasn't it for how the sounds broke against the skin pasted over their mouths, distorting it all into blood-clotting grunts.

"All it'll do is get me bones braided into the throne right next to ye," she said and pressed a palm against her forehead, releasing an exasperated sigh. "Ach, if me Master ever finds out the truth... Foolish, foolish girl."

My heart beat faster, no matter how I tried to breathe it into quiet compliance as I inched closer. Orlaigh had called Njala a foolish girl, but what truth was she talking about? And to which of the corpses in the throne?

Another step.

Another clank of my fangs.

Orlaigh spun toward me, lifting a smile too tense around the corners. "Ach, lass, I was about to get ye."

Arms wrapped around myself, I crossed the rest of the bridge and walked up to her. "Who did you talk to?"

Her belly shook with a chortle. "Talk? Dinnae have no soul to talk to in this place but ye."

Me, and two soul-bound corpses. "I heard you from the bridge."

She swatted the air dismissively. "Aye, time makes yer own head yer best companion. Dinnae mind me chattering to meself like a goose."

"But I—"

"Me Master has a surprise for ye, lass." She stroked her palm down my arm. "But ye cannae go like this, letting the autumn winds howl across yer neck."

Whatever suspicion my body held fell away, quickly replaced with a buzz of energy tingling my toes. "Enosh is taking me outside?"

"Aye, lass. Did ye eat the pudding I brought earlier?"

My pulse quickened at her question, then some more when I said, "I woke feeling a bit ill and had no appetite."

The way her eyes dropped to my belly roused an expectant flutter around my heart I couldn't afford. Probably nothing but an upset stomach. That, or the sad mind of a woman who'd always welcomed her monthly bleeding with tears. It was too early for me to have such signs of pregnancy, no matter how subtle.

"Wait here while I fetch ye a fur," she said, then made her way toward my room.

My eyes wandered back to the corpses in the throne. Enosh had the terrible habit of restoring them some, only to let them rot away until their faces crumbled off in pieces. If they had mouths, what stories would they tell?

Hesitant steps brought me closer. One more, and my shins pressed against the throne until they ached. I leaned in close enough that I caught a whiff of their subdued stench, like soured milk mixed with the fumes of burnt incense.

Lord Tarnem's eyes made a blood-curdling sound as they shifted to focus on me, like boots sinking into deep mud. Gray and woven with hairline cracks, his right jawbone shifted, and the brown skin across his mouth groaned as it stretched and—

"Hmmp... mhh."

I shifted back on a gasp as my heart thundered like the boom of hooves in my chest. His mumbles continued with such urgency, a tendon slowly frayed at the motion. Heavens, I couldn't make out a single word. What was he saying?

Back and forth, my eyes followed the movement of his tongue pressing against the skin from the other side. And if I cut into it, would I find a mouth behind it? Did I want to know what it had to say?

I clasped one of the fangs dangling from my bodice, pointed enough it might pierce the leathery skin. Seconds passed with nothing but the frantic rush of blood in my veins. What would this serve me, other than to feed this skin-itching curiosity?

It would gain me nothing. Trouble, perhaps. And still the fine thread of skin gave a *crk* as I ripped the fang off. I lifted it toward Lord Tarnem's mouth.

He mumbled faster, louder.

Sweat broke on my forehead.

I pressed the fang against the skin.

I pushed down, and—

"What are ye doing, lass?"

Letting the fang retreat into my palm, I trailed my finger over the brittle skin, then turned to Orlaigh. "Just looking if he still has a mouth."

"Aye, one full of lies." Orlaigh's heavy stare remained on me for another moment, the valleys beneath her cheekbones filling with patches of shadows. "Time has a way of twisting the truth."

Apparently, in a way that put her at risk of gracing the throne. For that reason alone, there was no point in pushing her for it.

She came up the dais as I let the fang clank to the ground on a cough, put a light fur around my shoulders, then ushered me toward the Æfen Gate. "I prepared me Master a satchel with enough food and drink ye dinnae have to find a tavern. Aye, ye best have yer wits about ye when ye go home."

"Home?" My steps echoed along the dark incline, toward where the first streaks of light appeared, which broke against the outline of Enosh beside a horse.

"Yer wife," Orlaigh said, "as me Master requested."

Enosh secured a burlap bag to the harness the brown horse carried, then turned and reached his hand out in invitation. "Come to me, little one."

I let my fingers intertwine with his. "Where are you taking me?"

He guided me beside the horse and let his knuckles stroke along my cheek, his gunmetal eyes fixed on mine.

"To Hemdale, so you may point out John's grave and visit your father. *Briefly*."

Weakness gnawed at my knees until they softened beneath me, and a sudden rush of joy blurred my vision with tears. Brief or not, I would see Pa at least one final time. He wouldn't have to spend the rest of his life wondering about me.

Unable to contain my excitement, I thrust myself at Enosh, arms struggling to wrap around the entirety of his upper body. "Thank you."

"Mmm, how nicely your heart stumbles over its cadence." He encapsulated me in his embrace, then let his hands shift to my hips. "Is my mortal pleased?"

"Very," I said, reaching for a handful of mane as he lifted me onto the horse's back. "You couldn't have given me a better wedding gift."

"Wedding gift?" He arched a brow at me, then mounted. "Oh, mortals and their customs."

Orlaigh cleared her throat and held out her rot-speckled hands. "Master, me flesh?"

"Upon my return. Hemdale is not such a far span away, and we shall be back by night."

Enosh let the horse trample over the carpet of corpses. One of them twitched, then another. Soon, several struggled themselves onto their battered legs to limp behind us, spears of bone forming in their palms.

"Did you see danger?" I asked as we rode up a winding path a recent storm must have carved into the hillside, the air moist with traces of moldy leaves.

"Nothing concerning or I wouldn't have brought you along, but we ought to have protection. They will follow at a distance as not to draw too much attention while we stay away from the roads."

I glanced back at them and how they shrank as the distance increased, their clothes nothing but tattered shreds here and there. One had a broken jaw, which dangled on a tendon bouncing against his chest.

Behind me, Enosh exhaled audibly. "You have no disgust for the dead, do you?"

A chuckle escaped me. "As a child, I cut more tangled corpses from Pa's fish cages than I could count. Orlaigh told me Njala didn't like the Pale Court."

His chest hardened against my spine. "No, she found no appreciation for the beauty it once carried."

The benevolence in his tone ached me somewhere, inching me toward a question I'd ignored for days. "Do you love her still?"

"Mmm, my dutiful wife, I am not as fickle-minded as my brother." He nuzzled my temple before he let his whisper break against the shell of my ear. "No, I do not. Perhaps I no longer possess a heart to gift you, but you own my loyalty."

Every single one of his words touched me in a million different places, stirring a concerning tingle underneath my ribs. "A simple no would have sufficed."

A chuckle against the top of my head. "Ah, but a simple no would not have inspired such a flutter in your core."

Heat crept into my cheeks. Damn him and how he stripped me of the ability to deny how he worked himself under my skin.

"Perhaps my woman's silence comes at little cost after all," he mused after a while, the slightly elevated pitch of his voice giving away his amusement. "I shall enjoy it for the few beats it lasts."

It lasted for what felt like an arse-numbing eternity, but likely was no more than three hours from the height of the late-morning sun. Dead horses traveled quicker since their hooves never mis-stepped and no exhaustion claimed their lungs, or so Enosh had once explained.

I shifted my dull muscles and peered back at the crown of the Pale Court as it disappeared into the horizon. "A traveler once told me he walked around the Pale Court, though we call it the Graying Tower, and he only ever found one entrance. How come, if there are three more?"

"I cannot say," Enosh confessed, steering our horse around tall birch trees, toward a clearing that twinkled ahead in a play of light and shadow. "When I came into existence, the Pale Court shaped around me as such, as did the Court Between Thoughts for my brother."

"And the third?"

"The world is Eilam's court." Shifting on the horse, he assessed the forest in all directions, then pointed at the lush patch of grass speckled with deep green shamrock and red clover. "We shall rest here so you may eat and... tend to your other mortal needs."

"What a fine way of saying that you know how badly I have to piss."

Something I executed promptly behind a nearby shrub. When I returned to the horse on straight legs, Enosh took the satchel from the harness and handed it to me.

"Did the old woman pack a blanket as well?"

Enosh huffed as if I'd insulted him, crossing his arms in front of his chest as streams of bonedust drifted around us on the wind. They came together in four sturdy posts, forming a rectangle, intricately tooled with motives of thorny vines swallowing creatures. Alabaster crossbeams appeared above us, with rings of bone from which the sheerest fabric weaved itself toward the ground on all four sides.

It wafted in the wind with an iridescent shimmer, its ends catching on the backrest of a large daybed. It formed at the center, beautifully shaped of the whitest bone, topped with pelts of gray mink.

I swallowed past a lump of awe. "Now I understand what you mean by the beauty of the Pale Court. You could create palaces... entire kingdoms."

He took the satchel from me. "These lands are ripe with flesh and bone."

Ripe.

The word caused a shift in my core, amplified by how Enosh placed a hand around my middle and guided me to the daybed. "May I ask you something?"

"You may."

"Am I... am I pregnant? You could feel it before my bleeding is due, could you not?"

He lowered himself onto the daybed, one leg outstretched and the other angled at the edge, and planted me in front of him. "I sense no child growing inside you."

My chest constricted.

I counted one shallow breath, two, three, waiting for a sense of relief, a lightness in my chest—hell, I would have done with a long exhale. Instead, old cracks of pain veined across my heart.

It was disappointment.

Disappointment and guilt, because my neck shortened in preparation for a "You have failed to conceive yet again, Adelaide," or "What a useless wife you've turned out to be, Adelaide."

But Enosh placed his hand on the diamond of my bone collar and pulled me back to rest against his chest as he whispered, "Patience."

That only made it worse.

He wasn't supposed to be this calm and unconcerned about something he clearly wanted so much. Just as I wasn't supposed to soak up the word and slacken, content with his conviction that I would soon carry a child I shouldn't want.

"Open," he said, bringing a little red ball of a fruit I had no name for to my lips.

My lips parted obediently as he fed me like he often did, all while his other hand combed through my hair, turning me soft underneath the skilled fingers of a god. And what if I wanted this child he promised? Did that make me gullible? Selfish? Did I have a reason left to judge myself so harshly when others had done it for years?

I contemplated on that throughout the meal until a cutting breeze wafted from the forest to the left, ruffling the feathers of my dress and pebbling my skin.

Enosh tugged on my shoulder fur, letting it thicken into the softest pelt, taking great care as he gathered my hair and lifted it over the fur with scalp-tingling tenderness. "Better?"

"Yes." Heat swarmed my belly at the concern in his voice, so I forced my attention to the blossoms carved into the backrest of the daybed. "The way your brother made it sound, the Pale Court was once a lively place with music and... and dancing. I can't picture it with you."

"My little wife, your husband is a formidable dancer, unmatched by any mortal man. When gods dance, time itself stands still, so it may watch us in our grace."

I couldn't help but grin up at him. "Oh, gods and the stories they tell."

A spark came to his eyes, followed by his telltale smirk of mischief. "I shall prove it."

"Wha—"

He promptly rose and pulled me against him. With his arm around the small of my back and his fingers intertwined with mine, my feet scrambled for footing underneath me as he swayed us into the first circle. At the second, the sheer fabric glided over us as he led me into the clearing. Shamrock and clover spun around us, dotting the edges of my vision as my feet found the rhythm.

Tufts of grass wafted around our steps, gently whispering a melody while the air filled with the earthiness of the moist loam beneath our dance. One filled with all the graces one might expect from a god, yet a sparrow danced about on a nearby branch, cocking its head this way and that as it watched us.

"Time is unimpressed," I said. "Seems to me you dance like any mortal man."

"Ah, my wife, but can a mortal man do this?"

At the next sway, white feathers drifted away on its current, some catching on the fabric while others flowed into the forest. In their stead, little buds emerged on my dress. When my feet left the ground—Enosh's hands firm on my waist as he lifted me—the buds bloomed into a thousand pale brown roses, only to wilt and waft into the branches. There, they reshaped into... into what?

I stared up at what appeared to be the flutter of wings, so mesmerized by the beauty of it all as joy illuminated me from within. Enosh let them form into butterflies, with spindly bones for their thorax and the sheerest skin for wings. They slanted into their capricious movement, rising and falling in an unpredictable pattern until, in one surge, they landed on the remaining roses on my dress.

"Do you see its beauty?" Enosh lowered my toes back to the forest floor and stared down at me from the gray storm of his eyes. "The perfection of flesh and bone when in the hands of its master?"

I looked up at him, barely a sliver of air left between our lips. "I see it."

When I placed my hand on his cheek, he moaned before he said, "You, my little one, were made for me."

I breathed against a quiver in my chest. "How can you say that moments after you told me I'm not with child?"

The faintest twitch tugged on his upper lip as his eyes slipped to mine, robbing all strength from my knees. "Child or no, you are precious beyond all, and you have my devotion for eternity."

Time ceased to exist as his words sneaked through the widening cracks of a wall built from hatred, touching me where I'd vowed he would never reach—certainly not before he returned to his duty.

But he did so with striking accuracy, letting the wall tremble until I swayed off balance. My center of gravity shifted until I clasped his neck, and his head lowered just as mine strained toward him.

Our lips connected.

The ground shook.

I kissed him. God forbid, I stroked my tongue into his mouth, tasting his masculine sounds. I lost myself in the trembling of our lips, the heat of our breaths, the support of his arm as he kept me from swaying even as he staggered toward me a step.

I palmed the muscles beneath his shirt, dove my fingers into his black strands. Heavens, I shook uncontrollably, my muscles torn between the instinctual reaction to pull away from this wrong intimacy and the devastating need to succumb to this fever surging between our bodies. To yield to the cruel god who promised me everything I'd ever wanted and surrender myself to his delicious corruption.

Clasping onto the fading memories of a world cast into darkness, I broke the kiss and breathed some sense back into my heated body. Whenever he said things like that, it was just too easy to forget that this was the same god who'd gnarled my legs. Who'd threatened to let his corpses hunt me down, and who was the reason graves carried grain sacks instead of headstones.

"We should leave." Before he twisted my head the way he'd twisted my bones. "We're still a good way from Hem—"

Gripping my collar, he cut my retreat short as his exhale stuttered against my lips. "Now, little one. I choose now."

CHAPTER 19
ADA

Now.

I shivered at that word, an invisible chain pulling me closer to him, strung together by three letters and forged in the fires of my foolishness. Of course, what he'd offered the night at the tavern had been too good to be true, and what he'd asked in exchange... not nearly so simple.

With his grip on my collar, he pulled hard enough that my head tipped back. He lowered his forehead to mine, locking our gazes as his mouth strained for my lips, pausing less than a hair-width from them before making contact. The tenderness of his kiss stole my senses as he ghosted his lips over mine—the touch so light, the air between them quivered.

He lifted me, cradling me against his chest as he carried me over to the daybed. "Did you believe, little one, that I would let you run from the heat in your cheeks or the flutter around your heart?"

Even as he spoke, his mouth remained with mine, rounding each syllable with a suckle of his lips or a swipe of his tongue. I moaned at the familiar taste, even as the trap around me snapped shut.

Its prey?

My heart.

Caught between the welded iron of a promise given and the lure of sweet words sitting at the center, its rapid pounding drew in the devil who wanted it. A devil who sensed its every sinful stumble, every wicked vibration, every squeeze around an organ that had wilted in my chest for too long. Enosh sensed everything.

Every.

Immoral.

Beat.

Letting him corrupt it as he'd done with my body would be weak. Selfish. Undeniably wrong.

I wanted it so badly.

Wanted to turn my back on the world like it had on me, and instead, listen to the wicked whispers of the devil whose words made me feel special, valued... damnit, perhaps even loved in the most rotten of ways.

I closed my eyes and filled my lungs, yet my voice cracked at the first sound. "I... I hate you."

"We shall rectify that. You, my wife, learned to love my touch, the hardness of my cock, the power of my thrusts, and the pleasure I bring you." He lowered me onto the mink, letting butterflies and petals burst into the air as he loomed over my naked body, his lips never straying far from mine. "And you will learn to love me."

I shook my head, yet our mouths refused to part, caught in a glorious kiss of stuttering breaths. "Not until you open your gates and rot the dead."

"Love comes unbidden and has no care for precautions, turning us into fools for liars and monsters." His swollen cock pressed against my heated center, telling me his breeches had vanished, but his hips made no further advance. "That much, I learned of love."

So he likely knew that Njala had never loved him, which ached me somehow. "Neither is it a decision."

"No, it is not. Love comes into existence between the flutters of a heart and grows awash in the heat at one's core." He cupped my face as our foreheads drifted together, submerging me in the scent of ash sprinkled over snow. "I dare you to look at me and deny how your heart beats faster at the undivided attention I give you."

Me and no other, making me feel like a woman desired, worthy of this devotion he promised. "I'm not denying it."

The ground trembled; it ran up along the trunks of the birch trees, letting the branches quiver until small twigs rained down. One caught in Enosh's hair, which I fumbled from his black strands, only to stare at it in mute shock. Perhaps the god held my weak heart trapped in this moment of intimacy, but his was not as unaffected as he had claimed.

My gaze went from the twig to meet his. "Return to your duty."

A smile curved his lips, quickly hidden beneath a kiss he pressed to my collarbone, and more toward my breast from there. His tongue trailed a circle around my nipple, rousing the bud into a hard pebble while he kneaded the heating flesh of both. My breathing quickened when his tongue trailed down along my belly. His hands splayed open my thighs, exposing me so fully out here in the forest, but only until his mouth covered the juncture between them in a warm caress of lips.

Arching my spine, I braced my heels against the bone, trying to escape the sudden onslaught of sensation only to shift toward it. His tongue stroked along my folds, lapped at my entrance, and circled my clit, each movement a smooth answer to my body's demand. I shifted away, and he eased the pressure. I spread my legs wider, and he buried his tongue ferociously inside my cunt.

I gave in to it all, allowing myself to succumb to the delirium of pleasure that was my husband's sinful mouth. Glorious shivers wracked my body as his tongue dipped inside, only to draw back and play with the soft, sensitive edges. When my breathing turned to panting, his attention shifted to my clit, where he gingerly lapped and suckled until a torrential wave of heat flooded my sex.

"Beautiful," he mumbled against my cunt as he kissed me there until my breaths lengthened and slowed. Then he climbed between my legs, cupped my cheek, and brought my gaze to his. "Look at me."

His eyes remained locked on mine as he reached between us, where his cock throbbed against my inner thigh. He placed the bulbous crown at my slickened hole, and then...

Nothing.

Instead of thrusting inside, he lowered his forehead to mine. He brushed his mouth over my cheek, allowing a moment between us not dominated by lust or overshadowed by my urge to escape it.

I was a willing captive.

He was a loving god.

Together, we were a man and a woman, making love in the forest, unconcerned with the snapping of nearby twigs or the passing of time as the sun peeked through the thinning forest canopy.

I clasped my legs around his waist, inviting him with a tug. *Commencing the act.* "Return to your duty."

"Ah, and ride the lands while my family awaits me at home." He slowly stroked inside me, adopting an unhurried pace void of his usual urgency. "My mortal wife shall sit on a throne of the dead, motifs of trees and birds and meadows carved into its bone. Is that what you wish?"

I moaned at the warm pressure as he worked himself deeper. "Yes."

"And there, on your lap, shall sit our son or daughter, black of hair with eyes the color of the sea between the Kilafa mountains." He nudged his pelvis tightly against mine, letting us share in a shudder that pebbled our skin. "And I shall embrace them, and kiss them, and take them into my arms. Yes?"

I swallowed past a constriction in my throat, only for it to form a knot of warmth beneath my sternum. "Yes."

"Then, I shall rock our child and place it to sleep between us on a bed of bone while my beautiful, kind, and stubborn wife looks upon me with such ardor, eternity will seem like a blessing. Mmm... your heart, little one." He pressed his hand against the valley between my breasts, letting the organ pound against the flat of his palm. "Right here is where it flutters, causing such warmth between the rapid flow of blood at everything I may lay by your feet... everything I could give you." A kiss to my temple before he whispered, "If only you would love me."

A task that seemed so easy as he let his words fill the void at my core, driving out this sad loneliness we shared. "If only you would treat me right."

He drew his hips back and thrust again, working my body to a higher ledge of pleasure with the measured stroke. "Have I not shown you my goodwill since we gave our vows?"

Yes, but Enosh was unpredictable in his godly whims—

a constant sway between delicate and domineering. "You hurt me many times."

"Mm-hmm, yes, I hurt you." He once more gripped my collar, exposing the sensitive skin above it, and laid siege to it with his teeth until it burned and set me ablaze. "And I would hurt you again. I would break your bones, sour your flesh, meld your skin to mine. I would do all that and worse, if only to have you for eternity. That, Ada, is how much I desire you."

The sound of my name was my undoing.

Anchoring my arm around his neck, I lifted my lips to his, letting them slam together with such ferociousness, they trembled on impact—as did the ground. Twigs snapped, birds took flight with rapid wingbeats, and somewhere, pinecones must have thudded to the ground. A *crk-crk-ckr* brought my attention to the hairline cracks veining along the backrest of the daybed.

I broke the kiss and snapped for air. "Enosh—"

"Shh." His lips reclaimed mine until they throbbed, only parting for one agonizing second as he pulled his shirt oven his head. "Nothing but the bone in the ground growing restless, eager to come to my aid. Touch me, Ada."

I let my fingers glide over the slopes of his shoulders, over the firm set of pectorals, and down the defined muscles rippling over his abdomen. "Tell me you're at least tempted to give in."

"More than ever before." Gradually, his pace quickened, making my insides convulse with a need for release that shook me to the core alongside the world. "Decades. Centuries. Eons. One day, you will love me. And on that day, when you become wholly mine and nobody else's, I shall open my gates and return to my divine duty."

At his next thrust, I pulled him deeper into me. Our

kisses lost precision, but my benumbed lips pressed down wherever they reached as I ground against him, meeting him beat for beat.

When my breath caught in my throat and my entire body tensed, Enosh's back rounded, strong hips pinning me to the soft mink beneath us. Snarls hissed passed his clenched teeth, cutting across my lips as a cry wrenched from my throat.

The world seemed to collapse around us, trees threatening to bury us beneath their branches as we peaked. Only when the tangle of our panting breaths calmed did the forest grow still.

Aside from the groans.

My eyes snapped to the underbrush and my heart gave a massive whomp. "Why are they here?"

Enosh followed my line of sight to the dozens of corpses looking at us from between shrubs and standing on fallen trunks covered by moss. Men, women, children... they bore their milky-white stare into us, their faces smudged, their hair covered in lumps of dirt, grass, and wilted leaves.

A bemused scoff rumbled from Enosh's chest. "They must have thought their master at great risk."

"You didn't call them?"

Enosh regarded me, his air of superiority vanished, the face beneath the mask laid bare to the almost sheepish grin on his lips. "Not precisely... but I am ever-so pleased with their eagerness to protect me."

Protect him from what?

The question fanned a little spark to life in my core. During our lovemaking, my husband had accidentally made the dead crawl from the ground. My temporary surrender had blown his mask off, right along with his control. Perhaps he was no less trapped than I, exposing a heart he claimed he no longer had.

I placed my palm against it.

A heart that fluttered wildly against my skin, long after his breathing had calmed, right where it bred love with no care for precautions. Should that scare me?

It scared him. I could tell from the way he fled my touch, disguised as no more than a shift to get comfortable.

"Perhaps we made a child now," I said.

"No, Ada. I'm afraid you will have to gather more patience for your womb is nowhere near its fertile state." He sat up as leather encapsulated his legs and a fur-lined dress of silky skin formed around me. "We ought to hurry now, so we may reach—"

Something hit my eye.

Both clenched shut on reflex, throwing me into darkness as my ears pricked at an onslaught of groans and whistles. I wiped a hand over my face.

Wet. Warm. Slippery. Blood?

"Stay down!" Enosh's bark resonated along with a barrage of quick *shk-shk-shks*, like spades cutting into the ground, and a heavy weight settled on my chest. "The corpses must have led them straight to us."

Them.

My heart burst into a sprint and my eyes shot open. I blinked once, fighting the burning blurriness in one of them. The outline of Enosh sharpened with the second blink. At the third, my stomach dropped.

Heavens, no!

Red rivulets ran down his abdomen, coming from a gaping wound between his shoulder and his chest, the flesh and skin shredded around the tip of an arrowhead. The feathered fledging of yet another arrow protruded over his shoulder, where they must have shot him in the back.

"Oh my god!" My shaky hand reached for his wound. "You're injured."

Enosh only hushed me and picked me up, my body so heavy I could barely lift my arms to clasp his neck. Because he'd once more given me armor, row upon row of bony scales that still formed around me as he hoisted me onto the horse. "One leg to each side, for we shall ride faster than ever before."

He reached behind and pulled an arrow out under curses. A sudden crack caught my attention, and that was when I saw it. A wall of bone had erected around us, shielding us from whatever wanted to come through.

Arrows, mostly.

Several punctured the bone here and there, though the biting *crk* of an axe also chipped away at the wall. The more the bone crumbled, the more shouts filtered in, sickeningly cheerful and underlined with the hiss of blades. Wafts of bitterness crept into our shelter, putting a knot in my stomach.

Was there... fire?

"Stay close to me." Enosh mounted behind me as easily as ever, but I heard the groan of pain as he wrapped his arm around my middle. "Shh... I will not let them harm you."

I did as told and pressed myself tightly against him, fighting the panic pounding in my chest. Everything happened so fast, yet time seemed to slow as the wall of bone thinned into a cloud of powder.

It surged toward us with the speed of lightning, only to burst into the forest shaped like a thousand bony daggers. They found their way into skulls and stomachs, replacing the twang of bowstrings with the blood-clotting screams of... soldiers.

My heart dragged heavy on its strings at the sight of studded armor, plated helmets, and green standards peeking from all around us. This was no mere mob of pitchforks and priests, but a formidable force barely thinned by those who sunk to their knees. Even before the men collapsed to their sides, they shot up again, taking up arms against their comrades.

Our horse spun, tore through a wall of swords, and dashed deeper into the forest. It weaved around corpses who bit into the necks of soldiers, while Enosh sent wave after wave of bone daggers at them or let ropes of skin strangle them. For a blissful second—not even half a breath—it appeared as though we might escape.

Until the forest floor caught fire.

It started as an orange spark, but quickly ran to the left and right, forming a wall of roaring flames. Thick and tar-black, billows of smoke turned the air rancid, burning my lungs with every inhale.

Our horse stopped.

Spun. Then spun again.

"Catch them!"

Soldiers armed with swords and torches poured in from both sides, cutting off our escape.

Enosh held me tighter. His other hand pressed against my face, blinding me as the horse shifted beneath us. Everything shook. A force thrust me upward. The horse disappeared from underneath me. Excruciating heat engulfed me, and the stench of singed hair crept into my nostrils just as my arse hit the horse's back once more.

"No..." The word tumbled from Enosh's lips as his hand slipped off my face, letting the blood chill in my veins.

Another wall of fire spread out ahead of us, letting the flicker of flames reflect on the studded shields of the soldiers before us. They gushed in from a hill to the right, took formation nearby a creek to the left, brought in—

Something thrust me forward.

I clung to the horse's neck as Enosh's thighs shook where they framed mine. At his scream, I swung around. All blood sucked from my arteries, sending a chill across my skin.

The bloodied tip of a heavy bolt protruded from beneath his collarbone, only a hand-width away from where my head had been. They must have attached a rope to it, which whipped against the horse's side each time it danced.

Enosh dug his shaky fingers into my hair. "I gazed through the eyes of the dead and the way home is empty after the last line of soldiers. Let the horse take you to the Pale Court and wait for my return while I fight them and ensure your escape."

Bile licked the back of my throat. "No! No, no, no—"

"Shh. They will not rest until I am captured or they are dead. It's far too dangerous for you to remain with me. The corpses will protect you." His forehead lowered to mine. "I will return to you, Ada. I will always—"

A strong tug unseated him, pulling him off the horse. Just then, a rope of skin braided itself around me, tying me to the horse until I leaned forward and clasped its cold neck. A brittle wall of bone shaped to my left and right. The horse thrust into a canter faster than the wind, nearly throwing me off if it wasn't for the rope. Hooves boomed underneath me to the whistle of arrows as they pierced and splintered the weakening wall.

It thinned into a thick cloud of bone, from where it

turned into a crowd of corpses. They lined my sides, running, stumbling, barraging through everything in their wake as they ensured my escape for what felt like a small eternity. The wind whipped around my eyes and tears blurred my vision. Something stood in our way, but the horse ran right through, and a *crk* echoed along with a yelp. The tension of the rope disappeared as my veins filled with liquid dread.

Oh no. No, no, no...

This was too fast.

My dress to heavy.

When the horse jumped something, I shifted back. Scales of bone, heavy and rigid, tore me sideways. I leaned forward. I grappled for the mane. Harness. Anything.

With a jerk that vibrated against my clammy palms, the thunder of hooves turned more hollow. Gravity ceased to exist for long moments. Suspended in the air, I was ripped sideways.

I hit the ground a moment later, my shoulder clashing with the massive root of a tree before I skittered over dirt. Pain exploded inside the joint and the skin along my arm burned as splintered bone chips cut into it. My eyes shot to the horse.

It kept running.

Without me.

CHAPTER 20
ADA

I snapped for air, pulling the autumn chill down my throat and into my dread-filled chest. What was I supposed to do now? The horse was gone. What remained were several dozen corpses who stared at me none the wiser.

As long as they kept standing, though, they hadn't overwhelmed Enosh. Still, I couldn't just sit here and wait for him. Soldiers might come for my head next. Devil be damned, where was I?

A loud rumble answered, along with the salt of the sea that seasoned my tongue each time I groaned in pain. I forced myself onto shaky legs, taking a quick assessment of my state. My cheek burned something awful. Cuts painted one of my arms crimson while the other hung limp and somewhat displaced from my battered shoulder. *Dislocated.*

I walked toward the deafening boom until my feet met the edge of the cliff. Below, violent waves threw themselves against ungiving rock. Seagulls drifted over the water where something bobbed on the surface...

A man.

A corpse, to be precise. Everyone knew a merchant ship had succumbed to a storm a winter ago, clashing with the rock before the current ripped the sailors asunder. Trapped them there to wiggle on each full moon.

Enosh must have called them to his aid.

My heart clenched and my legs threatened to snap underneath me. Calm. I had to stay calm and think. Panic would get me nowhere but onto a pyre, and Enosh couldn't die.

But he could suffer.

No, I couldn't think of that now.

Breathe. Breathe!

I knew where I was.

We called this place Beggar's Bay, and that name lifted some of the pain. Hemdale wasn't far from here, easily found if I followed along the cliffs before I cut inland toward the east. Ugh, the pain returned twofold. Hemdale was no safer than any other place out here, perhaps less so. Shouldn't I return to the Pale Court? But how?

The Blighted Fields lay... what? Half a day's ride away? Walking there would take me three full ones. I lifted the heavy bone train of my dress and cringed at the blooming bruises.

Make that four days.

I glanced over the quiet fields from which I'd escaped, spotting neither my husband nor a soldier. Still, who could tell what I would run into if I went back there? Enosh had sent me away for a reason.

Bile soured my tongue.

I was just as hunted.

Between the threat of running into soldiers—likelier having my throat cut by vagabonds before even setting eyes on the Pale Court—and a few hours to potential safety with Pa, the choice was simple.

After a quick glimpse at where the sun reflected from behind dreary clouds to make certain I would follow the cliff in the right direction, I looked down at my dress. Aside from the fact that bonemail would earn me suspicion, it was too damn heavy. Beneath it, the lined leather dress remained intact.

I ripped one of the splintered bone scales away from the sleeve, then cut through the strings of leather that held the rows of chips in place so I might slip out of it.

Turning toward the corpses, I gave a few shooing waves at them. "Go away. Or... I don't know. If you follow, just don't make it so obvious."

They followed.

And groaned...

Devil be damned, they stomped behind me for a while as I headed north with a slight limp in every other step. Toward home... or away from it?

My throat narrowed.

It didn't matter.

What good was keeping a promise if I died trying to fulfill it? A mule and provisions. A waxed, hooded cloak. A scarf to hide my face for good measure. That was all I needed to prepare for my journey to the Pale Court. Maybe three days of rest for my shoulder—

Thud. Thud.

Thud, thud, thud.

I turned back.

Panic surged, freezing my legs in place as I stared over the motionless corpses littering the ground.

They'd captured Enosh.

CROUCHING BEHIND BARRELS, I waited in the shroud of darkness, listening to the once familiar bellow of Hemdale's night guard as he called the hour and lit the few oil lamps. His voice faded into the thick fog lingering between the buildings, making room for the rapid *ba-boom* of my heart.

Three.

Two.

Now!

I slinked around the barrels and hurried steps carried me up the cobblestone. It changed into seashells crunching beneath my thinning soles as I snuck around my home and hushed into the shrubs beneath the window.

Snores came from behind the shutters. I pushed a twig through the gap and disabled the lock behind them. Hinges creaked when I opened the shutters, and I reached up in search of hold on the window's frame. Since my arm still hung limp and numb, it took several attempts to reach the sill. Once I did, I wiggled myself inside, ribs grinding along hard wood before my hip caught on it. I hit the wooden planks a breath later. Pain flared to life across my body once more, putting the ache around the blisters on my feet to shame.

Still, the snoring continued, and I patted the table down for a candle. Red embers guided me toward the hearth, where I lit the wick, letting a flame cast nervous flickers about the room. My handloom took up a large part of it, and I carefully worked around it toward Pa's bed.

My nose caught a whiff of musty straw, so foreign after two months of the softest pelts keeping me warm. Something inside me revolted. Everything smelled wrong; the air I breathed so void of the familiarity of ash sprinkled over snow, it sunk my heart. Would they burn Enosh at the stake?

My head shook on its own.

There was no point pondering it.

In the end, Enosh would be alive.

Though I might not end so lucky.

I kneeled beside Pa's bed, palm suspended above his mouth in case he screamed. "Pa." When he smacked his wrinkled lips but otherwise didn't rouse, I tried again. "Pa. Wake up. It's me... Ada."

He shot up with a groan, clutching his patched-up quilt. I hadn't needed to worry about him screaming. He pressed the quilt to his mouth, letting the wool muffle a violent cough that shook the tousled white strands at the top of his head. With it came the scent of blood, like a rusty nail warmed between one's fingers.

I brought the candle closer, letting the dim light cast across the many dark red spots that dappled the linen atop the straw. My stomach hardened.

It had gotten worse.

So much worse.

"Ada..."

Pa's voice, muffled beneath layers of bloody phlegm, brought my eyes to his. "We have to be quiet or the night guard will find me."

"Oh, child..." His blood-stained lips trembled, his eyes glassy. "Where have you been? What happened to your face? For days, we sent riders to search for the mule, but they never... never found you, and..." When his eyes narrowed on my neck, I suddenly remembered that I still wore my collar. "What in the name of Helfa is that?"

"Shh, I'll tell you everything." Even if I didn't know how. "First, I'll heat some water, then get a rag and strong alcohol for my wounds. But..." I peeled my shredded dress away from my badly bruised shoulder, "I'll need your help with this. You have to push it back, like I saw you do once with William."

His lips pressed into a thin line as he struggled age-stiffened bones from the bed. "Your cheek needs stitching, and even then, it'll leave an ugly scar. Where have you been, Ada? Why have you not sent word? So stricken was I with grief and guilt, but the mule, it... There was nothing I could do to hold him."

I shook my head, not knowing where even to begin. "No, Pa, there was nothing you could've done. But listen, I can't stay in Hemdale. Stitch me up as good as you can, and I'll try to explain while you do."

The silence grew pregnant while I heated water in the kettle by the hearth, stacked the fire, gathered needle and yarn. How could I possibly explain all that had happened if I could barely straighten my thoughts or overcome this hollowness swelling beneath my ribs?

Keeping my voice low lest the night guard might grow suspicious, I told Pa everything. Well, almost everything, leaving out the parts that would make any god-fearing man draw the sign of Helfa to his ashen forehead.

"We married in a little temple," I eventually concluded.

At that, Pa's bushy white brows knitted. "And have you been this... creature's wife in every sense of the word?"

Cheeks sucked between my molars, I nodded. "Not a creature, Pa. A god. And... I gave my vow."

"And before this terrible *god* coaxed this vow from you, for we all know of his cruelties..." There was a heavy pause as he held the needle into the fire, sending a shudder across my back. "Has he touched you? Has he... forced himself on you?"

I flinched twice.

Once at his question, the second time when the hook needle poked my skin, thread squeaking through the flesh around a weeping cut on my cheek.

Between the drafty gaps in the daub and the old straw in the mattress of my simple home here in Hemdale, the answer would have been yes. But nothing was simple about Enosh or how I'd gone from captive to wife to... to lover? Where had my obedience ended? Where had my cravings begun? What if I'd welcomed the desire in his touch, his attentions, using his power as a convenient way to wash my hands of sin and call it insanity?

Pa stroked my hair back. He must have read the confusion on my face, and that shamed me deeply.

I forced a smile. "Enosh said he would open his gates and rot the dead the day I loved him."

"Sounds to me like something the devil would say. And a pact with him is what you got yourself into."

My stomach clenched. "King. God. Devil. He brought rot to the girl Anna, and he agreed to do the same for all the children in these lands. Does that account for nothing?"

"My child, I simply don't know what to make of this." Pa sighed as he cut the thread with a sharp blade. He wiped a cold, wet cloth over the wound before the room filled with the balmy traces of marigold salve, which he dabbed onto my cheek. "John was bad enough. Oh, I never forgave myself for agreeing to his bride's price. Can a father be concerned for his—" A cough cut through his words, leaving a speck of blood on the corner of his mouth. "I worry about you."

"I know." But I worried about him more, and how his chest now vibrated with a constant rattle, as though blood collected in his lungs. "This morning, Enosh took me with him to stand by his promise. Soldiers attacked us. Maybe the corpses he raised put them on our tail. Maybe they'd watched the Æfen Gate all along. Who can say?"

"Ever since people reported his sighting, High Priest Dekalon issued all villages and towns to supply a militia for his capture for he would surely emerge again."

Something I'd warned Enosh about, but neither the god nor I had expected such force. "They used fire as though they knew what his weakness was, just like in that book someone told me about. I'd bet a silver coin that the Hight Priest knows exactly what Enosh is."

"Yes, a god, you say." Doubt carved itself into the wrinkles around his scrunched nose. "Has he spread rot? Have you seen the children rot in the ground, whatever that might look like?"

An itch started underneath my skin, growing more uncomfortable with each second I said nothing. "Well... we were attacked. He had no opportunity to do so."

"So headstrong, not even the devil could master it." He scoffed, but the sound held more accusation than amusement. "A man who broke your legs, collared you, had corpses keep you a prisoner, and did who knows what else to you... yet he has done nothing to lift this curse from what I can tell, aside from rotting one strange girl."

"*Twisted*. He didn't break them, but—" Damn it to hell, I should have kept my mouth shut or came up with a lie. Of course, all this made me look like a woman out of her wits. "I trust his word."

Pa frowned. "The devil is the father of all lies."

I rose and paced the creaky floorboards, not liking how this itch refused to ease. "Enosh is many things, but he's no liar."

He'd vowed no mortal shall find rest at the Pale Court,

and none did. He'd promised to make every one of my orifices his to play with, and he had. He'd threatened his cock up my arse if I wasn't agreeable, and he'd done that, too.

All perfect examples of his truthfulness, but even without saying them out loud, I sounded like a madwoman, even to myself. As much as those things proved his sincerity, all it did was make him an honest devil—one who likely burned at the stake at this very moment.

I let myself slump to the ground before the hearth and buried my muddled head underneath the tangle of my arms. Nearly two months with Enosh and what had I achieved? Very little.

That dark void in my core expanded, sucking all my remaining strength into its black nothingness until my chin hit my chest. All I'd accomplished was getting him captured. And for what? To rot the remains of my deadbeat, late husband? He could go right ahead and walk off the fucking cliff for all I cared.

Curse this mess to hell and back. I'd made everything worse. Days, months, years... eventually, Enosh would free himself. And once he did? Oh, my husband would listen to no talk of rot, and instead, he'd come straight for High Priest Dekalon. And if something happened to me out here...?

I shuddered at the premise of the looming destruction, forcing my head up to meet Pa's eyes. "I have to get back to the Pale Court."

"I don't think you should return to this man, whatever he might be," Pa said, his voice stern, but he eventually nodded. "But yes, you're not safe here. Talk about a woman who rode with him is spreading from village to village. Little did I know it was my own daughter. Stand up."

"I made a vow before God."

"A vow before a god you say is not real, so I can only wonder about its value." He gave me a come-hither motion. "Stand."

When I did, Pa grabbed my arm with one hand. With the other, he cupped my shoulder until, with a rapid push, it cracked and slipped back into its joint.

I hissed a dozen curses into the sleeve of my dress. "I need a mule. Better even, a horse."

"Weak and battered as you are, you'll fall right off at the first breeze catching on your hair. What you need is rest. A month to rest your shou— Haugh!" Another savage cough sliced through his words, speckling the fist pressed to his mouth with blood that ran along his wrist before it dripped onto the wood. He cleared his throat, wiped his hand on his gown, and tapped my collar. "This needs to come... come off, lest you want your head severed by some cutthroat to get to the stone. Some nippers should get through the bone."

I nodded, eyes going to the red stains on his white gown. Even I understood that one misstep of a hoof might cause such pain in my shoulder, it might throw me off the horse, never-mind the pounding beat hammering the joint at a canter. Yes, I needed rest. Gathering all provisions would take time.

Time I would use to convince Pa to come with me.

"He could heal whatever is wrong with your lungs, you know." I grabbed the wet rag from the kettle and washed the blood off his age-wrinkled fingers. "Come to the Pale Court with me, and Enosh can make it right again. I know he will do it for me."

He stroked my tousled tresses back but shook his head. "I look forward to reuniting with your mother."

Who was stubborn now? "You'll wander."

"Yes, your husband made certain of that."

My head turned on instinct, unable to face whatever objection I might find on his face. "I'll need ashes and walnut shells to darken my hair. We cannot use our names wherever we go, and nobody can know that we came from Hemdale or anywhere near it."

"There's a quaint fishing village upstream," Pa said, already reaching for his travel sack. "News is slow to reach there. Two days' travel. A month of rest for your shoulder."

"I can't afford a month." If Enosh escaped and found the Pale Court empty... "We'll go to that village to rest and prepare. If we bring your cages along, we can sell fish for coin and can afford a mule. Then we'll head to the Blighted Fields, but we'll take the long way around."

CHAPTER 21
ENOSH

There was that smell again—acrid, the mist of mortality wafting around it moist in my nose. My flesh sizzled. Blisters popped against the lick of flames underneath me. Its stench was second only to the sulfurous odor of my burnt hair. Still, I found reprieve in the fact that the dry, bitter reek of ash remained absent.

For now.

Because they'd weaved my broken bones through the spokes of a wooden wheel, allowing my skin and flesh to mend when I was at its highest point.

Ah, torture had come a long way.

Wood groaned.

I dove toward the fire.

Every muscle in my body strung tight until the iron chains around my wrists and ankles clanked. Violent trembles seized my body and a guttural groan lodged from my throat unbidden. *Tshhh* went my lashes as they singed away for the hundredth time to the bellow huffing air into the flames.

Pain... so much pain.

But I could not linger on it when I emerged from the flames, eager to leave this rotten place and return to my wife. Memories of our coupling in the forest spread through me, weaving a sanctum for my crippling mind, no matter how frail. My little one had wholly given herself to me, to us, to this inkling of sincere affection between us that went beyond lust and loneliness. Had that not been so?

Matters of the heart confounded me, but not that of flesh and bone. And my wife's had been pliable beneath me, not a single muscle offering resistance. I needed to return to her. Oh, she had to be so scared, shaken, terrified.

I forced my mind through the fog of agony and anguish, letting it roam over the dead scattered across the lands, commanding them to aid me.

Master. Master.

The dead called out to me forevermore, eager to do my bidding. I let them dig from their graves, rise from where they'd last collapsed, and march—

Fire engulfed me...

...and didn't stop.

"I need a break," the man beside me said through the roar of flames. "Turn him slowly in the flames and faster at the top, or he'll use his black magic."

Eager flames devoured me, opening my eyes to it all as it burned my eyelids away. Gray flakes soon drifted up and away until my vision first blurred, then speckled, until it finally darkened. My lungs smoldered from the heat; seared even more from how I wanted to scream but wouldn't allow such humiliation. Pain carried me within the reaches of death... but no further.

Wood moaned.

Iron fittings creaked.

Flames retreated.

My skin itched where it mended as I came up again, more violently around the charred flesh of my lips from which I drooled. For days I'd prepared my escape, but gathering bone proved tedious. Hardly did I bring it to the surface from the outreaches of my prison, did approaching flames cut my efforts short. Oh yes, Lord Tarnem had made certain of that.

Footsteps!

A set of two.

"We sent doves to all towns, villages, and hamlets, asking—" Flames crackled through the approaching voice, and sores hissed in their heat. "Witnesses have come forward, confirming the rumors, Your Highness. A piece of writing was found at a—" *Crackle. Hiss. Pop. Pop.* "...in the forest, but we continue our search for the woman."

Liquid rage poured into my veins. They would never take my wife from me, that I had ensured. No matter how many arrows had punctured my organs, knives had severed my tendons, or axes had chopped through my bones... I'd fought them long after the horse had reached the Pale Court.

Until they'd poured oil over me and set me ablaze, to be precise.

"Halt the wheel!"

Halt, it did.

The heat licked away at my feet, but at least my vision returned, faster once I was able to blink again. A man walked up before me, dressed in white robes heavily embroidered with golden suns. He pressed a hand to his mouth to mask the stench, and pearls of sweat formed on his bald head as he leaned toward me, scrutinizing me from all angles.

"Two hundred years, but you bastard had to emerge

during my tenure." A snarl flitted across his hard-cut features, his robes filthed with the signs of a false god. "I am High Priest Dekalon."

Of course he was. "Save your introductions for Lord Tarnem and Commander Mertok, mortal."

"Your Highness." The armored man beside him lowered his head enough the cast of flames glistened along the puckered scar that cut across the malformed bridge of his nose. "Fire indeed proves the only thing keeping him from shaking the ground and raising the dead. Soldiers are weighting down graves across the land at double the measure, but there are too many and the pits are full. We need to turn him."

Dekalon gave a dismissive swat at the air as he watched me rise on the wheel. "I had hoped Helfa would spare me your sudden appearance. But then again, so has every high priest before me. A fine dungeon, is it not? My predecessors..." his voice faded into the roar of flames, only to filter back in one turn later, "...built into the mountainside on the hardest rock, not a single grave over the span of many furlongs."

Which explained the scarce amount of bone at my disposal, gathered from insects, rats, and whatever other creatures had found their end between these stony walls. Escape would come neither soon nor easy, but none of that mattered as long as my wife waited safely at home.

My heart clenched.

I'd failed her so thoroughly. Had lost all control, so overwhelmed was I with ardor, corpses had dug from the ground by the dozens. An appreciated accident, given how mortals had attacked us moments later, putting my little one in grave danger. But she was safe now. The man's words confirmed as much, eliminating all doubt.

After another excruciating turn, Dekalon reached out his hand, palm up. "Your blade."

My throat narrowed.

The mortal beside handed over his knife.

A knife Dekalon brought to my shaky fingers. Carved handle sitting in the clasp of his hand, he rested the glinting blade against my blistering thumb. He pushed down, severing through red skin, flesh, and muscle. When the blade embedded itself in my bone, he brought his other hand to the handle for leverage.

Crk.

My bone gave, and my thumb dropped onto the filthy stone beneath us, only to roll into the flames with a wet hiss.

His eyes flicked between the disappearing digit in the fire and how it slowly reshaped around the bleeding stump of my knuckle. "I am... fascinated."

And I was starting to get angry. "Ah, yes, such is the simplicity of your mortal mind. Eternity in my service shall broaden it."

His green eyes narrowed. "You are quite arrogant for an immortal chained in a dungeon, stinking up its walls."

What could he do that had not been done before? "And you are quite bold for a dying man who will soon relinquish his bones to my keep. Mmm, what a fine adornment that polished head of yours will bring to my throne."

He lifted the blade to my face, taking his time as he carved a slash across my cheek. "Does this not pain you? It ought to... if old scriptures are to be believed."

As if I would confess such a thing to a mere mortal. "Pain and I are old acquaintances."

I held his poisonous stare, gathering bone from wherever my tired mind reached. It crushed into the finest powder, drifting on the wind along dark corridors. It passed torches, armed guards, hushed over the filthy stone, down several steps, up others, and through the gaps of the oaken door locking me here.

"All the scrolls, books, and stories kept at the High Temple... no simple tale after all. For two hundred years, the high priests of the realm have prepared to capture you, should you ever emerge." A smug grin tugged the corners of his mouth. "Still, even charred and pitiful as you are at this moment, I am... humbled to stand in your presence."

"Oh, I shall teach you true humble—"

"Turn him!" Dekalon leaned into me, his voice dripping with venom. "Turn him *twice*."

Fire engulfed me.

Agony scraped over my mind one degree at a time until I returned from the flames with a growl. "Oh, you foolish mortal. I shall—"

"Keep turning him!"

Blazing, burning, biting flames peeled away barely mended skin, chewing down to flesh still raw and sore. Spin after spin, the torment continued, and death passed me with each one. The air bittered further until, with a nauseating whiff, the mind-numbing stench of ash infiltrated the disfigured leftovers of my nose.

My mind shriveled, collapsing into madness as I gagged and choked on the stench of my charred flesh. I dug my teeth into my tongue until blood seasoned my gums and the organ severed between my clenching bite.

Oh, I would kill him.

I would kill them all!

Many turns later, when my taste of smell had long abandoned me, along with my vision, the wheel stalled once more. Slow footsteps tapped here and there, followed by the high priest's voice.

"By Helfa, he bit off his tongue. Say something, King of Flesh and Bone. Threaten me while the blood slobbers from the gaps between your teeth." A chuckle. "Oh... you no longer have much of a tongue for threats. You cannot fathom my hatred for you and the chaos you left in this world after you abandoned us." His blurred outline appeared in front of me. "People had nobody to pray to; nothing to hope for but endless wandering. Only with the help of Helfa were the temples able to save us from falling into a darkest age."

I strained my neck, lifting my new eyes to his as I tried curling my reshaped tongue. "Your gosh'a lie."

His imperious laugh fanned the rage in my blood. "True enough for the people since it got you captured, as the high priests had hoped we would someday. They built a prison strong enough to keep you contained until we burned the last tree, the last dried piece of pig shit." Lifting the hem of his robes, he squatted before me. "This world only has room for one god."

"Agreed."

He scoffed. "You think yourself so superior, yet you've failed to escape the soldier's ambush."

To save my wife.

I could have overwhelmed them, but not without putting her at risk of getting injured or worse. Pain, torture, cuts... I would suffer a million flames to ensure her safety—I had vowed as much. Ada had vowed to return to my side should we get separated, offering me a source of strength. I would escape this.

Dekalon scrunched up his nose. "An immortal charred black."

"A temporary predicament," I said, letting powdered bone rise and settle between the stones where the mortar had crumbled. "Unlike your punishment. That will be eternal. Let your mind think of my words, mortal. I shall offer up corpses to have your soul bound once the time comes."

His brow lifted. "You speak in riddles."

"I leave the riddles to my brother."

Now his brows knitted in all their mortal ignorance, his mind so unassuming about things far greater than he could possibly comprehend. Oh, how blessed my brothers were in being ignored by mortals, for I was the physical embodiment and its ability to suffer pain.

"Your Highness," the armed mortal beside us urged, gesturing the man with the bellow to feed the flames higher once more, sending plumes of smoke to the arched ceiling. "The fire. We need to turn him."

"Ah, yes, turn me."

Up I went, the itch along my skin unbearable, my scalp tingling where my hair grew back. Then I went down, diving into the sweltering heat of the biting flames. The moment I emerged, I focused on the remnants of the dead. Powdered bone, painstakingly brought here over the course of excruciating days, shaped into a first spike—

"Enosh."

At the sound of my true name, the spike settled in the crack between rock, and dust rilled onto the stone floor. My pulse quickened. What an unexpected surprise.

"It is your name, is it not?" A smirk tugged on Dekalon's mouth. "The priest who wed you wrote it in the book of bindings, along with your identity. Your wife is beautiful, from what I heard. Adelaide, correct?"

Book of bindings.

My molars ground together until they ached. "Mortals and their damned customs."

"Wherever might your wife be, Enosh?" When I said nothing, he sighed. "I had a wife once, many years before I stepped onto Helfa's path. Hilde. No woman in the village made better pie than her. The secret's in the browned butter, she used to say. She died during childbirth... on a full moon." He smacked his lips and slowly shook his head. "Seeing her go pale and lifeless was terrible to witness. Worse was how she then got up and scratched at the door, pacing bowlegged with my child stuck between her legs. I daresay heartbreak such as this ought to drive a man insane. Leave him in the fire for a bit."

Panic stitched through my chest.

Flames wrapped me in agony until my screams died away in my throat. They devoured all thought, all nerves, all senses, reducing my existence to nothing but pain that no immortal should survive. I needed this to stop. I needed to get back to my wife.

When the fire finally retreated, I couldn't feel my body anymore, couldn't think past the fury clouding my mind and this all-consuming need for my wife. Wicked, wayward mortals.

A ringing started in my ears or whatever was left of them, which soon took on the sound of words. "—wife might have escaped to the um... what did the scriptures call it? The Pale Court? With its master gone, perhaps we may finally enter. Maybe she'll even do us the favor and come out at some point."

No, Ada was no fool. She would stay inside the safety of our home. But what then, once food became scarce and her only servant rotted away while my wife succumbed to age?

A strange sensation came over my heart, like an odd beat of caution that didn't quite fit its usual cadence.

Out. I needed out of here.

"Oh, how your eyes widened for a moment, even as they rolled in their sockets." Dekalon leaned over, letting his whisper drill into my mind. "Several soldiers reported having seen you... consummate this union. As we both agreed, this world has no room for two gods, especially not one who breeds. Cut it off!"

Cold dread soaked into my muscles, chilling me to the bone until I was ready to beg for the bellow to hike the flames. Stabbing pain shot into my groin, ripping a scream from me that got stuck halfway up my throat, along with my breath. My back bowed and arched as they cut my manhood away. I trembled with such violence, the entire wheel shook.

"We certainly don't need three gods, should this woman carry the spawn of the devil," Dekalon snarled. "Priests across the land are spreading my word. Should this woman ever emerge, people are to bring us the wife of the devil and the spawn she carries in her womb."

I sought the high priest's eyes, no matter how mine faded in and out of darkness. "Hear me, m-mortal... your head will g-gr-grace my throne. Your bones w-will serve me for eternity, for I am your god."

"My god is Helfa," he said. "Watch and see, Enosh. Watch and see how my god will do his divine duty of keeping the world in line."

CHAPTER 22
ADA

I wrapped my calloused fingers around the thick rope. With each pull on the line of fish cages, ripples hushed across the water's surface. My breath rose in billows, more fervently with each strenuous tug against a weight that quickened the pulse in my veins.

Finally!

Rose looked up from where she sat on a boulder, a half-gutted trout in one hand and a knife in the other. "Heavy catch, huh?"

"Has to be," I said, sensing the chill creep into my cheeks the wider I grinned. "I'll give you one of the smaller trout if you help me pull them to shore. The last thing I need is a cage to rip from the line once they hit that current there."

She tossed the fish and knife into her basket, letting her arm brush a few auburn curls from her forehead where they'd escaped her wimple, and waddled over. "Would be a shame if you lost another cage. Better make it two."

"Two then." I nodded. "Now grab the rope. On three, we walk back and drag them all the way in. One." I braced against the river rocks underfoot. "Two." My stomach tightened. "Three."

Gripping the rope tightly, I shifted my weight back for leverage. My heels dug into the shifting rock as I fought for every inch, ignoring how exhaustion blurred the edges of my vision. Against the chill lingering in the crisp morning air, sweat broke along my spine. Heavens, this catch had to be worth quite a few coins.

I needed them.

Desperately.

When the cages hit the current and the one at the end of the line bobbed and tossed on the white cap of the surface, I hung my entire weight on the rope. "Pull harder!"

"I am!" Rose heaved behind me as a handful of curses tumbled from her mouth. "Make that three fish!"

She could have four and the rest would still bring me enough money that I could finally haggle with Thorsten in earnest, and get the flea-bitten gray in his stables.

Three loud cracks threatened those hopes.

One of the cages broke apart, and pieces of wood first tossed in the air before they hit the water. The current swallowed them whole, sending them down the falls where it would sink to the ground next to the cage I'd lost four damn days ago.

But I wouldn't let the rest go.

It was still heavy.

Against the tremble in my arms and the pain searing along my shoulder, I pulled, fighting backward against the current, until the first cage dragged over the rock. I counted two trout jumping in its belly. Another cage emerged with one more measly trout.

A knot formed at the back of my throat, but I swallowed

it down. "Careful with the last one. An entire swarm must've caught in that one."

One final pull and all resistance fell away as the cage tumbled to shore. I stumbled back, straight into Rose. We careened over each other, but she caught her balance while my knees hit the ground.

A rock cut through the cotton of my dress and scraped my skin, ripping a hiss from me. "Devil be damned, there better be an eel in there, too."

Rose scoffed and circled a hand over her pregnant belly. "Not unless they grow beards now."

When my eyes snapped to the last cage, my stomach bottomed out, sending a lap of bile onto the back of my tongue. "No..."

"I still want those fish you promised me," she said. "I pulled, Elisa. Not my fault you caught a corpse."

For a moment, I just sat there, listening to the treacherous sound of water lapping against the shore and how it distracted from the violent current hidden beneath its surface. A little over two weeks, and I was no closer to the Pale Court. Two weeks without a sign from Enosh, but all the more talk about how they'd captured the King of Flesh and Bone.

A sob built at the back of my throat, mixing with the acid that kept rising from my empty stomach. Three coins for the healer, two more for the tenancy on our little hut, and another for Pa's herbs... At this pace, I would never make it home.

Behind me, Rose groaned, one hand pressed against the small of her back. "Augh, this babe is killing me. When it gets like this, I can barely make it down the hill."

"Lean over and brace your thighs." I got up and positioned myself behind her, letting my thumb press against the nerve along her tailbone through the cotton of her dress. "His head is coming into your pelvis. Not much longer now. Better?"

She straightened, shifting her hips this way and that, humming with relief. "Curse this place and how we have no midwife. We women could do with someone like you who knows how to make the aches go away. Where did you learn this?"

"Saw it somewhere once." I walked over to the cages and pulled my knife from its sheath by my belt. "Idiot got himself so tangled during the full moon, I don't even know how to cut him free without damaging the rope."

Rose walked over and glanced down at the man, his blueish face waterlogged and swollen, algae woven through his red beard. "You'll have to bring him to the cellar so they can lock him up. Magistrate said it's the law now." When I cut her a glare, she shrugged. "Don't give me that look. Leave him here, and he might start twitching."

Something corpses across the land had reportedly done after Enosh's capture. They'd crawled from the dirt, only to collapse three steps later, and so it went on.

Rise. Collapse. Rise. Collapse.

"None of them have moved in at least a week."

My guts tied into a knot. I couldn't stomach what that might mean. That, maybe, whatever they were doing to Enosh was so gruesome, he no longer called the dead to his aid. Curse these lands and all these fools. I'd been so close. So close to fix this mess. And then they had to capture him, ruining *everything*! Perhaps Enosh was right about the depravity at our cores? Was there truly no fixing it?

"As if I could drag a grown man all the way there." I leaned over, feeling the corpse's arm for a joint to sever as I swallowed past a swell of bile. "My handcart's too small—"

My stomach heaved. My chest convulsed, strangling that swallow of bile straight back up. It burned along my throat, bittered the back of my tongue, clenched my gums until—

I retched onto the rock to the sound of Rose shuffling away from me as she said, "By Helfa, you better brought no sickness here."

Using the train of my dress, I leaned over and wiped the yellow strings from my mouth. "Just had no breakfast."

"You said the same thing yesterday when you retched behind the bushes. No village as small as ours takes well to strangers, but even less so if they come with a pestilence."

I took my starched wimple off, placed it on the rock beside me, and wiped the thin layer of sweat from my forehead. "It's no sickness."

It was worse.

For days, I'd woken nauseous, unable to keep much down, lest I nibbled on stale bread. It got better as the day grew older. Combine that with the fact that I was late on my bleeding, and you didn't need to be a midwife to figure out just from what condition I might suffer.

Joy.

Dread.

Two emotions warred at my core, pulling my mood from cheerful to scared. For so many years, I'd prayed for a child. The answer couldn't have come at a worse time. But how, if Enosh had sensed nothing? Perhaps it had been too small then?

"Maybe it's a sickness after all." Maybe I was finally going mad, my mind stuffed with head-spinning confusion about this entire ordeal. "I'll have to cut the rope, then see if my father can mend it. Take your fish from the cages."

She didn't.

Rose only stood there, her stare fixed to the dark streaks and onyx discoloration painted across the white cotton on the inside of my wimple.

Sheathing my knife, I quickly grabbed it with my other hand. I placed it back on my head and shoved escaped black wisps into it, forcing my gaze to look at her basket, a nearby oak, the crow in its branches. I looked at anything but her, anything but how her eyes narrowed on me in the corner of my vision.

I took my knife out once more and ran the blade along the fraying rope. "You don't want 'em?"

"Sure I do." She blinked out of her thoughts, then retrieved three fish from my cages, leaving only enough behind to feed Pa and me for perhaps three days, four if I made stew again. "I better hurry. Nobody trusts fresh fish once the sun stands too high, no matter how cold it is."

While Rose filled her basket and eventually left, I ruined the last of Pa's ropes. I detangled the corpse and took off the cages. Once I gutted the few fish I'd caught, I loaded everything onto my groaning old handcart and headed to the village, leaving the dead man behind.

The wooden wheels of my cart creaked along the muddy path that led through Elderfalls, a village with too many fishermen and not enough fish. A woman emptied a bucket of scraps into the pigpen beside her hut, the air ripe with the stench of piss and poverty.

When I passed the iron-studded hutch to the cellar, a biting odor crept into my nostrils, but it was gone at my next step. Instead of a pit, Elderfalls kept the dead in a dungeon beneath its courthouse. We no longer released them during a full moon. High priest's order.

"Elisa." Thorsten dipped his head as he raked a flake of

straw from the pile beside the stables. "Come to haggle with me again?"

I sighed and waved at my basket. "Only if you'll take the coin I offered last week and four small fish."

He chuckled, but the sound held a tone of kindness. "I want double the coin for the mule now."

I clenched the rough cart handles. "Are you joking? We both know the animal is lame on the right hind."

"Afraid not. All stablemasters raised their prices in the other towns and villages; why not me? We might be far out, but someone will find the mule. Temples are giving out coin so the militia can buy horses and mules."

My pulse throbbed at the tips of my fingers. "Such a fuss, still, even though they caught the King?"

He shrugged. "They're looking for someone... a woman."

I'd figured as much, but that didn't stop my heart from racing and a new layer of sweat to break at the nape of my neck. "What woman?"

"Can't say. Heard no name. No word of who she might be."

Still, a shudder chased across my skin, but it stayed the longest around my exposed neck, where my collar had been. On reflex, my fingers wandered there, rubbing, searching for the comfort of it, only to find it gone. Strange how the absence of something that had once made me feel like a prisoner now caused panic to settle at my core.

Where are you, Enosh?

My fingers itched to reach into my pocket for the stone Pa had cut from my collar, but I thought better of it. Yes, it would buy me a mule—a lame one, right along with a new set of problems. Even if Thorsten didn't ask how I came by such a treasure, others would once he traded it for coin. Might even think I had more of it. And if that happened faster than I could escape on a mule with teeth as long as my thumb...? The way my luck went with mules, the old thing might just die underneath me halfway across the stretch.

I took a deep breath. "Just... let me know if someone comes and wants the mule, and I'll see what I can do."

Maybe I needed to offer my services as a midwife, after all? But wouldn't that put me in even greater risk of being found out? How much longer until that woman the priests wanted had a name? A description? An occupation?

I needed to leave this place and reach the Pale Court, but how? Fear crippled me, making me doubt every idea I came up with. Then I doubted it a second time, asking myself if I was just making excuses, stalling to make good on my promise.

I'd tried to escape Enosh for over a month, and now that I had, I didn't know what to do. What to think. What to feel. What did I want beyond rest for the dead that might as well never come now? Curse this devil, what did I feel for my husband beyond sympathy? What was this heavy weight I dragged around in my chest? How did any of this make any sense, given how—

The cart stopped.

A splinter drove into my palm.

I pulled back with a hiss, shoes sinking into the mud as I tried to get the wheel unstuck. Life had never been particularly kind to me, but had it ever been this miserable? Perhaps it was a matter of perception, and mine had changed after two months of soft pelts, sweet berries, and always enough food in my belly.

When I finally reached the house at the end of the village, I brought my cart underneath its thatched overhang. Inside, dried herbs hung from the rafters, scenting the air with traces of rosemary and chamomile. Dozens of little drawers lined one wall, each labeled with whatever it stored behind, from mushrooms I recognized to names I couldn't pronounce.

But I could read most.

The healer lifted his gaze from a book that rested in his palm and pushed the spectacles higher up the bridge of his nose. "Yes?"

I cleared my throat. "My father's tea? For his lungs?"

"Ah. Yes." He placed the book on its wooden stand on a table beside him, then rummaged through a woven basket. "Has he coughed less blood?"

"He coughs less, though the blood comes in larger swells whenever he does."

I trailed my finger over the letters in the book, loving the feel of parchment against my fingers. What if I offered my help to the healer? Not many could read, and he might need someone to sort stock or mix ingredients for potions.

"Are you a piss prophet?" I asked.

"No. There's a piss prophet two villages over. I never studied the taste of urine during—" His magnified stare dropped to how my finger traced a letter, his disapproval so obvious in the arch of his brow that I abandoned my silly idea. "Your father's tea."

I took the pouch he handed me. "What do women do around here to find out if there isn't even a midwife?"

"These grains right here." Another shove on his spectacles, then he pulled a small bowl from a shelf behind him with two depressions, each filled with a different seed. "Urinate on both chambers. Cover it for five days in a warm place. If both kinds sprout with the same vigor, there will be a child."

"I've heard of this before." An ancient method for those who had nobody trained in the taste of a pregnant woman's piss. "How much?"

"With the tea?" A smack of his lips. "Two shillings."

I pulled the coins from my pocket, dropping them to the table with a *clank*. "I do this at any time of the day?"

"Morning is best," he said as he took the money. "Your husband works the mines? Died?"

My husband couldn't die. "Died at Airensty."

"My condolences to you, woman." He nodded, but his interest shifted back to his book. "I shall look in on your father in two days."

And waste me another coin.

Pa could barely get out of bed anymore without choking on his own blood, let alone travel to the Pale Court, even with the aid of a mule. I would have to leave him behind to die. Alone. In a strange village. All because I'd returned.

And what if I made it to the Pale Court only to meet my end there? Lord Tarnem had held Enosh captive for a fortnight. For all I knew, the priests might keep him locked up for months, years, even. Maybe I would sit on his throne for a decade, watching my skin wrinkle while I remembered the day I left my father to die in a bed of moldy straw.

My heart sunk in my chest. I had to make a choice. Should I stay with Pa? Use the stone and risk suspicion? Or spend the last coin on good shoes so I could walk the whole damn way?

My hand wandered to my stomach, daring one circling caress, then another. And I realized that, for the first time in my life, I might have to do what was best for my child.

CHAPTER 23
ENOSH

Black spots dotted my vision through the haze of pain. I wheezed, but I'd stopped thrashing against the fire long ago, letting the hot metal burn my wrists and ankles as my weight dropped toward the restless tips of endless flames.

When I rose to the highest point of the wheel, the priest standing on the scaffold dug his bloodied hand back into the gaping cleft on my abdomen. He rummaged through my organs with one hand, giving his nods and frowns, then let the quill in his other hand note all the peculiarities of an undying god.

"What a curious creature you are," he murmured, his robes drenched in sweat from the sweltering heat that radiated back from the ceiling. "A stab to the heart will do as little to you as the removal of your guts, aside from weakening you temporarily. Another turn, please."

A swell of blood oozed from the hole in my body, veining across the welts and pustules that covered my skin. How long I'd been here, I couldn't say—I'd stopped counting the days when they'd cleaned powdered bone and spikes from the furrows in the rock.

The high priests had gone through great trouble indeed, amassing enough knowledge to keep me here; reducing a god to a drooling creature with his guts dangling from a crater in his abdomen, while somewhere between hisses and pops, his penis shriveled away once more.

When the fire engulfed me, again and again, I couldn't think past the dense fog of misery. One turn blurred into the next, and the only thing keeping my mind from descending into hysteria was the memory of Ada's vow. I needed my little one; I needed to return to my wife. I was growing more and more willing to scream for it, beg for it, to throw myself at the goodness of mortals I knew did not exist.

I emerged from the flames to the creak of hinges. An armed mortal entered my dungeon, his trembling hand wrapped around the pommel of his sword. Sweat glistened on his forehead and his shoulders bobbed with each studded step of his metal-plated boots.

"What is this about?" the man by the wheel said. "High Priest Dekalon ordered that nobody—"

His words died on the sword as it sunk into his ribcage, only for the blade to sever his spine and let him collapse to the ground at an odd angle.

A spark of hope.

Until the wheel shifted, slowly at first, only for my weight to rip me down into the fire once more. Coals seared into my chest to the sound of metallic clanks. The stench of burnt blood ripped a scream from my throat until my voice died at the scorching, scalding heat that flayed my lungs from the inside.

Die.

I wanted to die.

Wanted to die...

Wanted to—

"Ew." Yarin's familiar voice wafted through the thick smoke of charred hair as I lifted toward the ceiling once more. "Let me tell you, breathing through the stench alone calls for at least fifty corpses, sixty if you need me to stuff your guts... Oh my, is this truly my brother? Hard to tell with half your face carved down to the skull—" A hiss. "Bastards cut your pecker off. Oh, I do commiserate with you on that particularity."

I blinked him into sharpness as he climbed over me and lifted the heavy chains to thread them through the spokes. "I... called... for you."

"Yes, about that." He brushed a rust stain from his tailored green jacket before he set to work on another chain. "See, I wanted to come to your aid sooner, you have to believe me. In fact, I was at a brothel when thoughts about your torture reached me. I wanted to come immediately. Right after I finished. But then Eilam showed up. Oh, what a mess it was. Uh... do help me with breaking this chain."

Against the weakness in my limbs, I braced my heel against a spoke and fought the constraints of iron. "Pull harder..."

"That's what she said, but then Eilam came. And as it so goes with our brother, everyone dropped dead. There I was, my hands on this woman's hips, about to pull her onto my length..." He ripped through the chain with a spark, then let it clank down along the wheel. "So confusing. What does one do in such a moment? Should I stop? Should I finish? What are the divine rules here? After all..."

His voice faded away.

My mind spiraled on its wobbly axis as I sat up and stared down at my gnarled legs. Their bones had healed into the weave of the spokes, leaving me no choice but to break them once more. Nine pounds of my fist shattered them into a hundred pieces, allowing me to pull first one, then the other, from the constraints of the wheel.

"I dare say I had an onslaught of... morality of some sort," the God of Whispers continued as he climbed back onto the scaffold. "Such a lovely woman. Anyway, Eilam threatened to follow me to every whorehouse across the realms should I aid you. What a waste of fine women that would be. Oh, you vexed him so, Enosh. The drowning didn't help our thoroughly dysfunctional family. Oh, you do look rather beaten. Good thing I convinced that archer to kill most of the guards."

Saliva pooled beneath my tongue as I pushed my liver back where it ought to be for faster healing, only one thing on my mind. "I have... have to go home."

Back to my wife.

Nothing else mattered.

Not yet.

"Home. Yes, of course. You ought to rest." Yarin made his descent, his voice like fangs digging into my brain. "In the end, I mentioned balance. There has to be balance, but how, if our brother is being carved up like a pig?"

I inched toward the scaffold. My legs refused to obey; still broken enough, I had to lift and drag them by hand. No matter. Out. Just out. I let myself roll over the edge. My arms paddled the thick air, and I sucked in a sharp breath before—

Crack.

My skull shattered on the rock, and all air burst from my lungs. Blood seasoned my teeth as the dungeon spun around me, and Yarin's chatter faded into blissful silence. A ringing followed, then the pop of flames, and finally...

"Ah, ten corpses should be appropriate," Yarin said. "I am not a greedy god, and I can only divide my love and attention between so many."

As my senses returned and my skull mended, I glanced around my prison. The priest lay beside me on the ground, his eye nothing but a black, oozing socket where the sword must have thrust through his head. The armed man kneeled not far from him, the blade embedded in his own chest.

I jutted my chin toward the lot of dead men and let them rise for my protection. "You may have them once they have ensured my escape."

Yarin lifted a brow at me. "I said I have no preferences; I didn't say I have no taste."

"Suit yourself," I said, and let them march ahead of me toward freedom.

I crawled over the stone like vermin, up a short set of stairs and through the oaken door, dragging my useless legs behind me. Once I reached the light of day, its brightness stabbed into my head. Bile soured the back of my throat and my stomach cramped before strings of vomit driveled from my lips. It tainted the air with bitterness and saturated the seashells beneath me.

Streaked blood-red at the horizon, the chaotic morning sky matched the color of the flayed skin flapping from my chest. Naked to nearly bone, I rose, blood still dripping from my crotch. Torture had certainly changed over the span of two hundred years, each new instrument an attest to mankind's depravity.

I sent the corpses to clear the area, some sort of temple

grounds surrounded by walls carved from the rock. "High Priest Dekalon?"

"Not here, I'm afraid," Yarin shouted over the screams of the remaining soldiers as the dead turned temple to tomb, biting through arteries and breaking necks. "Oh, I do understand how eager you are to chain his soul. Bring him to me, and I shall do this for you in exchange for the corpses."

He would die many gruesome deaths. But not yet. I had other priorities. As promised, my wife was waiting for me. And as promised, I would return to her.

Forever return to my Ada.

Letting armor form around me from the skin of the dead guards and priests, I walked over to a chestnut mare that stood saddled beside a weapon rack. A bucket of water sat by her side, showing me the reflection of something that looked nothing like the man Ada knew, but all the more like a monster.

Ribs exposed and charred black on one side, half of my face peeled down to the bone, my hair a tattered mess of singed strands and new growth. No, I would not let her see me like this. I needed to heal before I could dare hold her, kiss her, sink into her arms.

"How long?" I asked. "How long was I held captive?"

Yarin shrugged and grinned down at the corpse of a dead woman. "A little less than a fortnight, perhaps."

I cut the mare's throat with a bone knife, only to let her rise moments later, turning her toward the Pale Court. I needed rest. Perhaps I would even find much-needed sleep in my little one's arms, so I may wake and pretend that this had been nothing but a terrible dream.

"This one," Yarin said. "The rest... mmm, nothing but

brutes with hairy arses. I shall call on you once you are... Wait, where are you going?"

"To my court." I raised the woman, her soul already shackled to her form. "My wife is waiting for me. Perhaps you should come with me and ease her mind. She has to be terrified."

"Oh, she was. So overtaken by panic, fragments of her thoughts resonated in my head over the span of towns." He reached for the confused woman, helped her onto shaky legs, and pulled her into his embrace as he hushed her. "But your wife is not at the Pale Court." A chuckle. "Not unless you have recently acquired a new servant named Rose and fish cages."

Your wife is not at the Pale Court.

I froze, rendered utterly dazed and confused by his words. Fish cages? My jawline stiffened as doubt and distrust tore the veil that hid old memories shaped by vile betrayal and set into my core in the shape of a broken heart.

I gulped past a lump of blood and ire. "Where is my wife?"

"How would I know? I have more important things to do than to listen to your wife's internal ramblings about frayed ropes and what to put in her stew."

Frayed ropes?

Stew?

Raw and violent, mistrust crackled through every fiber of my being, an emotion I was too familiar with. Why was she not where she ought to be? I had *ensured* her return to the Pale Court, yet she was not there. Neither could she be held captive if she pondered fish cages and stew. I stumbled back a step, my mind suddenly spinning again.

How...?

Why was she not...?

None of this made sense.

I'll hide in the back of beyond until my hair's gray, Ada's words infiltrated a mind already standing at a crumbling edge, with the black void of madness gaping below. *How could I not want to leave you? Any woman in her right mind would. I hate you.*

A feverish chill crept over my mending skin, tightening around my skull until my temples throbbed. Had this not happened before? Had I not been snared? What if my wife had escaped me after all? What if this wicked woman had played me for a fool like—

No!

She'd promised.

Had given me her vow!

My wife had come to care for me, had she not? At least some? Had I not tried to please her? Had put my doubt aside and trusted her? But I had trusted before. Had tried so hard to please, and what did I get in return? Betrayal. My child taken from me. A return to loneliness.

I hate you. Hate you so much, not even your brother is powerful enough to change that.

Somehow my legs gave out underneath me, and I sunk to the ground. No, none of this made sense. I just wanted to go home to my little one. My flesh was exhausted, my mind muddled from—

She had not returned...

"I thought you knew," Yarin said. "After all, you can sense her flesh and bone."

All I'd sensed for weeks was pain, bought with the assurance that Ada would be safe at the Pale Court. Assurance that she would wait for me. But she was not there. She was...

Where was my wife?

Closing my eyes, I disentangled my mind from the clank of stones shifting on the mountain and the flaps of wings on the breeze above. Instead, I listened to the beating flesh of hearts and the *ba-boom-ba-boom* of their cadence. I searched its undertones for that one out-of-tune beat, that particularity that was my wife's—

Ba-boom-boom.

An echo.

As though Ada's heart called to me, my senses steered themselves northeast. Was she in Hemdale? And would that not make sense after—no. Not Hemdale. My mind traveled higher. Higher yet. All the while, my heart sunk deeper into the raging pit that was my stomach. A fortnight, and my wife wasn't even a furlong closer to the Pale Court. Instead, she'd gone north.

Away from it.

My fingers itched.

Away from me?

My nostrils flared, faster the closer my senses came to her form. Her heart drummed its odd beat, her hand gently stroked around... something. Comfortable warmth encapsulated the skin of her arm, whereas I had boiled in fire for weeks. A smile curved her lips where mine had been charred away hundreds of times. Her chest was lighter than ever before, whereas mine had suffocated in the stench of my burnt flesh.

I sensed everything on her.

Everything but despair.

Everything but heartache.

Everything but the agony of something being amiss or the pulse-quickening dread of prey in hiding. My wife's body felt lighter than it had since she'd come to the Pale Court, as though she'd unburdened herself of her shame, her guilt... unburdened herself of me. Her happiness overwhelmed my senses. How could she be this happy when she must have known of my dire circumstances? How?

A roar built at the back of my throat, my ribcage not large enough to contain this brutal pain, like a thousand fires burning within me. "Listen to her thoughts. I want to know what she's thinking *right this moment*."

Yarin peeled his lips over his teeth and sucked in a hiss of air, tilting his head this way and that. "She is far away from here, brother, giving me nothing but fragments."

"Tell me!"

"She is thinking of going farther north, where fewer people pray to Helfa," he said, letting me choke on a spike of anger. "Something about a mule. And, um... Elric. It comes into her thoughts often. *Elric. Elric.*"

Farther. North. Mule.

Elric.

Joah. Oh, where is my beloved Joah?

It started as a slight tremble in the ground, that moment where the truth of her betrayal stabbed between black ribs and squeezed my heart—twisted it, ripped it out, and held it before the eyes of a fool. No, she'd never even tried to return to my side... wicked, wayward mortal.

Liar!

The word dug its nails into a mind racing back, clasping, clawing, containing, but the madness at its core swelled until it spread across the lands. It shook the bone in the ground until the mountain behind me roared, rock crumbling as it sent billows of dust into the sky.

Yarin held his arms out, fighting for balance as he stared at the shaking ground. "Ah, we have no luck with women, brother. Mine run into my arms, only to slit their wrists; yours keep running away from you, only to have their throats cut."

I mounted, letting an army of corpses rise so they may protect me while I hunted down my wicked, wicked wife. "Oh no, brother... death will offer her no escape from me."

CHAPTER 24
ADA

Elric.

Elric.

Yes, I liked that.

Pure, unadulterated joy soared through my chest as I smiled down at the sprouted grains, dozens of bright green stems emerging from the seeds. And if she was a girl? Amelia... after her grandmother.

I pressed my hand against my belly, stroking the child growing beneath my palm. Even before the grains had sprouted, I had no doubt I was pregnant. Still, seeing the growing proof soothed over the feeble remnants of guilt and shame, banning it to the deepest, darkest crannies of my core.

Folded cloak in hand, I walked over to the table and placed it beside the provisions I'd stacked there. "I'll head farther north at first, where fewer people pray to Helfa, which means fewer priests. That way, I can come down this passage here." I grabbed the map I'd traded for salted fish with a traveling merchant, held it out to Pa, and tapped the crooked line that read *Willow Road*. "It'll take a day longer, but I can avoid Hemdale. There's a small tavern along this road, should I need it."

Pa offered me a weak smile where he rested in bed, his features as pale as his hair. "Best avoid it... right along with people."

Because I had no friends out here.

Only small groups of priests who supposedly rode from village to village, spreading word of the woman who might carry the devil's spawn in her belly. On instinct, my hand went back to my stomach, drawing another protective circle around my baby.

My baby.

No matter how dire my circumstance, another smile stole over my lips. I couldn't help it. When the morning sickness had refused to abate and my breasts started to ache, making a choice had become simple. It was one thing if I remained with Pa and ended up burned at the stake, but quite another if they wanted to burn me with my child growing beneath my heart.

Another circle.

I'll keep you safe.

"I'll bring everything to Thorsten and tell him to ready the mule and lead it here." Cloak, pouches with dried fish, filled waterskins; I arranged it all in a wicker basket. "All I'll have to do is climb onto its back and ride off. Even if he boasts about the stone down at the stables right after, I'll be on my way." A shadow came over my mood and I quickly kneeled beside Pa's bed. "I'm so sorry. I should never have come back. You'll be in danger."

"Oh yes, they'll come and cut me down from my youthful prime," he mumbled, letting his jittery fingers stroke over my cheek. "But perhaps I won't have to wander after, should you succeed."

"I don't know if I will." Almost a month without a sign from Enosh didn't exactly inspire confidence. "All I know is that I have eternity to get him to calm down. Per my estimation, it'll take two hundred years for each month they hold him captive."

Maybe more.

"Still too good, carrying the weight of other people's problems, of the entire world, on her shoulders." His throat bobbed with a stifled cough before he swallowed the blood right back down, as though it would burden me any less with doubts of leaving him behind. "Go now. And don't let that god husband of yours ruin your damn tenacity."

I reached my hand beneath his head to fluff the straw in his pillow, then gently lowered it back down, tugging the spit rag to rest right beneath his mouth. "We're not saying goodbye yet. I want to find this bowl empty when I return from the stable." I pointed at the fish stew on the stool beside him, tried myself at a stern look, then rose. "I'll be back soon."

Knitted scarf draped around my shoulders, I left our crooked hut behind. I headed down the trample path toward the heart of the village. The handle of the wicker basket dangled from my arm, holding everything I needed to make my way back to the Pale Court. Except for my knife, which rested in its leather sheath on my belt, along with a small purse of coins.

Lonely snowflakes drifted on the biting breeze that cut inland from the sea. Not enough to accumulate on the frozen ground, yet their scent climbed into my nostrils. It reminded me of Enosh, crisp and clean, with a cold undercurrent that rose the fine hairs at the nape of my neck. What would he say once he returned and noted my condition? Perhaps he would come when the child was already born? Would he be happy? Even angrier for being kept from it?

At my next footfall, a strange sensation ran through me, as though I'd stepped onto the heave of a boat with one step, and back down at the next. My legs slowed as I lowered my gaze to the ground. And there, right between the toes of my boots, did veins of white crack through the frosty layer atop the hard mud as though the earth wanted to gape open.

Had the ground just trembled?

My gaze shot to a nearby maple, its crown bare, and all the thin branches and spindly twigs did was bend to the wind. Nerves. Nothing but nerves, and it wouldn't get better if I wasted more time.

The moment I turned toward the stables, my nose scrunched at a sour whiff. What had started as an unpleasant but faint smell three weeks ago now wafted around the few houses and stores, so gagging it put the stench of fish and manure to shame.

Rose stood at the corner of an empty merchant stand, watching how a man wheeled a corpse on a handcart toward the cellar. Another man squatted over the open hutch, yelling something at whoever was down there with the corpses.

Against the quiver in my stomach, I walked up to her. "What's happened?"

"By Helfa, so many times I told Sigward to shovel the shit from his pig's sty." Fanning her face, she jutted toward the cellar. "Now they found a corpse somewhere in a ditch. The moment they opened that hutch to toss him in there... Oh, that stench! I've never smelled anything like this before. What is it?"

All blood drained from my face as I inched toward the

cellar, my muscles so stiff that my lungs struggled to expand. Good thing they did, because the stench turned more nauseating the closer I came, yet the foreboding twitch of a smile tugged the corners of my lips. No, this couldn't be...

A man emerged from the cellar, a rag wrapped around his mouth and nose. He shook his head and hiked his shoulders in nothing short of shocked disbelief. Across his arms lay a small body, its spindly arms speckled in dark patches of... of...

I froze.

Had he truly...?

"It's the boy!" the man shouted, muffled through the fabric covering his mouth as he lowered the child to the ground, stepped back, and shook his head yet again. "Devil be damned, that stench. I've never seen anything like it. The bloated belly, the black fingertips, the... the green and gray on his skin. By Helfa, what is this?"

A whisper escaped me. "It's rot."

Tears swelled behind my eyes as I breathed through the heart-splintering sobs that built inside my chest. I'd seen enough rot that I could tell that this child had decomposed in there for a while—likely from the moment Enosh and I had left the Pale Court.

I heaved through an onslaught of warmth in my chest. Hating Enosh seemed impossible right then. Perhaps I even loved him in that moment, where my worth took on the shape of a rotting child. He'd stood by his word. All this time, children had been at rest across the realm, all over a vow of 'til death do us part to my husband undying.

Rose hesitantly walked up beside me. "What is this?"

"I have no idea," I said and turned back toward the stable, while more villagers poked their heads out of their homes, watching the commotion. "I have to speak to Thorsten."

Had to return to the Pale Court and stand by my promise as Enosh had. No more delays. No more doubts. Pa hadn't raised a daughter who broke vows, yet standing by it ever so faithful had never seemed as right as it did now.

Somewhere, a bell rang.

I found Thorsten just as he emerged from the stable and leaned a pitchfork against the filthy wall beside the muck heap. "What's all this about?"

"Just the corpse of a child. A sickness, maybe. Who can say?" I unhooked the basket from my arm and reached it out to him. "I'll take the mule saddled, with all these things stored in properly stitched saddle bags if you have them. If not, a harness will do. Just make sure it's secure."

He folded his arms in front of his chest and cocked his head. "You have the coin?"

"Something worth more than the coin you want." When he took the basket, I glanced over my shoulder to ensure nobody was looking, then fingered the stone from my pouch. "Bring the mule to our hut, watered, fed, saddled, and ready. Do this, and you'll get this stone." A glint came over his eyes, but the moment he reached for it, I dropped it into my pouch. "If anybody sees me with this, I'll have my throat slit around the next corner. You'll do well keeping it to yourself until you take it to Airensty and sell it there for more coin than any militia would ever hand over for a mule."

He pursed his lips for a moment, and his head tilted from side to side as he considered my proposal, but he eventually gave a curt nod. "Before the sun stands at its highest, I'll bring him up to your hut. You better still have the stone then, or I'll keep the mule and all your—" His attention shifted to something behind me. "And then I'll sell the mule straight to them."

I turned.

The blood stilled in my veins.

A robed priest led a black donkey toward the courthouse, while another sat on its back with a bell in his hand, letting its *ca-lank-ca-lank* resonate through Elderfalls. Everyone came together in earnest, torn between the gossip about the odd corpse and the shouts of the magistrate calling for order and silence.

Not good.

"Are you quite alright, Elisa?" Thorsten asked. I didn't notice the sway in my legs until he gripped my elbow and steadied me. "You've gone ashen."

"I'm fine." The scratch in my voice betrayed too much fear. "You know what? I changed my mind. Toss a saddle on the mule and bring him here. I'll do rest on my own."

His brows knitted, but he turned away and disappeared into the stable, leaving me with my heart clanking against my esophagus. Damn it to hell and back, I'd waited too long. One wrong move, one flicker of suspicion, and they would be on my tail.

"Good people of—" The priest leading the mule turned to the other, exchanging mumbles before he returned his attention to the gathered crowd. "Yes, Elderfalls. High Priest Dekalon issued the capture of a woman. Fifty pieces of gold—" At the communal gasp, the priest raised his arms in an appeasing manner. "Yes, yes, fifty gold pieces shall be rewarded to whoever arrests her and brings her to the nearest temple, a priest, or any loyal servant of Helfa. Preferably alive."

My throat narrowed to the width of a hair. Dead or

alive, I had no intention of being handed over to the high priest.

I turned toward the stables, only to bump straight into Thorsten. "What about my mule?"

"Shh. I want to hear this." He leaned against a wooden post and flicked a finger at the priests, then let his baritone shatter through the village. "Who is this woman?"

Dozens of eyes shot to us, slowing the beat of my heart as if the organ didn't dare another beat. What was I supposed to do? Wait? Tell Thorsten I had changed my mind yet again and to bring the mule? If I walked away now, everyone would stare at me even harder. Some might even grow suspicious. Who didn't want fifty gold pieces?

"The woman's name is Adelaide." The priest's shout hurtled my pulse into helpless panic. "Blue eyes and of bearing age, with crooked legs."

A sigh of relief parted my lips, but only until a voice asked, "What color is her hair?"

"She is light of hair," the priest said. "The woman comes from Hemdale, is a knowledgeable midwife, and likely travels with her elderly father."

I stared down at the mud.

Still, I felt them, the few eyes that wandered over me as mumbles rippled through the rows of people like the foreboding whispers of a storm. No, I was just imagining those nervous pricks needling my skin, urging me to run. My legs were straight, and I was a fisher. A poor one, to be certain, but my hair was as black as tar.

Without consent, my eyes flicked to Rose.

She stared right back at me.

I offered a smile.

She didn't smile back.

Instead, she rounded the merchant stand and leaned

into her brother, Henry, letting whispers hush between them. He straightened his spine, shifting his balance from one leg to the other.

Don't look at me.
Don't look at me.
Don't look—

His eyes captured mine.

My muscles tensed, and I turned toward Thorsten. "You know what? I've changed my mind. Bring the mule to my hut. Hurry, and I'll give you the stone, along with all the coins in my purse."

I didn't hurry away.

I walked, slowly enough as not to seem in a hurry, but fast enough that the cold air brought tears to my eyes. Or perhaps it wasn't the wind after all, but the pressure that pounded inside my skull. I wasn't safe here anymore. My baby wasn't safe.

Just then, the priest's voice chased behind me. "This woman has wed the devil, the King of Flesh and Bone." Groans of disgust resonated through the crowd, but it turned into the roar of chaos when he added, "It is believed that she carries the devil's spawn in her belly. Find her, good people of Elderfalls. Find her or this woman will cast the world into eternal darkness."

CHAPTER 25
ADA

My heart slammed against my ribs.

I pressed a hand onto my belly, letting sheets of ice that had formed in the furrows crack beneath my steps as I hurried toward the hut. A sudden gust tore the scarf from my shoulders and when I turned to grab it, I saw them.

My heart stopped.

Henry followed me, staring at me from beneath the brim of his felt hat. Another man walked beside him, and Rose waddled not far behind. There was no way I could outrun two men—or fight them off should it come to that—but I wouldn't let them harm my baby...

Oh god, my baby... my—

Why did everything spin?

Calm.

Breathe.

Despite the panic surging in my chest, I forced my expression to remain blank and turned my gaze back to the hut. Not far now. And once I reached it, what then?

Ignoring them would do me no favor. I had to get them to leave. Damnit, how long until Thorsten brought the mule?

I hastened my steps.

Too fast!

I slowed them.

Forced my breath into an even rhythm.

The moment I reached for the door, still many steps away from it, Henry said, "Elisa. A word?"

His low rumble stilled my heart, but I turned and battled a slight curve to my lips. "My father is ill, and I need to look after him. What is it?"

He flashed the smile of a wolf as he pushed the brim of his hat up, giving me a good look at his narrowed brown eyes. "Well, Rose and I reckon you sound just like that woman the priests are looking for. This... Adelaide."

"Me?" I tried myself at a chortle, saliva pooling beneath my tongue, but I didn't risk swallowing it. "She sounds nothing like me. My father's just a fisher, as am I."

"A lousy one," Rose said, casting her eyes over my belly. I needed to stop touching it. "She helped me with the baby pain. Knew just where to push and how. Sounds like something a midwife would do."

The other man sidestepped and slowly walked around me, circling me like prey chased into a trap. "Legs look nice and straight to me."

Rose snorted a laugh. "Maybe she broke them and they healed. Might've twisted an ankle. Her hair isn't black, either. I saw it. Saw the false color rub off in her wimple."

The stranger ripped my wimple off faster than I could dodge it, glanced down at it with a faint whistle, then gave Henry a single nod. "Looks like soot rubbed off on the inside."

"I'm not the woman they want." My voice trembled. "Now leave me be so I can look after my father."

"Why hide your hair then, huh?" Rose asked. "You're a stranger who suddenly showed up here with your *elderly* father, right after they caught the King."

Enosh. Internally, I screamed his name, pleaded for him to help me, to protect my baby... to kill them all! Damn them. Damn all of them and how they shoveled their own graves. But they wouldn't shovel mine!

I lifted my chin and straightened my spine. "I am not that woman!"

"Maybe you are, maybe you're not." Henry sighed. "Either way, fifty gold coins buys us better land upstream where there's still fish. You'll come with us without a fuss, and we'll let those priests decide."

I took a step back. "No."

Henry took a step toward me, placing his hand on the handle of a knife where it protruded from its sheath by his belt. "Or make a fuss... Preferably alive, they said. I'm no man of fancy words, but I reckon than means dead's fine, too."

My eyes flicked between his and how he slowly unsheathed his knife, letting horror freeze my muscles, my stiffening hand shifting to cover my child.

Big mistake.

"Told you she's pregnant," Rose said. "Retched behind the bushes more times than I went to piss."

Hinges creaked.

Pa leaned against the frame and poked his head out, glassy eyes widened with shock. "Wh-what is this? What do you want with—"

"Go inside!" I shouted, and when Pa didn't move, I turned toward him. "I said go—"

The stranger lurched at me.

I stumbled back a step, pulled my knife from its sheath, and pointed it straight at him. "Come closer and I'll gut you!"

Anger seethed beneath my skin at the unfairness of this, my foolishness over wanting rot for the likes of them. Enosh could turn the three of them into cups for all I cared, and I would drink from them gladly. Wicked, wayward mortals!

"We should kill her," Rose hissed. "We can tell the priests she attacked us and fell onto a knife. If she's the one, they won't care. And if she's not... they won't care, either."

Pa whimpered.

I gripped my knife tighter.

Henry smacked his lips. "Might get us into trouble with the provost. Let's just grab her and march her straight back."

"And what if she makes such a ruckus that others snatch her from us, huh? It's bad enough that I have to share with the two of you."

"Almost don't care about those coins anymore." The stranger shifted his weight back as he pulled a knife from his mud-crusted leather boots, pointing it straight at my belly. "I say we kill her. Who wants to take chances when she might as well have the devil's babe in her belly? World's bad enough without the King's spawn."

"No!" Pa thrust himself away from the door. "By Helfa, how can you—"

Henry pushed against Pa's chest. "Stay out of it, old man."

Pa's spine crashed against the wooden frame, ripping a bloody yelp from him before he collapsed to the ground.

"Pa!"

I hurried toward him.

Pain seared across my scalp. One tug, and the stranger pulled me back by my hair, nearly ripping me off balance.

Cr-shk!

Stabbing pain shot into my belly. It reached all the way through to my spine, from where it spread across my entire body. My knees wobbled and specks of darkness clouded my vision.

What... what was happening?

The ground shook.

I shuffled back.

I stared at the man.

He stared at my belly.

My gaze dropped to the frayed cotton of my dress, soaked red a hand-width to the right of my navel. Coldness encapsulated my skin, numbing me into the paralysis of shock.

My baby...

No.

No. No. No.

"Something's not right," Henry mumbled as another tremble shook the earth beneath my unsteady legs and screams resonated from the village center behind him. "Ground's shaking like it did when they captured him. What if she's truly his wife? What if the King's sending corpses after us?"

The stranger tightened his grip where he still held on to my hair. "Then we best make sure the child's gone."

Another stab.

And another.

At the third *csh* of metal gliding into flesh, my legs gave out underneath me. My back hit the quivering ground to the sound of the blade clanking onto the frozen mud, shuffling feet, and screams... so many screams. The ground ripped open beside me. Trees swayed. Birds took flight.

Darkness hushed around the edges of my vision as the weight of the world squeezed down on me.

Cold... so very cold.

Pressure expanded within my chest. Iron seasoned my tongue. Hair clung to my cheeks. The ends tickled my lips as I trembled, the chill of winter sucking all warmth from my body.

"Ada."

I blinked but saw nothing but an eagle circling the sky. And snowflakes, so many snowflakes. Beside me, before me, around me, next to the man—

I groaned, fighting how my eyes wanted to flutter shut on the man kneeling beside me. Wind swept through his long white hair, framing eyes entirely black. He had neither white nor brown in them, yet I sensed his stare.

"Come into my light, give me your breath." Gentle fingers stroked along my jawline as he crouched over me, his thumb stroking blood-painted lips. "I cannot let him extend it a second time."

"Eilam." His name was a dying whisper on my lips.

Lips he suddenly suckled between his in a stiff kiss. It lasted only the fraction of a breath before he pulled back, his mouth and chin smeared with blood. My blood.

He dragged his tongue over it, licking it, tasting it, before he shook his head. "No, I do not understand. Now, come to me. Let me ease your pain. Life is precious to me, but I will not allow him to steal you a second time."

"Come into my light," his voice beckoned from where darkness faded into pure brightness. *"Return to me what I let you borrow."*

Lightness settled upon my body as my head lolled to the side. One step of my mind, and light encapsulated me.

Pain. Sorrow. Grief.

It all vanished.

The earth shook with rage.

"How extraordinary," Eilam's voice wafted around me. *"There is more life in you than in any before. More than I need to sate this hunger existence has cursed me with."*

The light faded away, leaving me with no pain, no warmth. Coldness gnawed on me from the inside, along with an overwhelming need to find warmth in Enosh's arms.

I tried to call for him.

Lips refused to open.

My mind called to him instead, saying only one thing.

Master.

Printed in Dunstable, United Kingdom